Trouble in the Cotswolds

By Rebecca Tope

THE COTSWOLD MYSTERIES

THE WEST COUNTRY MYSTERIES

THE LAKE DISTRICT MYSTERIES

Trouble in the Cotswolds

REBECCA TOPE

Allison & Busby Limited
12 Fitzroy Mews
London W1T 6DW
www.allisonandbusby.com

First published in Great Britain by Allison & Busby in 2014.

Copyright © 2014 by REBECCA TOPE

A CIP catalogue record for this book is available from
the British Library.

First Edition

ISBN 978-0-7490-1443-8

Typeset in 12/17.2 pt Sabon by
Allison & Busby Ltd.

The paper used for this Allison & Busby publication
has been produced from trees that have been legally sourced
from well-managed and credibly certified forests.

Printed and bound by
CPI Group (UK) Ltd, Croydon, CR0 4YY

For Tim

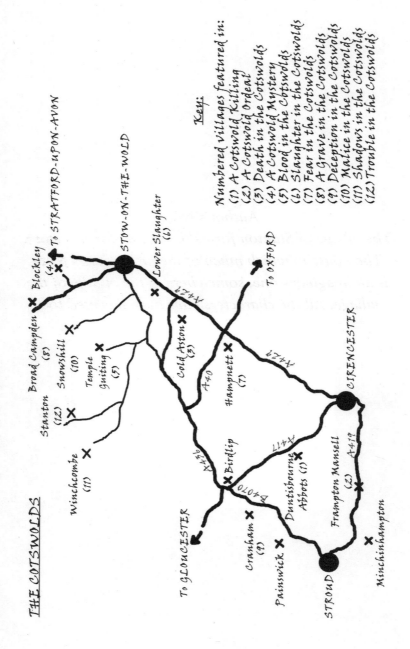

THE COTSWOLDS

TO STRATFORD-UPON-AVON

Blockley (4)
Broad Campden (8)
Stanton (12)
Snowshill (10)
Temple Guiting (5)
Winchcombe (11)
Cold Aston (3)
Hampnett (7)
Birdlip
Cranham (9)
Painswick
Duntisbourne Abbots (1)
Frampton Mansell (2)
Minchinhampton

STOW-ON-THE-WOLD
Lower Slaughter (6)

A429
A40
A429
A417
A419

CIRENCESTER

STROUD

TO GLOUCESTER
B4070
B4236
TO OXFORD

Key:

Numbered villages featured in:

(1) A Cotswold Killing
(2) A Cotswold Ordeal
(3) Death in the Cotswolds
(4) A Cotswold Mystery
(5) Blood in the Cotswolds
(6) Slaughter in the Cotswolds
(7) Fear in the Cotswolds
(8) A Grave in the Cotswolds
(9) Deception in the Cotswolds
(10) Malice in the Cotswolds
(11) Shadows in the Cotswolds
(12) Trouble in the Cotswolds

Author's Note:
The village of Stanton forms the setting for this story.
The house in which much of the action takes place
is an imaginary one, somewhere in the middle of the
village. All the characters have been invented too.

Chapter One

Philip and Gloria Shepherd were going away for Christmas, leaving their house containing a large dog, three pet rats and a lot of glossy potted palms to the care of Thea Osborne, house-sitter.

'But, Mum, you *can't*,' protested Jessica, her daughter, when she heard about it. 'You can't spend the whole of Christmas in a strange house by yourself.'

Thea's first reaction had been the same. 'It does seem rather awful,' she agreed. 'But when I thought about it, I decided it would be quite nice in some ways. I can go to the local carol service, and maybe there'll be some sort of happening at the pub. There's a very characterful pub on top of a hill at the end of the street.'

'What about *me*? Where am I supposed to go?'

'You could probably come and join me in Stanton,' Thea offered doubtfully. She had not asked the Shepherds whether a second person would be acceptable. It had been hard enough to convince them to allow her spaniel to spend ten days in their house. 'Except—'

'What?'

'They've got rats. Nice friendly pet ones.' Jessica's rat phobia was legendary in the family, thanks to an unforgettable incident when she was seven and had come face to face with a dying one on the front lawn.

'That clinches it,' she said decisively. 'I'll go to Auntie Jocelyn's. She'll take me in.'

Thea felt a pang of envy and remorse. Her younger sister had five children, making Christmas at their house a wild orgy of traditional celebrations. The Osbornes had never managed anything approaching such wholehearted zest. Jocelyn made scores of mince pies, filled five stockings with magical goodies and cooked a vast turkey with all the trimmings. Even when Carl had been alive and Jessica an enchanting six-year-old it had all been slightly flat. Carl had deplored the materialism and Thea had never been much of a cook.

'I'm sure she will. You'll have a lovely time there.'

That conversation had taken place in the first few days of December, when plans for Christmas had become suddenly urgent and Thea had been forced to decide about the Shepherds. They had approached her in September, offering extra payment for working over the holiday and assuring her that Stanton was a thoroughly splendid place to spend the holiday. *So why are you going somewhere else?* Thea wanted to ask.

The dates had been vague, and somehow Thea had failed to fully grasp the implications of actually being in a strange village for Christmas Day itself.

Now it was the 21st December, and they were off in their car to catch a flight to Bermuda. The weather was damp and grey, so there were no worries about snow on the runway or ice on the wings. 'We're due back early on the 31st,' said Philip superfluously. 'Just in time for the New Year party down the street. Don't want to miss that. And with any luck the flu scare will have died down by then.' News headlines were aflame with hysterical predictions of a pandemic just in time for Christmas. Earnest spokesmen warned against gathering in large groups, ignoring the realities of festive parties and crowded trains.

'You'll be all right, won't you?' asked Gloria, with the familiar anxiety that people so often manifested as they left their house in Thea's care. 'Blondie's going to pine for a day or two, I'm afraid. She's an awful wimp.'

Blondie was a white Alsatian, with a habit of curling her lip to reveal immense teeth. 'It's her way of smiling,' Gloria had explained. 'Don't let it scare you.'

Thea wasn't scared. She was extremely fond of dogs, even ones who appeared to be snarling at her. Blondie was gorgeous, her coat thick and clean, her big pointed ears demanding to be played with. 'I expect Hepzie will cheer her up,' she said.

Hepzie was a cocker spaniel, thoroughly accustomed to sharing quarters with assorted creatures in a succession of houses. She had a chequered history behind her, in which she had run off with two absconding dogs, helped to find a missing snake, quailed at abuse from a parrot and endured the contempt of a number of cats. Rats, however, were new, and she found them deeply alluring. She stood to attention below their cage, wagging her long tail vigorously and emitting small yelps of excitement.

Gloria had watched worriedly. 'Would she kill them, do you think?'

Thea paused. 'Not once she gets used to them and realises they're pets,' she said bravely.

'The thing is, we generally let them out for a run in the evening. They'd miss it if they had to stay in the cage.' The awkwardness had been palpable. The Shepherds – quite understandably – had jibbed at the presence of a strange dog, for this very reason. Gloria's affection for the domesticated rodents was plain to see. Here, thought Thea, was a trophy wife who had brought some of her earlier interests with her into this affluent Cotswold environment, and good luck to her.

Thea had made firm promises about keeping her spaniel under control and never letting dog and rat come together. But Hepzie's behaviour on this final morning of departure was not creating at all the right atmosphere.

'I'll shut her out of the room when they have their run,' she promised. 'I assume Blondie's all right with them?'

'Oh yes. She thinks they're miniature dogs,

apparently. They run all over her sometimes.'

Thea eyed the rodents speculatively. They were pale in colour and had palatial quarters in a room at the back of the house. It was furnished with a wall of shelves containing books and ornaments, a large table on which a Royal Worcester set of china was arranged in a display that was surely seldom seen by visitors, and carpeted with a faded wool Persian affair that looked as if it could have been handmade five hundred years ago. Did the rats not nibble the books, or knock into the china or pee on the Persian? Gloria pointed out a sort of trail around the room that was the rats' habitual exercise run. 'You just open their door at about seven, and leave them for an hour,' she instructed. 'When you come back, they'll have gone into the cage again of their own accord. It's fun to watch them, but you don't have to.'

'I expect I will. They do seem to be friendly.'

'They'll ride on your shoulder if you invite them.'

Thea smiled tolerantly, thinking she was unlikely to make such an invitation, if only because her dog might take real exception to a shoulder smelling of rat when they snuggled together in the living room on Christmas Eve.

Philip Shepherd turned out to be an incorrigible list maker, although he left it until after his wife had taken Thea through everything verbally, before presenting his ten printed sheets of information. Blondie's bedtime routine figured prominently. *Turn off the light in the*

*living room, and say 'Time for bed and widdles'. She'll
go to the back door, and you let her out, watching that
she relieves herself. When she comes back, give her a
small biscuit from the blue tin, and leave her in the
kitchen with the door closed.*

The rats got half a page of their own, echoing much
of what Gloria had already said.

The locations of the fuse box, stop tap for mains
water, time switch for heating and other domestic
matters were meticulously listed. There were instructions
regarding keys and phone numbers for doctor, vet,
police, emergency electrical breakdowns, and a builder.
Thea didn't ask why she might want to phone a builder
over Christmas.

And unlike many of her employers, Philip gave a
detailed itinerary of where they would be on any given
date, and how best to get hold of them. Getting hold
of homeowners was something Thea very rarely did,
even when there was news for them. She worked on
the basis that they should be allowed to enjoy a restful
holiday while they could, because virtually everything
could wait until they got back again.

On the last page there was a list of local events that
she might wish to investigate. A Dickensian Christmas
Revel was scheduled for the Sunday before Christmas;
and a Boxing Day Special Supper at an enterprising
nearby pub sounded good. There were details including
how to get to the venues and who to phone for further
information.

Never since her first house-sitting commission in Duntisbourne Abbots had she been so comprehensively advised. To the best of her recollection, she had never felt the need to locate the fuse box in a house she was looking after or to know exactly how to put a dog out before bed.

Husband and wife both dithered on the doorstep for longer than was comfortable, plainly trying to remember whether they'd told her everything of importance. There was always a hiatus, sometimes of a month or more, between the initial visit in which the nature of the work was assessed, and the actual handover when the owners finally disappeared. In this case it had been almost three weeks since she had driven to Stanton for a guided tour of the house and its occupants. The Shepherds had sung the praises of The Mount public house and its spectacular views, as well as the delights of Stanway and Snowshill and several other nearby places. 'I know Snowshill,' said Thea. 'I was there only a few months ago.'

'Ah, yes,' said Philip, with a knowing look. 'We did hear something about that.'

'Did you?' Thea readied herself to explain how nothing of what had happened had been her fault in any respect, but it seemed her defence was unnecessary.

'We've done a little bit of research on you,' he went on apologetically. 'And it does seem as if you've landed up in some sticky situations over the past year or two.'

'You could say that.' She heard a note of bleakness

in her own voice that surprised her. Had the past two years really been so dreadful? She thought perhaps they had, on the whole – worse than she had fully realised.

'But we also heard how good you are with animals and that you cope well in a crisis.'

She wondered where such accolades could have come from, but felt it wise to refrain from asking. 'I have had plenty of practice,' she smiled. 'I just hope it doesn't snow while I'm here.' She looked out at the broad level village street, and added, 'But even if it does, I suppose it wouldn't be too disastrous.'

'The neighbours will see that you're all right,' he assured her. 'Whatever happens.'

'Nothing's going to happen,' Gloria interrupted. 'When did anything ever happen in Stanton?'

'Except for poor old Douglas, of course,' muttered Philip.

Gloria waved a hand sharply at him, in a gesture plainly designed to silence him. She turned smilingly back to Thea. 'You'll be *fine*,' she said emphatically.

They left eventually, and Thea experienced her usual mixture of anticipation and abandonment. She had recently begun to suspect that her career as a house-sitter might not be doing her basic character very much good. She had noticed only gradually that she had no real relationships any more. There had been her friend Celia in her home town of Witney, but with so many prolonged absences, Celia had moved on, found herself a new man and showed little continuing interest in Thea. Jessica, now twenty-three, was focusing intently on finishing her period as a police probationer and finding favour as a fully fledged constable. There were phone calls every week or so, and weekends spent together from time to time, but Thea understood that the ties had loosened, not least because of her own distracted behaviour. She had immersed herself in some of the house-sitting commissions, and when calamity had struck, took it upon herself to resolve the chaos and discover the truth behind various terrible events. When Jessica had suffered her own personal trouble, her mother had not been anywhere near as supportive as she ought to have been.

And then there was Drew. At some point during the previous six months or so, she had found herself thinking more about Drew than about her own daughter. When she entertained visions of Christmas Day in Stanton, they included Drew Slocombe playing Scrabble with her in front of a roaring fire, not Jessica.

But Drew lived in Somerset and had two young children in his care. His wife had died that summer, and the demands of family and work meant that Thea had heard very little from him since her stay in Winchcombe in September. His colleague, Maggs Cooper, had watched the blossoming friendship with initial suspicion, followed by outright hostility and finally acceptance. Thea was made fully aware of these evolving reactions, unsure of what significance they might have. Maggs was somehow in the way, obstructing any natural developments that might otherwise take place. As were the children, of course. As a solo parent, Drew was seriously unavailable. And that was a pity, because he liked the idea of himself as an amateur detective, fleetingly joining up with Thea to ferret out the facts in Broad Campden, Snowshill and helping via the telephone when there was trouble in Winchcombe. She had very much appreciated the presence of somebody to share the thrill – if that's what it was. More often it felt like utter chaos and confusion, laced with pain and shock.

The Stanton house was constructed of the ubiquitous Cotswold stone, facing boldly onto the single street that comprised the village. History leaked self-consciously from every facade, the square entryways constructed for coach and horses carefully protected. There were quirks, as Thea had come to expect, this time in the shape of wicker animals fixed onto the ridges of a few thatched roofs on the western edge of the settlement. A fox strolled bizarrely along a rooftop, silhouetted against the sky. An owl attracted the curious attentions of other large – and living – birds. Thatch itself was uncommon in the area, somehow not quite fitting with the honey-coloured stone. Where it did occur, it was obsessively preserved in perfect condition; a statement that Thea was still attempting to interpret.

The Shepherds had struck her as classic Cotswolds inhabitants: affluent, self-assured, friendly, she in early middle age and he ten years older. An unkind observer might add complacent and privileged to the epithets, she supposed. Their garden was tidy, their possessions of indisputable quality. Gloria was evidently well adapted, despite showing signs of not having been born to the life. She wore Cotswold-coloured clothes, made of wool and linen and well looked after. Even her hair had the same honey-and-caramel hue. Philip had a slightly unfocused gaze, as if perpetually calculating the value of his stocks and wondering which sort of car he should buy next. There had been no mention of children, until Thea had made a casual remark about her own daughter. 'Ours is in Japan,' Gloria had replied. 'Her husband's Japanese. We're going out there at Easter.'

The only anomaly that Thea had so far observed was that at least one of the Shepherds – and she supposed it was probably Gloria – was a dedicated smoker. There were ashtrays in every room, with the telltale grey-brown singe marks that betrayed constant use. The unemptied swingtop bin under the kitchen sink smelt powerfully of old smoke. On a shelf in the larder there were two boxes of Marlboroughs, with the health warnings in French. Thea knew people who smoked, of course, but they were a dwindling band and the smell of tobacco was unusual enough to be noticeable, especially inside a building.

It was eleven-thirty on a Friday morning, and she had little or nothing to do until the rats were to have their constitutional and Blondie to have her supper. Although there was no fixed pattern to her various commissions, she generally did some preliminary exploring on the first afternoon. Acutely aware that this was the shortest day of the year, with barely another four hours of proper daylight left, she chirped at the spaniel and suggested a walk. Inevitably ecstatic, Hepzie jumped up at Thea's legs, long ears flapping, tail waving.

Thea had momentarily forgotten Blondie, who stood a few feet away, staring hard at the spectacle of the spaniel's exuberance. 'Gosh, sorry!' Thea said. 'You can come as well. Of course you can.'

There was no sign of gratitude or enthusiasm. The heavy dog seemed to droop, the thick tail brushing the floor. Depression was all too evident, barely twenty minutes after its people had left. 'Come on,' Thea urged. 'It's not as bad as that. They'll be back before you know it. Let's go and have a look round, okay?'

Gloria had drawn her attention to a drawerful of small plastic bags in the hall, essential equipment for dog walking, along with Blondie's smart lead hanging on a hook. 'You have to bring the bag home and put it in the bin,' Gloria explained with a sigh. 'Makes you wonder, doesn't it, when dog poo goes into the landfill. There's a man across the street who flatly refuses to do it. He's got two corgis and insists their poo is natural and good. Slugs eat it, apparently.'

'They do,' Thea confirmed. 'But do we want to make life easier for slugs?'

Gloria laughed. 'Good point,' she said.

So Thea pocketed a couple of bags and attached leads to both dogs. There was unlikely to be anywhere for them to run free in the centre of the village. Tomorrow, she promised herself, they would venture onto one of the footpaths that branched in every direction. The chief one was the Cotswold Way, which made a deliberate diversionary loop to take in Stanton, so charming was the village deemed to be. The footpath meandered like a river along the bottom of the steep escarpment to the east of Stanton, before surging up the hill to an ancient settlement and turning sharply northwards, following the ridge along the top of Shenberrow Hill. The landscape undulated drunkenly, with patches of woodland serving to disrupt any attempt at a direct walk. Thea had been slightly unsettled to see from the map that Snowshill was less than two miles distant. It felt much further away, and much longer ago than the five months since she was there. That had been a violent and distressing experience, leaving her shaken and sad. She had no desire whatever to go back to Snowshill. To her relief, she ascertained from the map that the footpath headed for Broadway without going near the scene of disagreeable memories. She could take the dogs along it without fear of reliving the misery of what had happened.

There were no shops in Stanton, but she had enough provisions for a few days. She had stocked up at a busy supermarket the day before, astonished at the crowds of people buying extraordinary quantities of Christmas fare. Would they really eat it all, she wondered? Caught up in the frenzy, she found herself dropping mince pies, nuts, dates, and a large bag of satsumas into her basket. She did not buy a turkey or a Christmas pudding, but she selected some chicken legs, sausages and ham. The resulting bulging carrier bags that she stashed in the boot of her car were far bigger and heavier than she had planned.

She let the dogs lead the way, and tried to concentrate on the beauty of the village, mentally comparing it with Winchcombe, Blockley, Naunton and other Cotswolds settlements. Their triumphant variety was one of the main sources of her admiration. Nobody could mistake Painswick for Chipping Campden, or Northleach for Stow. A single glance would identify any one of them, as they devised their own individual methods of adapting to the topography, positioning the church and the main hostelries accordingly, curving their streets or bravely situating them on a contour which necessitated one side being several feet higher than the other. The smaller places were even more distinctive, and very much more numerous. She had tried to count them a few times, with no definite conclusion, other than it had to be between a hundred and a hundred and fifty, if you included everywhere with at least ten properties clustered around a church. Perhaps more. It depended, of course, on where you drew the boundary. Some people insisted that Banbury was in the Cotswolds, which Thea was doubtful about. Others pulled a sceptical face when she talked of Winchcombe as a Cotswold town. Her own home in Witney felt decidedly beyond the invisible line.

She had been house-sitting for two and a half years, widowed for three and a half. She was in her mid forties, another birthday looming in six weeks' time. Her future was a disconcerting blank, with no ideas other than some decades spent in a similar pattern of taking over other people's homes for a brief spell, and dealing with whatever aspect of those people's lives might arise in their absence. She usually grew fond of the animals in her care and did her best to keep them happy and safe.

They crossed the wide street and walked along a stretch of raised pavement that was well clear of the road. Blondie walked beautifully on the lead, gliding smoothly at Thea's side without pausing to sniff the ground or scan the scenery. By contrast, Hepzie pulled outrageously, always wanting to be onto the next thing, darting from side to side to investigate smells. With a dog in each hand, Thea could do nothing but maintain a civilised pace and hope the exercise was sufficient for them all.

She could see the narrow spire of the church close by, with a turning leading to it. For want of anything more enticing, she took the dogs that way, observing a stone cross on a broad area of pavement that might merit closer inspection. Christmas lights glowed in several windows, even in the middle of the day. Thus far there had been no sign of anybody in the open air, but she felt sure she was being watched from some of the windows, and wondered how widespread the news of the Shepherds' absence was. Blondie was surely a giveaway – she had to be a familiar figure throughout Stanton.

There were two cars parked outside the church gate, leaving very little space for any other vehicles. Residential houses stood opposite, needing access in and out of their own gates. Something was apparently going on, she decided, seeing a small group of people in the church doorway. Preparations for a carol service, most likely. No chance, then, of having a quick look at the interior – something she mainly did from a sense of completeness rather than genuine interest.

She turned back towards the main street, where an estate car was drawing up just around the corner. She watched a woman of roughly her own age climb out and walk to the back of the vehicle to release a very large dog. A dog bigger than Blondie by some way. It was a Great Dane, its legs much the same length as Thea's, its neck long and strong, holding up the handsome head. 'Wow! Look at that!' she breathed in admiration. 'What a beauty!'

The woman must have heard her. She turned and

stared unsmiling at the little group. She had wide cheeks and wavy hair fading into the neutral colour that came between blonde and grey. She wore well-cut grey trousers and a short black jacket. Her dog – which Thea noted was a castrated male – raised its nose and sniffed the air with a haughty serenity that went some way to dilute Thea's esteem. This was not an animal that would gush and romp and slobber over her. Blondie gave a tiny throaty sound that was not encouraging. A fight between the two big strong dogs would be appalling – although she had a notion that Great Danes were amongst the least aggressive breed of dog. All the same, Thea didn't think she could hold the Alsatian if it decided to exert itself. And the other woman looked equally unfit for the task. 'It's okay,' Thea called. 'We'll go the other way.'

'Thank you,' said the woman as if nothing less was to be expected. 'I'm afraid I've learnt to avoid that dog as far as possible.'

Then why did you let yours out in plain view of Blondie? Thea silently asked. Normally she would have voiced the question aloud, but in recent months she had been making a concerted effort not to make sharp comments to people who might take them badly. It had slowly become apparent to her that the world at large required a level of politeness that was oddly new. Something to do with political correctness, she assumed ruefully.

'Oh?' she said neutrally.

'She has something of a reputation. Haven't you been told?'

'Actually, no. She's been absolutely fine with me so far.'

'They took her on some sort of training course, earlier this year. Gloria insists she's completely reliable now, but "once bitten", as they say.'

'Did she bite you?' Thea glanced down at the white ears, which were pricked alertly. Hepzie was sitting unconcernedly, nibbling at her own rear end and ignoring both the other dogs.

'Well, no. Not quite.'

'Come on, then,' Thea invited both dogs. 'Let's go and see what's this way.' She threw a last look at the Great Dane and its owner. 'My name's Thea Osborne,' she said, before the distance between them became too great for conversation. 'I'm here until New Year's Eve.'

'I'm Cheryl Bagshawe,' came the response. 'I live in Stanway. There's a nice long circular walk we often do, from here to Laverton and back. This is Caspar.' She pronounced her name with a soft *sh* sound, rather than the usual hard *ch*. Thea heard it as Sheryl with an S.

'We'll probably do it ourselves one day, then,' she said, with a forced smile. Cheryl kept her lips together, and glanced back towards the church in an attitude of calculation. 'Just time for a quick stroll today,' she muttered, contradicting Thea's assumption that she was about to embark on the circular walk she'd described. On further examination, it became obvious that she was not dressed for a substantial trek through wintry countryside. And the car would not have been required, either. Thea's natural inquisitiveness suggested several questions, but she could see there was no prospect of posing them. The woman said nothing more and Thea walked westwards nursing a lonely sense of rejection.

Chapter Two

She took the dogs along the main street another fifty yards or so, and then turned into a branching road that offered a new set of views to the south and west. Stanton had a pleasingly informal air, which it took some time to associate with the sporadic provision of pavements. Along many parts of the street, the road simply stopped at the front walls of the houses, the edges blurred by flowers planted in shapeless clumps. At least, there would have been flowers in any other season. All that remained were chopped-off stalks and a few naked rose bushes. Thea's imagination had little difficulty in fast-forwarding six months, when there would be verbena, montbretia, hollyhocks, lupins and penstemons: tall self-confident plants that would enhance the handsome houses and force pedestrians to keep their distance. A few houses had low stone walls to fend off any traffic, and some had wider grass verges. The very variety held an old-fashioned charm that Thea remembered from Winchcombe in particular. The Cotswolds were peopled by individualists, and had been for centuries. They didn't want to emulate their neighbours, but instead preferred their own property to stand out as especially lovely and therefore desirable.

The street itself was more like a country road that happened to have buildings along both sides. There were very few straight lines. There was a sense that traffic only came through on sufferance, and would be expected to stop for a loitering dog or child. Stanton was not on the way to anywhere, the residents would reason – and therefore only those with business in the village ought to visit. In summer there would be tourists in cars, but likely to be greatly outnumbered by walkers, with rucksacks and sticks and stout sensible boots. Stanton was in the books and on the maps as a detour for the Cotswold Way footpath. If you wanted to see it, you really ought to do it on foot.

Thea turned herself and the dogs around and dawdled back to the Shepherd house after twenty minutes or so of fresh air. To her surprise, this final leg of the little walk turned out to be a wholly different experience from the earlier part. As if responding to some inaudible call, people had emerged on all sides, and were gathered on the roadside in small groups or walking towards her. 'What's happening?' Thea muttered to the dogs in astonishment. Neither expressed an opinion.

On closer inspection it became apparent that the people were dressed more smartly than might be expected for an ordinary Friday afternoon. Long dark skirts, black suits, and even a woman in a boxy hat with a veil – 'My God! It's a funeral!' she finally realised. The population of Stanton was making its way towards the church where one of their number was to be despatched. As if in confirmation, just as she drew level with the Shepherds' house, the bell began to toll.

Dimly, she recollected that there had been a time when a village church bell would announce a death in coded form – indicating the age and gender of the deceased, so anyone hearing it would have a fair chance of guessing who had died. No such practice existed now, when telephones and emails and tweets could inform the world that the death had happened almost before the last breath had been exhaled. Except that Thea had no idea at all whose funeral it was, and whether she should care, and what if anything it might imply for the coming days.

She could hardly stop one of the townsfolk and ask. It wasn't her business, after all. She couldn't have known the person being disposed of. But the sense of exclusion was strong as she faced in the opposite direction from everybody else, and would be going into a house when they were all leaving theirs. There could have been no more powerful indication that she was an alien, an intruder, knowing nothing of recent events and what they might mean for the inhabitants. She thought of the woman Cheryl, leaving her car in a spot likely to be needed for a hearse, and was oddly gladdened by this suggestion that at least one other person had no idea what was happening.

She stood by the Shepherds' front door and watched the faces of the people walking towards her, and thought about tight village communities clustered around the church, and how they had existed for a thousand years and more. Here was a local brother, known to them all, dead in the deeps of winter – and they all suspended their busy lives to mark his passing. It was nicely medieval, she decided, particularly the way they were all proceeding on foot. And then, there were motor vehicles coming down the street. An unmistakable hearse, followed by two sleek black limousines, crawled along at walking pace. Thea had plenty of time to stare in through the car windows and make what she could of the chief mourners.

In the first car was a woman wearing a black hat and dark glasses. Obviously the widow. With her were two men in dark suits in their late twenties or early thirties, as well as a young woman. In the second car was another youngish couple with a boy who looked about ten. They all kept their eyes straight ahead and seemed not to be speaking to each other. Thea constructed a rapid family tree from what she had seen. The deceased was a man, in possession of probably three offspring, as well as partners in two cases, plus a single grandchild old enough to attend the ceremony. How had they divided up the seats in the limousines, she wondered? The little family in the second one gave the impression of lesser importance. Perhaps a daughter, rather than the two sons in the leading car. Or simply the fact of the young boy had ordained the separate limousine, in case there was a last-minute change of plan, or worries about what he might witness in the company of his grief-stricken grandmother and uncles. The coffin itself had been lavishly adorned with flowers, which was pleasing to Thea. It implied a burial rather than a cremation, and her acquaintanceship with Drew Slocombe had taught her that burials were infinitely preferable.

It was almost one o'clock, which was plainly the time scheduled for the start of the funeral. There were no more people on the main street – they had all turned the corner into the little road containing the church, and would be rapidly settling into the pews, ready for the procession up the aisle. Thea went into the house and released the dogs from their leads, hoping the walk would keep them satisfied for the rest of the day. The poop bags had remained unused. They could go out in the garden later on, just before it got dark, and then help her through the long evening to come. The fact of Christmas approaching so closely was more intrusive than she had expected. She had sent the usual twenty or thirty cards, and received a slightly lower number. More would arrive while she was away, and that now struck her as a shame. They would lie unopened until the last day of the year, by which time their message would be superfluous. They could be displayed for a week and then thrown away. Philip and Gloria, by contrast, were evidently hugely popular. In the face of all predictions that astronomical postage costs would kill the habit, the Shepherds had festooned their living room with cards. They were strung on slender silvery strings across the considerable space, from corner to corner of the large room, crossing in the middle. Idly, Thea counted them, finding the total to be an impressive one hundred and seventeen. And there would be yet more, no doubt.

There was no Christmas tree, however. Again, this struck Thea as a source of vague sadness. The previous year she had spent the festivities with her mother, and had not gone to the bother of setting up a tree in her own house. The trappings of Christmas died unwillingly, trailing so many associations, so much symbolism, hyped up so mercilessly by every commercial outfit in the land. Without it, the winter would seem much longer, the darkest days infinitely more depressing. With it, the obligations and expectations could give rise to their own sorrows when they failed to come up to scratch.

And just down the street there was a funeral service

going on for someone who had not survived to see this particular Christmas. Someone known to virtually everybody in Stanton, if the turnout was anything to go by. Likely to be a relatively young person, then. Thea's natural curiosity circled around the question of who it was who'd died. Had that Cheryl woman been planning to attend, first walking her dog and then leaving it in the car? Would there be a new grave in the churchyard, or were they driving off to the nearest crematorium after the service taking all those flowers with them? She thought, on balance, that a burial was more probable. With utter inevitability, thoughts of funerals led to thoughts of Drew Slocombe and his alternative burial ground in Somerset. Drew was an undertaker, albeit an unconventional one. He would like the picture of a whole community turning out to bid farewell to one of their number, on the shortest day of the year. He would draw meaning from it even now, after the death of his wife had shaken some of his deepest convictions.

The puzzle was solved in moments, at two o'clock that afternoon, when Thea came across a local paper from the previous week lying on an oak chest in the large hallway. It was folded over, with the lower half of the front page showing. 'LOCAL BUSINESSMAN FOUND DEAD' was the unimaginative headline over a lengthy report to follow. A quick perusal disclosed that a man by the name of Douglas Callendar, aged fifty-six, long-time resident of Stanton in Gloucestershire, father of three sons, had been found dead in his bath. Post-mortem investigation revealed that he had been electrocuted by a radio he had been in the habit of listening to in the bathroom. It was plugged in with an extension cord from the landing outside. His wife claimed to have warned him persistently that this was a dangerous thing to do, but he had insisted there was no risk. An expert in electrical accidents had confirmed to the police that only in the most rare and exceptional circumstances could a person be killed even if the radio were to fall into the water. It was a freakish thing to happen and Mr Callendar had been extremely unlucky. He was founder and managing director of Callendar Logistics, an international company dedicated to the transportation of urgent medical supplies. No foul play was suspected.

So that was that, Thea concluded. A silly accident, waiting to happen. A waste of a life that might easily have run another thirty years. Douglas had obviously been well liked, depended on for local employment and engaged in a business that nobody could find objectionable. The word 'businessman' conjured somebody worthy, slightly dull, comfortable amongst other men rather than women. All outrageous stereotypes, she felt sure, but persuasive just the same. She congratulated herself on having only the most limited acquaintance with anyone liable to be termed a businessman. Nobody could use the word to describe

Drew, for example, even if he did run a business. Her brother Damien was definitely no such thing. But neither Drew nor Damien would be daft enough to perch a radio on the side of the bath whilst it was plugged into the mains. Douglas Callendar must have really liked his music, or football reports, or reruns of old sitcoms, as he wallowed in the tepid water – itself a somewhat unpopular pursuit for men of his age, these days. How had the radio come to fall in, anyway? Had an errant cat jumped onto the side of the bath and sent it tumbling? Had the man fallen asleep and flailed his arms when he found himself almost submerged? And it seemed from the words of the expert that the radio would have had to be defective in some way for the current to escape its casing and flow lethally through the bathwater. Did the usual rules about making a circuit in order to create an electric shock not apply when water was involved? Had Callendar only died when he touched a tap or a handrail? Had it been a cast iron bath?

Such questions were meat and drink to Thea. She relished the vivid scenarios that her imagination conjured out of the few newspaper lines. She felt the cooling water, and then the sudden desperate shock of the electricity. She thought herself into the wife's shoes, perhaps hearing a splash and venturing cautiously into the room to discover its cause. Did the Callendars have their own bathrooms, his 'n' hers? Did Douglas lock her out while he took his bath? Did she try to revive him, or simply screech hysterically and dial 999?

Eventually, she caught herself up with a little shake. Such musings were unwholesome, and possibly disrespectful. There were elements to the story she found almost amusing. She could not pretend to be shocked or sorry, not knowing the man – nothing more than a gentle regret for the missing thirty years washed through her.

A yap from Hepzie drew her attention to the street outside. People had appeared, and were slowly walking up to the front door of the adjacent house, on the same side as the church, so they had no reason to pass by her window. But they milled around outside the door, so she had no trouble working out what was happening. Even so, she thought in frustration, a big bay window would have come in useful instead of the simple glazed hole in the facade of the house. On the whole, Cotswolds architects over the centuries had eschewed bay windows, which seemed to Thea rather a pity. She tried to catch sight of the owner of the Great Dane, at least, but could see no sign of her. Would such a large dog be welcomed as a guest, or would he remain for hours in the car?

The funeral party was adjourning to the house next door. That suggested that Douglas Callendar had lived there, and was therefore a close neighbour to the Shepherds. Had they not felt bad about missing the funeral? She remembered Philip's muttered reference to a Douglas, to be quickly hushed by his wife. As always, she felt the bafflement of knowing nothing about the interactions between the people she was amongst for the short spell of her house-sit. The newspaper had mentioned three sons – did that mean the new widow was delivering tea and sandwiches with the aid of daughters-in-law? How rotten it must be for her, so close to Christmas. Perhaps, when everybody had finally gone, Thea should approach her and offer some sympathy. She shook herself reproachfully at this notion. The woman would have plenty of people around, any of whom would do a better job than a strange house-sitter. The idea was ludicrous.

The stream of mourners took several minutes to get themselves inside the house. The loud chatter in the street could be heard through the closed window as the usual release that came after a funeral exerted its influence. *Douglas might be dead – but we're alive*, was the inevitable message flowing amongst them all. Not just alive, but still able to function. They'd escaped the reaper's scythe for the time being, and owed it to themselves, and even somehow to Douglas, to make the most of it.

Thea retreated to the kitchen at the back of the house and made herself a mug of tea. Hepzie pottered after her, as she always did, especially in a new place. 'Here we are again, then,' Thea said to her with a sigh. The spaniel gave a slow wag of agreement.

The first sip of tea was the precise moment when

it began. From one second to the next, she knew it was coming. Not just the taste, but the consistency, the momentary scratch that came from swallowing, the unavoidable awareness of her own throat. She was getting a cold! This had not happened for at least three years, but nobody could forget those insistent warning signs. Firmly, she resolved that it would be gone as quickly as it had come. She would turn up the heating and go to bed early, and in the morning it would have retreated under the unyielding resistance of its victim. Thea Osborne did not get ill. She had no patience with it. Besides – who would look after her if she did? As a house-sitter, she was obviously not allowed to be poorly.

She carried on with the allotted tasks as darkness fell, focusing on feeding generous quantities of top-quality tinned tripe to Blondie, and trying to get to know the rats. They came to the bars of their cage, whiskers quivering as they sniffed the new person who was meant to release them for their evening frolics. 'Sorry,' said Thea. 'I don't think I'm quite ready for it tonight.' The prospect of the creatures hiding from her, teasing their new custodian, like children with a supply teacher, was too nerve-wracking on the first day. 'Tomorrow, maybe we'll give it a go,' she promised. 'When you've got to know me better.' Having made sure the door to the room was closed, she unhooked the cage door and delivered a handful of the mixed corn they were to be fed. The darkest of the three animals put a small naked paw on her finger, in a gesture that seemed friendly. Cautiously, Thea stroked the dense coat, catching the intelligent eye and letting thoughts of vermin and Hamlyn and sewers sift through her mind. Rats were a good bet for long-term survival, after nuclear devastation or pandemics or another ice age had eradicated the humans from the world. They were organised, adaptable and cunning. They would eat anything and produced dozens of babies every year.

Her daughter's terror of them had come as a surprise. The incident when she was seven had involved little more than a wounded creature, mauled by a neighbour's dog, dragging itself pathetically over the grass in the Osbornes' garden, in Jessica's direction. The child's screams had brought people running from all directions. 'Take it away!' she had howled. 'It's after me.'

Carl had donned thick gardening gloves and scooped up the wretched animal. 'But Jess, it's poorly, look. It's been hurt. You should feel sorry for it.'

But the hysterical child shrieked and turned her back. 'Take it away!' she repeated. 'It's horrible.'

Carl, sensitive to the genuine fear, had disposed of the rat somehow, returning to his wife and daughter with a matter-of-fact air. 'Nothing to be scared of, sweetheart. You shouldn't let yourself get into such a state.' He and Thea had assumed his words would overcome the irrational reaction, only to find Jessica increasingly petrified as she grew up. She would never go into a shed or a cellar until someone had checked it first for rodents. She left the room if rats appeared on a TV programme. She went white at sounds of rustling or scuffling behind a skirting board.

'I rather like them,' Thea would always say, as if this would change anything. 'They're so intelligent, and clean and they've got lovely little faces.'

Despite her claims, even she found it a trifle unsettling that people could keep them as pets. Especially middle-class affluent Cotswolds people, who might be expected to regard rats as enemies in the struggle to maintain civilisation at all costs. Unsettling and mildly endearing. She liked the quirks and eccentricities of people when it came to relationships with animals. She had encountered geckoes, rabbits, a donkey, a snake and all the usual dogs and cats, in her house-sitting career. They all said something about their owners, and a quiet defiance of convention that pleased her. It was something she suspected Drew did not fully understand. Drew didn't really engage with animals, she had discovered. But then he had more than enough with his children and his house and his dead people.

The notion of going next door to volunteer her friendship in a time of sadness took another knock at the suspicion that a cold was starting. She knew from experience that sudden shocks were liable to lower a person's immunity. When Carl had died, she had developed a variety of minor ailments, including an outbreak of very unappealing acne. She had been tired and headachy for months. If the woman next door was anything like the same, a cold was all too likely to take advantage of her, given half a chance.

She reviewed her plans to seek out and join in with Christmas festivities in the village. By no means a churchgoer, she nonetheless relished a carol service, especially all the old favourites belted out with fervour. Whether she could face a Christmas lunch at The Mount Inn, at a table by herself, was a different matter. She was well provisioned for spending it in the house, if necessary. With the weather predicted to be nondescript – somewhat damp, perhaps, but no snow or ice or downpours or gales – she could take the dogs out for a good run, and savour her release from the routine rituals that had lost almost all their meaning for her when she was about sixteen.

But that was still four days away. First she had to dispel the cold germs, get to know the dog and the rats better, and perhaps read up on some local history.

It was six o'clock and dark when she heard someone at the back door. A muted thump, followed by a gentle voice calling, 'Hello? Can I come in?' Before Thea could push Hepzie off her lap and step over Blondie, the voice had come closer. 'Gloria – you there?'

'Who's that?' She wasn't scared, but she did feel a surging irritation. It was extraordinarily rude of this person to just march in without an invitation. If she was such an intimate friend that this was acceptable, then surely she knew that Gloria and Philip had gone away. And why hadn't somebody thought to lock the door?

'It's me, Juliet.' A soft laugh concluded this introduction, and a tall slender figure came into the room. 'Oh!' She stared in evident terror at Thea, but made no move to flee. Afterwards, Thea could not have precisely identified what it was that alerted her to this woman's condition, but she knew within seconds that there was something askew. The grey eyes that met hers contained panic, but over that lay a sort of resignation, as if fear and unpredictability were the natural order, only to be expected.

'Hello, my name's Thea Osborne,' she said calmly. 'I only got here today. Did Gloria not tell you about me?'

'Th-Thea,' stammered the woman. 'Oh.' She stared around the room. 'Is there a man with you?'

'No.'

'Good.'

'Where do you live, Juliet?' Aiming for a natural relaxed tone, Thea found herself speaking stiltedly, and wondering frantically what she was supposed to do.

'I live in Laverton.' She smiled at the assonance, moving her tongue as if tasting it again. 'With my mother. We went to the funeral this afternoon, you see. A fiendish funeral, with tears and tantrums. Poor Eva has died. Do you know Eva?'

Thea shook her head in confusion, thrown by the mixture of ordinary conversation and rogue lapses of

44

logic. 'I thought it was a man who died. Mr Callendar.'

Juliet frowned. 'No, it was Eva. She was my cousin and she had cystic fibrosis, the poor girl. Makes you question it all, don't you think?'

'Did she live in the house next to this one?'

'Oh, no, she didn't.' Another frown and then a careful laugh, as if there might be a joke somewhere that she'd missed.

'Was her funeral in the house next door?'

'Of course not.' Again a flash of suspicion. 'What do you mean? It was in the church. How can you have a funeral in a house?'

Thea understood that she had worded her question badly, and that her curiosity was undoubtedly misplaced anyway. 'You're quite right, of course. I meant the gathering afterwards. A lot of people came to the house next to this one, this afternoon, in funeral clothes.'

'Did they? Two funerals, then. Eva was buried in Willersey which is five miles from here. They're Methodists, you know. Very devout people. They actually believe in God. Don't you think that's strange, when science shows us so plainly that such a thing is impossible?'

'Well . . .' Thea was struggling to remain relaxed, to overcome the atavistic fear of insanity that she had not thought existed in herself. Juliet was in her thirties, at least. She was very unlikely to present any danger. She was clearly intelligent. She was also beautiful, with a long Pre-Raphaelite face and very pale skin. She looked delicate and insubstantial, both mentally and physically.

'No, but *don't you?*' she repeated urgently.

Thea floundered, quite unprepared for a theological discussion. 'I think science leaves quite a lot yet to be explained,' she ventured.

Juliet's face brightened. 'You're right!' she applauded. 'I was thinking about the flowers. Everybody sent flowers. Red ones, from Africa. Tulips. Roses. Lilies. They all mean something to people. But they're false as well – do you see? Because they're grown indoors and flown here on planes, and kept alive artificially. And I thought – they're the same as religion.' She lifted her chin triumphantly, as if waiting for an accolade. 'They'll just lie there on the grave until they rot. And that'll be the end of it.'

Thea felt weak. The woman's words contained plenty of sense, but the delivery was too forceful for the occasion, the facial expression not in balance with the words. 'Does your mother know you're here?' She tried a new topic in cowardly desperation.

Juliet shrugged. 'I'm later today, because of the funeral,' she explained. Her accent was pure cut-glass Queen's English, reminiscent of female newsreaders from the 1950s. Thea felt irritation towards the Shepherds, who had not mentioned the probability of this visitor, who was implying that she showed up every afternoon.

'It's dark now,' she noted. 'Perhaps you'd better go home.'

'No, not yet. I can't go yet, can I? I haven't played with the girls.'

'Um . . . ?'

'Sally and Maisie and Petulia. *You* know.' She waved an arm at the door into the room at the back of the house. 'I always come and play with them.'

'Oh!' Light dawned. 'You mean the rats. But Gloria never said anything. She never told me they had a friend.' Juliet ignored this. 'What exactly do you usually do with them?'

'As I said – I play with them. But now it's so late, it must be their supper time. Will you allow me to feed them?'

'Actually, I've already done them,' said Thea. 'But you can go and talk to them, I suppose. Just don't let my dog in with them. I'm not sure what she might do.'

Only then did the visitor give the spaniel any attention. 'A spaniel,' she nodded. 'Cocker spaniel. Blue roan. Long tail. Mum wouldn't like that. They really shouldn't have a long tail. It ruins the look of them.'

'They don't dock them so much these days. There are boxers and rottweilers and all sorts with long tails now.'

'All wrong,' dismissed Juliet. 'They look ridiculous.'

This normal-sounding exchange came as a slight reassurance to Thea. Her initial unease began to abate. 'Shall I make some tea?' she offered.

The frown returned. 'Would it be too much to ask you to make some hot chocolate? It's rather a habit with me and Gloria. I think you'll find some in the kitchen.'

'Okay,' said Thea slowly. 'Made with milk or water?'

'Milk,' said Juliet firmly. 'Now I'll see the girls.' She went through to the rats' room, closing the door behind her.

Thea stared after her, aware of a growing resentment at not having been told of this woman's existence. It was a gross oversight on the part of the Shepherds, by any standards. Was this going to become a daily occurrence? And was Juliet to be trusted with the rats? Blondie had effectively ignored her, which suggested a bored familiarity. And how was she going to get rid of her?

Before even more unsettling questions could arise, there was a brief tentative rap on the front-door knocker, as if a finger had delicately lifted and dropped it. Blondie heard it loud and clear, however, and sat up sharply, giving a staccato bark and kinking her ears forward.

'Stay here,' Thea ordered both the dogs, and shut them in the living room. The sense of a series of closed doors, protecting animals from each other and people from them all, made her sigh. She opened the front door slowly, bracing herself for whatever might happen next.

A woman of perhaps seventy stood there, face creased with emotion. 'Oh, sorry,' she breathed. 'But I wonder if you've seen my daughter? She comes here sometimes. We were at a funeral, and—'

'Juliet,' said Thea. 'Yes, she's in with the rats. She asked me to make her some hot chocolate.'

'Oh, my goodness. I'm *so* sorry. What must you think? She hasn't done this for *ages*. It's the funeral, you see, upsetting everything.'

'Don't worry. There's no problem. It's just . . .' she tailed off at the woman's expression. 'What? What's the matter?'

'We try to keep her away from the rats. They set her off, sometimes. You can understand it, can't you?' The woman had a pleading expression. 'One minute they're just cute furry pets and then they suddenly seem so sinister. And Juliet's very sensitive to that sort of thing. Especially today, with the funeral . . .' She heaved a profound sigh, as if it was all too much for her.

'Well, come in and sort it out, will you?' Thea felt tired and helpless, a mere onlooker in some complex drama that made scarcely any sense.

The woman slowly entered the house and went directly to the back room, evidently quite familiar with the layout of the house. 'Juliet?' she called in a voice that suggested more authority than had first been apparent. 'Come on out of there. You're not supposed to be here, are you?' When there was no response, she went into the room. Thea stayed back, hoping she would not have to do anything.

There ensued a muted anguished argument in the rats' living room that set Blondie whining in the doorway and Hepzie slinking cravenly behind the sofa. Thea forced herself to go and see what was happening. Juliet, with a rat held tenderly on her forearm, fingers entwined with its tail, became incoherent, quoting lines of poetry and casting her gaze to the sky like a rather exasperated medieval saint, with her mother chivvying her, for all the world like a harassed helpless mother in a supermarket, afraid to shout at, least of all smack, her recalcitrant offspring. There was an unreality to it that set Thea's teeth on edge and her stomach churning. Juliet presented a tragic figure, with the light of reason now increasingly unsteady behind her eyes. Thea feared for the Royal Worcester if Juliet made any wild movements, as seemed all too possible. The presence of her mother had dramatically knocked her off balance, making Thea wonder whether the whole genesis of the trouble lay in the relationship between the two. *It's always the mother's fault* came a rueful little voice in her head. Cruel and unfair as it might be, there was an irresistible truth to it. Who else had the power to drive their child into madness? God, she supposed. Or genetics. The same thing in essence, she suspected. Either way, it absolved the parent, which was doubtless a good thing.

She caught herself up, aware that she was echoing some of Juliet's own disjointed lines of thought. Did her mother refuse to engage with any of her musings? Did she mock and dismiss and belittle, as mothers tended to do? Whatever the facts of it, she had had enough.

'Listen to me,' she said loudly, standing in the open doorway, not caring if rats escaped or got eaten by dogs. 'I'm in charge of this house, and I don't think either of you should be here. Please go now. Both of you.'

It worked like a miracle. Juliet fell silent, and carefully replaced the rat she was holding into its cage. 'Good girl, Petulia,' she breathed.

'Right,' said Thea. 'That's right. Thank you.'

The older woman was red-faced and breathing hard. She headed grimly for the front door, not looking to see if her daughter was following.

'Eva died,' Juliet remembered. 'Poor Eva.' She tilted her head. 'But she's better dead, isn't she, Mummy? That's what you said. Sometimes it's better to be dead.' There was rage and reproach and challenge in her voice.

Her mother ignored her. 'Thank you for being so understanding,' she said to Thea. 'My name is Rosa Wilson. We live in Laverton. It's been a difficult day.'

'Was that not your relative's funeral, next door?' Thea could not help but ask. 'I saw there was a big service on at the church, and then everybody came back here. It looked like a good turnout.'

'Oh, no.' Rosa confirmed Juliet's information. 'That was something quite different.' Her lips grew thin and pinched. 'That was a man called Callendar. Nobody bothered themselves about our little tragedy.'

'Juliet said it was in Willersey. I'm afraid I've never heard of Willersey.'

'It's only a small place.'

51

'Well, I'm sorry for your loss,' Thea said tritely.

Juliet followed her mother out of the house, giving occasional twitches of her head, as if conducting an internal argument. 'I am so very sorry,' said Rosa again, on the threshold. 'As you can see – Juliet goes her own way whenever she can.' She gave her daughter a vindictive look.

'Don't worry about it,' said Thea wearily. She did not add any softening remarks about seeing them again or being pleased to meet them. When they'd gone, she went straight to the back door and very decisively locked it.

Chapter Three

She felt obliged to check that the rats had not suffered any ill effects from Juliet's attentions, and such was her relief to find them alert and apparently in good spirits that she gave them a handful more of their corn before bidding them goodnight. Three whiskery faces lined up behind the bars of the cage and tried to persuade her that they really needed exercise, and should be released for their evening run without delay. 'Sorry,' said Thea. 'I can't face it just now. I don't feel strong enough.' Her headache had got worse in the past ten minutes, and she had a nasty feeling she might be running a temperature.

She had eaten scarcely anything all day, but the prospect of food was not appealing. 'Maybe some soup,' she muttered to herself. Amongst her extravagant supermarket purchases there had been no fewer than four packets of soup mix. Onion, minestrone, mushroom and leek offered themselves. Mushroom, she decided and poured the powder into a pan with a pint of water. Easy cooking, which had become more and more of a habit since Carl had died. The idea of making a cake or pie from scratch had never even crossed her mind in the past few years. Not so long ago, she had managed to burn a shop-bought pie to a cinder when attempting to provide Drew with a meal. Definitely not the way to impress a chap – although he hadn't seemed to think much the worse of her as a result.

A cold was always worse in the evenings, she told herself. By next morning, she'd feel much better and be ready to go out and discover what Christmas jollity was on offer in the village. With the two funerals out of the way, people would be focusing on their family get-togethers and the last-minute shopping. And if she was still suffering a bit, she could simply turn up the heating and snuggle with the dogs, earning money for doing hardly anything.

The soup was soon ready and she poured it into a big cup she found, designed specifically for the purpose. It was warming and easy to swallow, but it did nothing to diminish the headache. Never needing to take pills, she had no paracetamol or codeine in her luggage. What was the protocol, she wondered, of raiding people's medicine cabinet in search of analgesia? Not really the done thing, she concluded. The best treatment would be an early night, anyway.

Hepzibah could keep her feet warm, as always, and all would be well next day.

It turned out to be a restless night. When she did sleep there were dreams involving escaping rats, hundreds of them, swarming down Stanton's main street and over the thatched roofs. In the dreams, she was oddly wet, as she tried to catch rats in a big fishing net. When she woke it was to realise she was drenched in sweat, and her knees were aching. *How funny*, she thought, *why my knees?*, before drifting off again into another nightmare world of clanging church bells and great swooping birds that pecked at the top of her head.

When she finally surfaced, the sky outside was still dark and her head still ached. It was half past seven. 'Damn it, Heps,' she mumbled. 'I think I must have got flu.'

Her initial reaction was anger. Those germ-ridden people in the supermarket must be responsible. She, Thea Osborne, who never got ill, had been wantonly contaminated by thoughtless Christmas shoppers. And now what was she meant to do? The anger morphed into mild panic, which she fought off determinedly. Getting out of bed, she tried to assess her condition. Not so very bad, really. She could walk and dress herself. She'd be able to let the dogs out into the garden at the back, if no further afield. She'd get them their food and see that the rats got theirs. She'd be better in a couple of days, in any case. It wasn't such a big deal. Except that everything seemed to *ache*. Head, knees, back, shoulders – they all felt heavy and sensitive and sore.

Outside there were people who would surely lend her a hand if she asked them. All she would have to do was stand at the front door and shout, if things got seriously bad. Which they wouldn't, of course. Women everywhere were valiantly making mince pies and wrapping presents, even if they did have a temperature of a hundred and a crashing headache. Once she could find herself some painkillers she'd be all right, and maybe a bottle of whisky, lemons, honey . . . she wilted at the list. None of those things would be obtainable in Stanton. She would have to drive somewhere – Broadway probably – and get them all. Well, so be it. Driving was easy. And at least she wasn't sweating any more. If anything, she felt rather cold.

She gave no more thought to the electrocuted Callendar or the Eva woman with her cystic fibrosis. An accident and a fatal condition – the normal causes of death that brought sadness and reproaches but not the desperate depth of feeling that came when there was a murder. She had had entirely too much close experience of murder in the past few years. People persistently took advantage of the changed circumstances that involved a house-sitter being in residence – or else her own deplorable curiosity led her into trouble, where another person might cheerfully have let it all pass her by without any sort of involvement.

Breakfast was minimal. Even the coffee tasted

horrible and left an acid residue in her mouth. The sore throat had abated slightly, to be replaced by sporadic pains in her armpits. For a crazy moment she wondered if she had the plague, with buboes developing. Anything seemed possible in her reduced state. Delirium could set in at any time.

Outside it was still not properly light. Thick cloud hung just above the hilltops that surrounded the village. She could see no people at all out in the street. Not too surprising when she realised it was only eight-thirty on a Saturday morning. There were at least five work-free days ahead for most people, which ought to give even the most dedicated celebrator of Christmas more than enough time to get everything done, without leaping out of bed before the sun was up. Even so, it made Thea feel lonely, there in a strange village where she knew nobody and nobody cared about her.

The headache made it difficult to think clearly. It hurt all over, like one big bruise. Perhaps the so-called flu epidemic was actually something much more serious, and all the people of Stanton were lying dead and dying in their beds, in a cataclysmic outbreak of a deadly contagion. All sorts of extreme trouble seemed possible in the absence of any evidence of normality.

Moving around proved to be slightly therapeutic. She let Blondie and Hepzie out into the garden and noted that they both relieved themselves. Neither seemed especially eager for a long hilltop walk, which was fortunate. The Alsatian disappeared behind a screen of

57

bamboo at the end of the garden, which Thea hoped meant further lavatory arrangements had been attended to. The animals might have a boring day ahead of them, but at least the floors should remain unsullied.

Time moved jerkily. It took hours to reach nine o'clock, and then suddenly it was twenty to eleven. If she was going out, she ought to get on with it. Traffic would be heavy, parking difficult, shops crowded. Well-stocked little local groceries were very thin on the ground these days, put out of business by the supermarkets. No way was Thea going to tackle another supermarket. She could all too vividly imagine herself passing out in the aisles and being rushed off to hospital.

Muzzily, she remembered a substantial garage shop on the outskirts of Blockley, about six miles away, and decided she should aim for that. If whisky proved unavailable, she would raid the Shepherds' stocks and confess when they came home. There was a modest shelf of bottles in a cabinet in the rats' room, which Gloria had shown her on the initial explanatory visit.

After a brief deliberation, she decided to leave both dogs in the house. If she had an accident due to her headache, it would be better for them not to be aboard. In the event, driving turned out to be much as usual, all the necessary instincts taking over, and a painful head no impediment. The lanes were quiet, contrary to expectation. She drove south, through Stanway, to the 4077 and turned left, thinking that took her eastwards. She should then take another left turn towards

Snowshill, and locate the road into Blockley that she could clearly remember.

But something went wrong. The 4077 was not very familiar to her, and she found herself gazing about, driving at a crawl, wondering what Cutsdean was like, and then spotting a sign pointing to the right, saying Temple Guiting. She knew Temple Guiting, but had not realised how close it was to Stanway. Perhaps, she thought, she should go there instead, and patronise the community-run shop that would at least have honey and lemons for sale. Before she could decide, she had somehow overshot the turning, and was carrying on eastwards. The road ran straight for two or three miles and her speed increased. The throbbing in her head was affecting her sight, with spots of silvery light flickering crazily like sparklers going off inside her eyes. It had been difficult to turn her neck when she looked both ways at the only road junction she had so far negotiated, because something at the base of her skull was painful.

'I'm really quite poorly,' she muttered aloud. It was frightening, but also slightly exciting. She was in the grip of a drama of a new kind, with a wholly unpredictable outcome. She would have to dig deep for her own inner resources. She would have to be sensible and stoical, because there was nobody around to help her.

She had to turn left, though. She should already have turned left. There was a map on the back seat, but she couldn't reach it. She didn't think she'd be able to focus on it anyway. The yellows and browns of the roads, the dotted greens of the footpaths and the thin black lines that outlined every blessed field would all swirl around in a mocking travesty that would leave her stranded in Burford or Stratford without a moment's warning.

And then there was a little crossroads, with a sign pointing to a trout farm to the left, and for no good reason, she took it. It had to lead northwards, and Blockley was definitely to the north – even though she could hardly remember now why she'd wanted Blockley to start with. Doggedly she followed the road, which was neither too narrow nor too twisting for comfort, so was a perfectly good road, as roads went, at least for the first mile. Then it indulged in a little wobble, with bends that required concentration, and then, with criminally inadequate warning, it deposited her at a T-junction with a big road full of speeding traffic. A sign informed her that it was the A424, and offered her the choice of Broadway to the left or Stow-on-the-Wold to the right.

This could be what she'd wanted, she supposed. Wasn't this the road that took you to Blockley? Or had she got Blockley and Broadway confused? She shook her head. No, of course she hadn't. They might look similar when written down, but they were *completely* different as places. She didn't like Broadway. But was she safe on a busy main road? A car behind her tooted questioningly, forcing her to take a deep breath and turn left.

Once again instinct took over and she covered a mile

or two without incident, despite a growing difficulty with her sight. Shards of silvery light were flashing chaotically before her eyes, apparently all part of the persistent headache that plagued her. When she turned her head at the junction, her neck hurt even more than before. She repeated her shopping list to herself: *lemons, honey, whisky, painkillers*. It seemed insuperably difficult to remember, and even more so to actually obtain the goods.

Suddenly there was a petrol station approaching on her left. Perhaps this was the one she'd been aiming for all along. In any case, didn't they all have some kind of shop attached, these days? Probably, if she'd had any sense, she could have found one a lot closer to Stanton in the first place. But now she was here, she could top up with fuel as well, even though the tank was still showing nearly half full. Never waste an opportunity, as Carl would have advised her.

Jerkily she indicated and pulled off the road, drawing up beside the pumps. Her body felt heavy and uncooperative as she crawled out of the car and grabbed the nearest nozzle. *Lemon, honey, whisky, pills*, she muttered. If there weren't any fresh lemons, she might find some juice, or Lemsip or something. The motor whirred as fuel gushed into her hungry tank, and before she knew it the sum owing had reached forty pounds.

'Oops!' she said. 'That's plenty.' It was more than she would usually spend on filling up, she thought crossly. They must have put the prices up for Christmas. Normally, half a tank would come to much less than that.

There was a small shop, as hoped, with local honey on offer and a selection of analgesia. No whisky, though. 'Have you got any lemons?' she asked the girl behind the desk.

'Sorry.'

'Lemsip?'

A languid finger pointed at a distant shelf. Thea couldn't understand why the stuff wasn't kept with the aspirin and paracetamol, until she realised it was actually the same shelf from which she had taken a pack of pills a minute earlier. Clutching her purchases to her chest, she fished in the bag she had luckily remembered to bring with her and extracted her purse.

Remembering her bank card number was another exhausting challenge, but it all went through, and she returned to her car with a sense of triumph. All she had to do now was retrace her steps and get back to the sanctuary of the house in Stanton.

The road was still busy and her neck still hurt, but she pulled out into a brief lull and set off southwards, wondering how in the world she would recognise the little right turn into the road that took her back to the 4077. No matter, she told herself. She would find it from Stow if necessary. She remembered the complicated junction where you had to do a sort of zigzag, right, then quickly left. It would take her through one of the

Swells, Upper or Lower, she wasn't sure which. In a welcome moment of clarity, she could visualise the route in surprising detail.

But she found the little turning, after all. She turned into it, recognising a bare oak tree beside a gateway a hundred yards along. She would have no difficulty from here on. She would take two painkillers and raid Philip's drinks cabinet and sweat it out. It was sure to be better next day. By Christmas Eve, two whole days away, she'd be thoroughly back to normal.

At first she thought the juddering came from her, and not the car's engine. But the truth was quickly apparent. It coughed and slowed, and gave every impression of a dying horse as she kicked down on the accelerator. In a narrow stretch of road, with a blind bend only a few yards ahead, her car came to a decisive halt. She turned off the ignition and then on again. It fired and caught, and she felt a wary optimism. But when she put it in gear and released the clutch, it merely gasped and stalled. *Perhaps this is a dream*, she thought. If it was real, then she was in danger of some vehicle coming round the bend and hitting her. Even travelling at thirty miles an hour, it would be hard-pressed to stop in time. *Thank goodness I haven't got the dogs with me*, she thought next.

In her purse somewhere was a card issued by the AA. There was also a mobile phone in the bag. She had all the modern necessities for getting out of a crisis with minimal inconvenience. All she had to do was call the number on the card and report her situation. A kind man in a truck would appear and either mend the car or tow her home. *First things first*, said her inner voice, and she took the pack of painkillers from the front passenger seat and opened it. It wasn't easy to swallow the tablets without any water to wash them down, but she did it. They left a bitter tangy aftertaste that was at first revolting and then oddly pleasant. If she could quell the headache, everything would be very much less complicated.

Then she tried to make the phone call. There was a long number across the middle of the card, which she carefully keyed into her phone. When nothing happened, she did it again. Only on the third try did she realise she was using her membership number and not the 0800 telephone number that appeared in even larger figures on the back of the card. An automated message eventually filtered through to her throbbing head, to the effect that all operatives were busy, but they would attend to her at the very earliest opportunity. The voice told her that if she was in danger of being struck by traffic, she should leave the car and stand well clear of it. That made sense, and she got out of the car, thinking how lucky she was not to have been killed already.

At last a real person spoke to her. She had to give her name and membership number, plus mobile number and car registration. Then she had to try to explain where she was and what the trouble was with the car. 'It just conked out,' she said. 'For no reason at all.'

Directions to the exact spot turned out to be infinitely more difficult. A small country road off the A424, to the west, leading down to the A4077, seemed clear enough to Thea, but the person on the phone thought differently. 'Haven't you got a *map*?' Thea demanded. 'It should be obvious, from what I've told you.' The effort had drained her, and she felt tears of frustration lurking somewhere.

The woman made soothing noises and asked a few more questions. When it was ascertained that she was there on her own, as well as leaving little or no space for other traffic to pass, she was promised priority attention. She would be called back with an estimated time of arrival, but should expect someone to be there within the hour.

That wasn't good enough by a long way, to Thea's mind, but it would have to do. Unless she walked back to the main road, scarcely a quarter of a mile distant, and tried to flag down a likely rescuer, she was doomed to a nervous wait in the cold, afraid to sit in the car in case something came along and hit it. *I'll probably die out here*, she thought melodramatically. *One way or another.* The pills had not made any discernible difference to her headache, and the way she felt, death was not such a terrible prospect.

The bare hedges on either side of her bordered featureless fields, with no sign of habitation. Patches of woodland on skewed hillsides were visible away to the right, where she guessed Snowshill must be.

She remembered abrupt ridges and sweeping stretches of fairly level ground on the approach road to that village. Little roads ran in every direction, making it all too easy to get lost. She had been there in summer, everything green and lush. Now it was bare and brown and she was put in mind of her stay in Hampnett, when it had snowed and she had been scared. That was a year ago now, and she had never gone back there. Perhaps she should have done, to check on the poor mindless dog she'd taken care of, and the inscrutable donkey.

She slapped her hands together, although she wasn't cold. This had been an easy winter so far, with no hint of snow and hardly any ice. Her own internal thermostat was badly misbehaving, and she could feel sweat running down her body under the three layers of clothes. When she touched her face, it was clammy – the skin warm under a layer of chilly moisture. She should have told the AA woman she was ill. It hadn't crossed her mind to do so.

She heard the approaching car from some distance away, but her slow wits prevented her from acting until it was too late. She should have gone to the bend, and waved them down. That's where she should have been standing from the start; it was obvious now. They'd come round it at forty miles an hour and hit her poor little Astra, as it sat there so helplessly. The driver would shout at her. There might be a small child on the back seat, thrown against its restricting belt and damaged. Ever since she'd been obliged to strap Jessica into a confining contraption, she'd had a vision of a neatly quartered infant, sliced up by the beastly constraints when the car hit something unmoving and sent physics into a new cosmos where none of the usual rules applied. Or perhaps there would be a dog, not restrained at all, sitting up tall on the passenger seat and mashed face first against the windscreen. The visions flashed feverishly through her mind in the seconds before the vehicle came into view.

'Stop!' she called uselessly. 'Oh, *stop*.'

It did, with a generous six inches to spare.

Chapter Four

By some dreamlike chance, it proved to be a police car. Not only that, but she recognised the man in the passenger seat. 'Higgins!' she gasped. 'Jeremy Higgins.'

He frowned uncertainly up at her through the car's open window. 'Um . . .' he began, before realisation dawned. 'Mrs Osborne!' he remembered. 'Lower Slaughter . . . your sister . . .'

'That's right,' she laughed, wanting to hug him. 'And Phil Hollis. Don't worry – it's okay to mention that. It's been more than a year now.'

The ginger-haired, bull-necked Detective Inspector got out of the car. 'Is this yours?' he indicated to the Astra.

She nodded ruefully. 'It conked out. The AA are coming.'

'We can't leave it here. Kevin – come and help me push,' he ordered the uniformed officer in the driving seat. 'What's wrong with it anyway?' he asked Thea.

'I have no idea. It was fine – and then it just died. I'm staying in Stanton,' she added helpfully.

Jeremy went to the front of the car and peered in at the scatter of shopping, purse and bag on the front seat. 'Just died, eh?' he murmured, sniffing the air. 'With no warning?' He straightened and looked at her. 'Is that a garage receipt I can see? Did you just fill her up?'

'Yes. At the garage on the main road, a mile or two away.'

'Does your car take diesel?'

'What? No – it's unleaded. Oh!' She put a horrified hand to her mouth. 'No! Surely I can't have been so stupid. I wasn't thinking. My head – I'm not very well, actually. But – oh, God – what happens now? How did you know?'

'I *am* a detective,' he grinned at her. 'I can smell diesel, can't you? It'll have to be towed to a workshop and drained. That's a job for the AA. Have they said they'll take you home afterwards?'

'I think so. Isn't that what they do? I've never called them before.' She had a thought. 'But I don't want to go home. They have to take me to Stanton.'

'You'll be in trouble without the car, if you're house-sitting,' he observed. 'With Christmas coming.' He looked at her more closely. 'And you're ill, are you? What's the problem?'

'Flu, I think,' she said miserably. 'My head's killing me and everything aches. And I'm all hot and cold.'

'We'll have to sort you out, then,' said the kindly man. Thea recalled how gentle he had been with her in Lower Slaughter, and how he probably knew much more about her than she realised. 'I'll have a word with the AA people and then we'll take you back to Stanton, and let the mechanic chap deal with the car as quick as he can. He'll probably just tow it to a garage.'

'That's very nice of you,' she said. 'Thanks.'

'First we'll have to move it. There'll be a pile-up if we're not careful.' Higgins issued instructions to the wordless Kevin, and within two minutes the Astra was on the narrow verge and the police car had reversed around the bend to provide ample warning of an obstruction. They had scarcely finished before a blue Transit van materialised and had to be helped through the narrow gap between Thea's car and the opposite hedge. Then a phone in the police car warbled and Kevin hurried to respond. He briefly reported their rescue mission, and told the DI, 'We're wanted in Broadway, but no great rush.'

Higgins nodded, and addressed Thea. 'Get in,' he ordered. 'It's cold out here.'

The car was snug and airless, with a male smell that Thea could detect even through her virus-ridden senses. Coffee, clothes, self-importance. Even the benign Higgins could not avoid this last. People were at his mercy, whether he liked it or not. Within seconds she was huddled in a corner of the back seat and her eyelids were drooping. Somebody else was in charge now. It felt like heaven.

She was faintly aware of Higgins walking back round the bend to her car, talking as he went. He seemed to be gone for some minutes, while Kevin sat stolidly in the driving seat, saying nothing, for which she was grateful. She sank into a mindless state, waiting passively for whatever might happen next.

A door closed with a muted thunk, then the car reversed and turned in a wider part of the lane, bumping slightly on a muddy rut. 'Makes you think of Lower Slaughter, doesn't it?' said Higgins, looking over his shoulder at her.

The events they had shared had involved a muddy country road, it was true, but Thea couldn't see any real connection. 'Mmm,' she said.

'Hey! Don't go to sleep on me,' he said sharply. 'It's bad enough waking my kids when they go off in the car. A grown woman with flu would be a lot worse.'

'You'll get my germs,' she mumbled. 'Just in time for Christmas.'

'Occupational hazard,' laughed Higgins, but Kevin gave a sort of squawk and started to lower the window beside him. 'Stop it, Kev,' said the detective. 'If you get it, you get it. There's not a lot you can do about it.'

'So what's the Stanton story?' he pressed Thea. 'Nice house, is it?'

'Average. A lovely big dog. Rats.'

'What? Where?'

'In a cage. Pet ones. One of them's called Petulia.'

'And the dog doesn't eat them?'

'Nope.'

'Man near Stanton died. In his bath,' volunteered Kevin. 'Silly fool.'

'I saw it in the paper,' Thea agreed. 'I'm in the next-door house.'

'No, no, that can't be right. Doug Callendar lived halfway up a hill in a mansion, with no neighbours for a mile in any direction,' Higgins corrected her.

'Oh.' She forced her mind to work. 'But the funeral was next door. I saw all the people. Yesterday.'

'Blimey!' laughed Kev. 'So the girlfriend got her way, then.'

The others were silent for a moment. Then 'Explain,' Higgins encouraged.

'Come on, sir. You know the story. Everybody this side of Oxford must know about it by this time. Callendar's wife is Marian Callendar the magistrate. He lived with her, but he's also got – had, I mean – a girlfriend in a house in Stanton. Bold as brass he was, making no secret of it. Marian's always put a brave face on it, making her own life and getting all her rightful perks as the wife. When he died, all the talk was whether they'd both sit up at the front for the funeral. Surely you've heard about it?'

'Sorry. Unless there's a crime I mostly ignore gossip.'

'You shouldn't,' said Thea softly. 'Stuff like that

often leads to crime. And it certainly explains a lot, after a crime has happened.'

'You think the wife – a very respectable woman, I might add, who I do know rather well – bumped him off?' Higgins grinned at her. 'You would think that, I suppose.'

She tried to summon some protestation. 'What do you mean?'

'Well, you're very often around when something like that happens. It must make you suspect foul play every time a bloke dies. Worse than a copper, you are.'

It felt very unfair. 'I'm not,' she said childishly. 'I never said anything about the wife killing the man in the bath. That was you, not me.'

'The question is – did Marian go to the wake at the girlfriend's?' Kevin summarised. 'You know what women are like – they'll surprise you every time. You never know, they're probably best buddies now.'

'Could be they bumped him off together, then, and shared out the loot. Plenty of it, from the sound if it,' said Higgins, belatedly entering into the spirit of the conversation.

'Nearly there,' Kevin alerted them. 'This is Stanway.'

'Stanton, not Stanway,' said Thea.

'Right. I know that. But there's barely half a mile between them. Look at that place!' He slowed as they passed the elaborate entrance gate to Stanway House, with the church modestly set back behind and to one side of it. 'Ever been in there, sir?' he asked Higgins.

'Once, years ago. Don't remember much about it.'

'It's got lots of history,' said Thea, struggling to focus.

'I prefer the cricket pavilion,' said Higgins, bizarrely.

Thea wondered if she was momentarily dreaming. 'Pardon?' she said.

'Haven't you seen it? You must have driven past it. It's here, look.' He pointed out a large wooden shed on the edge of a big field, with handsome old trees standing guard over it.

'I didn't notice,' she said. 'When I'm better, I'll come for a look.'

'You do that. Oy, Kev – watch out for the great hound.' Walking along the side of the road was the dog Thea had seen outside Stanton church the day before, with its woman holding it on a short chain.

'It's a Great Dane,' she said. 'I met that woman. Sherry, she's called. Something like that. She doesn't like Blondie.'

'Blondie's a dog?' checked Higgins.

'Right. I wonder if she did go to the funeral. She was dressed for it. But what about the dog?'

'You're delirious,' Higgins said kindly. 'The sooner we get you indoors, the better.'

'Oh! I forgot my shopping. And my bag. Oh, damn it.' She almost wept at the thought of the honey and Lemsip left behind in her car.

'No, you didn't. I've got them here. And I phoned the AA for you, telling them what's what. They should manage to see to everything without you being there, even though it's against their usual practice. I pulled a few strings. They've got your mobile number, so they'll keep you informed of what's going on. I hope,' he added almost inaudibly.

Thea blinked in bewilderment. How had she missed all that? 'Oh,' she said. 'Thank you. That's fantastic.'

'You'll be hungry,' he went on. 'It's well past lunchtime.'

'No, it isn't. I set out early. I'm sure I did. It must be only a bit after eleven.'

'It's half past one,' he corrected. 'These dark days, it feels like dawn at nine in the morning. I bet it was after eleven before you even left the house.'

'Could be,' she said dubiously, trying to remember. 'But I'm not hungry.'

'Feed a cold and starve a fever,' said Kevin, still eyeing the massive dog in his rear-view mirror. 'Isn't that what they say? If it's half one, we ought to be in Broadway soonish,' he added.

'What's in Broadway?' asked Thea, thinking she'd missed something else of significance.

'Some bit of bother at the Methodist church. Flowers missing from a grave, would you believe?'

'Willersey, not Broadway, to be completely accurate,' said Kevin.

'Another funeral,' Thea mused. 'Eva. That'll be Eva. How can people steal flowers? That's beastly.'

'Beastly,' echoed Higgins in a gentle mockery.

76

'Perfectly beastly. What do you mean – that'll be Eva?'

'I had a visit yesterday from her relations. Aunt and cousin, I think.'

Higgins hooted in disbelief and astonishment. 'Hollis was so right about you,' he crowed. 'You're like a magic talisman – always at the scene of a crime ten minutes before it's even happened. That's what he said.'

'Rubbish,' she snapped crossly. 'That's a horrible thing to say about me. It just so happens that they're friends with the people who own the Stanton house. The daughter's not quite right – whatever you're supposed to say these days. Schizophrenia or something.' She slurred the word drunkenly, hearing it rebound inside her foggy brain. 'Gets into very complicated arguments. She likes the rats. The cousin died. Cystic fibrosis, apparently.'

'And do you know who stole the flowers?'

'Of course I don't. Besides, isn't it slightly beneath your pay grade?' she wondered. 'Aren't you're an inspector?'

He cocked a cautionary eyebrow at her. 'Yes, I am. The fact is, this is Kevin's shout. I'm just along for the ride. Where he goes, I have to follow, at least for today.'

'Here we are,' she pointed to the Shepherds' house. 'It's called Woodside House, officially, in case you need to make a report. Not sure which wood it's supposed to be beside, but there you go. Most house names are daft when you think about them.' She was rambling. She could feel her own voice drifting along with scarcely

77

any conscious thought behind it. 'You can leave me now.'

'I'm not sure we can.' Higgins was suddenly showing serious concern. 'You've got a temperature, that's obvious. Your car's going to be out of action for at least the rest of today, so you're stuck here.'

'How will I get it back?' she wondered. 'Will they bring it for me, when it's mended?'

'The AA won't, but the garage might. Keep an eye on your phone. There'll be a text any time now, I shouldn't wonder, telling you where they've taken it.'

'Oh, Lord,' she wailed. 'How could I have done such a stupid thing? Will it need a new engine, do you think?'

Kevin snorted and gave an exaggerated look at his watch. Higgins made reassuring noises, but was obviously losing patience, as well as his colleague. Thea opened the door and started to climb out of the car. 'I'll be fine,' she said, more to herself than to the men. It was extraordinary how heavy her arms and legs had become. 'I don't have to do anything or go anywhere. The dogs can make do with the garden for today. I'll be much better tomorrow. Thanks, Jeremy. I don't know what I would have done without you.'

'Given your germs to the AA man,' Kevin muttered with ill-concealed resentment.

Higgins continued to look concerned, as he had done since he'd first found her. 'Tell you what,' he said. 'I'll just pop next door and tell them the situation, get them to keep an eye on you. They're neighbourly

78

people round here, especially at this season of good cheer. You've got to have some sort of safety net. Unless you've got somebody who'll come and stay with you?'

'My daughter's scared of rats,' said Thea. 'And Drew's got children. And my sister . . .'

'Yes, I know about your sister,' he said gently.

'No – not Emily. The other sister, Jocelyn,' she corrected earnestly.

Higgins waved the subject aside as irrelevant. 'I'll just be a minute.' He was addressing Kevin, who sighed theatrically.

'Not that side,' Thea told him, pointing to the house where the funeral party had gathered the previous day. 'That's where the dead man's girlfriend lives.' *See*, she wanted to boast *I'm still keeping up with everything.*

'Okay.' He gave the house a long slow examination that surprised Thea. Then he trotted to the door of the one the far side and rang the bell. Thea stood unsteadily beside the car, aware that her dog was scrabbling at Gloria's net curtains in the living room.

A man came to the door, listened gravely to Higgins' explanation and threw a somewhat unengaged glance at Thea. 'I'm afraid I'm going away myself tomorrow,' he said, quite loudly. 'But of course, if there's a problem in the meantime, do give me a shout.'

Higgins thanked him and went back to the car. 'Come on, then,' he said. 'Let's get you inside. Where's the key?'

'In my bag.' The bag was still in the car, and Higgins

retrieved it, handing it to her with a patient smile. She fished for the door key, which was on a ring with several others.

'No burglar alarm?' he asked.

She shook her head, noticing for the first time that the painkillers had finally worked. Instead of the sharp stab that any movement had caused, there was now a sort of muffling fog. 'It's all quite simple,' she said. 'They've got the dog. She looks as if she's snarling. A burglar would be scared stiff.'

He unlocked the door for her and ushered her in. Hepzie flew down the hallway at them, hurling herself at Thea's legs, in a flurry of long coat and plumy tail. There was no sign of the Alsatian.

'I have to go,' the detective said, apologetically. 'Get in the warm and have something to eat. I'll get back to you if they tell me what's happened to your car, but they'll send you a text about it, as well. You might have to contact the insurance people. I don't think the AA are going to cover the cost of draining the engine.'

'It'll work all right, will it? I won't have to have a whole new engine or anything?'

Higgins smiled. 'Should be okay,' he said, with a slightly uncertain nod.

Thea heard herself and frowned. 'I asked that before, didn't I? I'm scared it's going to land me with a massive bill.'

'Worry about that after Christmas,' he advised. Then he was back in the car, much to Kevin's relief.

She heard him drive off with a low-geared flourish, heading northwards to Broadway. Or, more accurately, Willersey, which Thea thought was a little way north again, just beyond Broadway. On a fine summer's day, it would be an easy walk along the well-trodden footpaths and country lanes, to Willersey and back again. Always, on her house-sitting commissions, she promised herself she would use her feet more and get to know the pathways. Somehow, it rarely happened as planned.

She was thirsty, but not hungry. Blondie was curled up in the kitchen looking miserable. Hepzie was stir-crazy, wagging furiously and jumping up at Thea's legs. Her own feathery limbs were in need of a good brushing, as usual. Thea did a concentrated inventory of the situation. It was nearly two o'clock. Her car had died. She had been lucky with the way Jeremy Higgins had got her out of trouble. It could all be a lot worse, she concluded.

Outside the village was oddly silent. The heavy cloud had not lifted all day, and there was no breath of wind. She opened the back door and chivvied Blondie outside. The big white animal slouched reluctantly to her special corner, cocked her ears briefly at a blackbird on a low branch and then came back again. She sighed deeply. 'Oh dear,' said Thea. 'You're not happy, are you? I'm not doing a very good job, am I?' She remembered what the Great Dane woman had said – that Blondie had been to correctional classes, or something of the sort. Had they somehow taken all the spirit out of her, in the process? She should be out in the open stretches of central Europe, herding cattle or whatever her breed had been intended for. Presumably she was a variation on the German Shepherd, which suggested work with sheep in Bavaria. Or Alsace, she supposed, wherever that was.

Rambling again, she told herself. The lurking fever that was making her alternate between sweating and shivering was also doing weird things to her thought processes. She boiled the kettle and made a mug of Lemsip with added honey. It was soothing, at least. Later on, she'd make more soup.

Higgins had been very kind. He'd always been nice to her. He knew Phil Hollis very well, of course, and she had no illusions about the degree to which the men had discussed her, when she and Hollis had been an item. Thea knew a number of police detectives in the Gloucestershire constabulary – her favourite being DS Sonia Gladwin. But Higgins had probably been unwise to tell the man next door about her flu. She would become a pariah, especially if nobody in Stanton had yet succumbed to the epidemic. Nobody wanted to be ill at Christmas. If it hadn't been for that, she might well have enjoyed a visit from some local proselytiser who would invite her to carol services or sherry parties. Now they'd all shun her and leave her to wallow in her own viruses.

She felt lonely and abandoned and not fully in control

of herself. She might dissolve into tears without warning, or fall downstairs, or forget to switch something off. She tried to focus on something outside herself, and landed on the woman next door – paramour of the dead Douglas-the-businessman. Thea had to revise everything she had first assumed about the owner of the house. How old was she? Did she have children? What was she doing for Christmas? Had she and the wife forged an unholy friendship and were at this very moment celebrating the demise of the man they had shared? Had they, she wondered irresistibly, indeed colluded in his murder, as had been suggested by one of the men in the police car? Which one, she had already forgotten. The conversation in the car had faded into a sort of dream, where she could not have accurately reported who said what, or indeed whether much of it had taken place silently inside her own head. Higgins had said something upsetting about her association with violent crimes during her various house-sitting jobs. It was possible, she told herself sternly, to achieve an entire house-sit without getting involved in anything criminal or violent. She had actually managed it a few times. This time, she could simply ignore everything to do with Callendar and his complicated life and death.

She was in the front room, stretched out on the sofa, which stood with its back to the window. Hepzie had used it to perch on while she scrabbled at the curtains. There was a small tear in one of them, Thea noticed, caused almost certainly by her dog. As she fingered it, thinking it would probably show more if she tried to mend it than if she left it alone, a confusing figure came into view on the pavement outside. Blinking it into focus, Thea recognised the Sherry woman and her huge dog, standing barely a yard away and staring in at her. 'Can I come in?' she mouthed exaggeratedly.

Thea hauled herself up and went to open the door. She made no attempt to restrain either of the dogs in her charge, but the woman snatched at her animal's chain when she saw Blondie in the hallway. 'Can you shut her in the kitchen or something?' she asked.

Thea sighed exhaustedly. 'I'm sure she won't be a problem,' she said. 'She's too depressed to pick a fight.'

'Well – if you're sure.' She came tentatively into the hall, and Thea shut the door behind her. 'You don't look very well,' the woman commented. Her spine straightened in a businesslike fashion and she removed the blue coat she was wearing, indicating an intention to stay. She hung it on an empty hook which was one of a row, near the front door, and turned back to Thea. 'I can see you need somebody to help.'

'No, I'm not very well. I seem to have got flu. You might want to keep your distance.'

To her credit, Cheryl – Thea had finally remembered her name – did not recoil. 'You poor thing,' she sympathised, with apparent sincerity. 'That must make things awkward. Anyway – listen. I saw you just now, in that police car. Did something happen?'

The change in demeanour made Thea wonder

whether her own fuzzy condition was somehow deceiving her. Hadn't this been a stand-offish person, exuding disapproval, only the day before? Now she was all attention and concern. 'I put the wrong fuel in my car and it died. Stupid. I've never done that before.'

'I imagine it's something a person only does once.'

'Yes.'

'So what are you going to do? Won't you need somebody here with you?'

'I'll be all right. It's not very demanding. Blondie can survive without a walk for a day or two.'

'What about neighbours?'

'There's a man on that side, who's going away tomorrow. And on this side there's just been a funeral. You knew that, I imagine. Did you go to it?'

Cheryl was scrutinising the room, including the strings of Christmas cards and the well-tended house plants. 'No,' she said. 'I had to be somewhere else.'

'Did you know the man who died, though? Douglas Callendar. He must have lived right next door, because that's where everyone came afterwards.' Then she remembered the gossip in the car and knew she'd got it wrong. There was a complication that would normally present no difficulties. But now her understanding seemed to be clouded with something urgent and physical.

'Yes, I knew him – not that I ever saw much of him. He never had a lot of time for socialising.' She sounded slightly bitter to Thea's ears. 'But his house isn't the

85

one next door,' Cheryl corrected. 'He's got a great big property up towards Snowshill, in the middle of nowhere.' She was speaking slowly, appearing to Thea to recede in an oddly dreamlike fashion.

'Yes,' said Thea weakly. She could feel her knees buckling, as she tried to stand up straight and conduct a normal conversation. 'Um . . . I think . . .' She felt herself swaying, a rushing sound in her head, and the world went a curious pinky-grey colour.

Chapter Five

It wasn't a proper faint, she insisted to herself. She felt the floor hit her quite hard on her bottom and shoulders. She felt Cheryl's hands on either side of her head, pressing and shaking in a decidedly unpleasant and unhelpful fashion. She opened her eyes and saw a nightmare vision of a massive dark-grey head, with loose lower lips showing flashes of pink. A long tongue was coming towards her. 'Caspar – get back,' said the woman. 'That's not going to help, is it?'

But Thea was more grateful to the worried dog than she was to its mistress. She looked into the liquid eyes and wanted to stroke the huge head. 'Pity he's not a St Bernard,' she said, idiotically.

'You fainted,' said Cheryl accusingly.

'I didn't. I just . . . I didn't pass out. I'll be all right.' A wave of energising anger swept through her at the situation. She could not permit herself such weakness. It was embarrassing, humiliating. She sat up. 'I didn't have any lunch,' she said, by way of excuse.

'You're shaking. Your skin's all clammy. You're incredibly pale.' Cheryl listed the symptoms dispassionately. She pulled her up and half dragged her onto the sofa where the strings of Christmas cards seemed to cut out the light and loom threateningly over her. 'Lie down,' Cheryl ordered. 'Now, you really must have somebody here with you. What if you fall downstairs or something?'

Thea's rage grew hotter. 'There isn't anybody,' she said furiously. 'The world is full of women managing on their own. It's what we do. Have *you* got somebody to look after you if you catch my flu?'

'Actually, no,' Cheryl admitted. 'A son, with a wife and a child, in Norwich. An ex-husband, with a wife and a child, in Manchester. A sister in Devon.'

'There you are, then,' said Thea. 'We manage on our own. Like I said.'

'No we don't. We help each other. Especially at Christmas. It's a religious festival, after all.'

Thea imagined the woman and her dog moving in for Christmas, she and Thea feverishly cooking a turkey together and pulling crackers. There was a look in her eye that reminded Thea of her brother Damien, who had embraced the Christian life wholeheartedly, some years before. 'Do we?' she said, appalled to find herself close to tears.

'Of course. Aren't I helping you now?'

'I'm not sure,' said Thea, too poorly to prevaricate.

'Listen – I'll make some tea. I'll take that dog out into the garden for you. I'll make one or two phone calls, if you want me to. I'm sure there must be *someone* you can find. Otherwise, the people will have to come back. Gloria and what's-his-name. Where've they gone, anyway?'

'Bermuda,' said Thea, with a flicker of satisfaction. 'They can't come back. That's ridiculous.'

'So . . . ?'

Thea avoided Cheryl's eye and said nothing. In an odd way it no longer felt like her problem. She was prepared to struggle on by herself – it was other people who kept saying she couldn't. After a pause, the woman went into the kitchen and started clattering much more officiously than necessary. Thea let her go, and let her head flop back on the cushions. Cheryl was mid fifties or so, and bossy. Further than that, Thea had not observed, unusually for her. Questions began to form dimly, many of them childishly dreamlike and irrelevant. Why did she possess a Great Dane? Why had she not been at work in the middle of a Friday, instead of walking the dog, when Thea first met her? How well did she know the people of Stanton? Somewhere, behind everything that had happened, there simmered an awareness of the usurper next door who had to be interesting and worth getting to know. Even through her embarrassment at what she'd done to her car, and the headache and the impatient Kevin, the snippets about the girlfriend of the dead man had taken root in her mind. They waited for her attention. And when she had accorded it, she would want to tell somebody the story.

Not just any old somebody, of course. There was only one person who would properly appreciate the intriguing implications of a mistress taking over the funeral of a man who already had a perfectly viable wife.

When Cheryl came back with two mugs of tea and some fruitcake, Thea stared at her for a moment, wondering whether she would dare ask her to phone him on her behalf. What would she say? What would *he* say? What possible good could come of it? 'Thanks,' she said. 'So you don't know the girlfriend, then?'

'Who?'

'Next door. Where they had the funeral party.' She wasn't sure how much of this she had already said – or had she just silently thought it? Memory of recent events felt blurred and unreliable.

'Oh. You were saying something about that when you fainted.'

'I didn't faint.' It seemed important to win that point.

'I know who she is, but we've never had any real contact. I think I should maybe go and talk to her – tell her you're here and not too good. What did you say about Douglas Callendar? Something I didn't understand.'

'After his funeral,' Thea said, with an effort. 'They

came back here for the wake. Except, it's not technically the wake, you know. There isn't a proper word for what people do these days. The wake is meant to be *before* the burial. It's a sort of vigil over the body. It's nothing to do with all that noisy stuff that happens afterwards.'

Cheryl made a sound that hinted at disapproval. Thea suspected she was rambling again, and lapsed into silence. They both drank their tea thirstily. *Must keep up the fluids*, Thea thought, with a sense of obeying an ancient edict. Cheryl finished first and slapped down the mug with an air of firm decision. 'Right, then. I'll leave Caspar here for a minute, and pop next door for a word. Won't be long. You just lie there and rest.'

Thea shook her head half-heartedly. 'I don't think we should bother her, though. She'll be busy with . . . you know . . . all that stuff that you have to do when a person dies.' Then she thought about it. 'But she won't, though, will she? She's not the wife.'

'You've got that right, anyway. But she'll be a backup for you, if you need someone. It's down to me to alert her.' Cheryl spoke with a nurse-like certainty, bringing her hands together in a decisive grip that seemed designed to strengthen her own resolve. 'You don't want to have to go the other side if you can help it.'

Thea was puzzled. 'He seems all right,' she murmured, but Cheryl wasn't listening.

'I'll go now, all right? I'll leave the door on the latch. You stay there. Caspar won't be any bother.'

The three dogs, left to their own devices, had

91

evidently come to an amicable understanding, out in the hall. Hepzie could be an effective peacemaker at times, squirming submissively on her back, exposing the pink underbelly and causing other dogs to mellow by means of her silliness. Mostly, they just sniffed disdainfully and proceeded to ignore her. Blondie and Caspar might have history, but Thea suspected that Cheryl had exaggerated it. People might be frightened of Alsatians, but in her experience they were generally pretty soft. Blondie's deceptive snarl must have done her reputation no good at all.

And Great Danes were scarcely dogs at all, by any normal standards. Embarrassed by their own size, only lightly endowed with brains, they strolled along beside their owners thinking their own thoughts and being very little trouble. Thea had known one as a child, and remembered the huge head towering over her, gazing into the middle distance and declining to play.

She couldn't stop Cheryl, even if she wanted to. Just as she couldn't stop Higgins going on the same errand to the house on the other side. Passing the buck, essentially, in both cases, she thought irritably. Calling on strangers to watch over her and make sure she lived through the next twenty-four hours or so, when she'd insisted she'd be all right. The whole thing was humiliating. The strangers wouldn't take kindly to the request – why should they? For a start, they would understandably shy away from the risk of contagion.

She glimpsed a figure passing the front window,

vaguely brown in colour, and assumed it was Cheryl on her mercy mission. Then she closed her eyes for a moment, noticing how giddy that made her feel, and how strange swirling shapes were lurking on the back of her eyelids. She watched them as if hypnotised.

Cheryl was back in what seemed like barely a minute. Thea heard the door slam, and a slight rustling sound which she supposed must be the removal of her coat. Seconds later, she was in the sitting room, breathless and with a puzzled frown on her face. 'She's not answering the door,' she reported. 'But I can hear voices inside the house.'

'Maybe the bell doesn't work.'

'It does – I heard it. And I knocked as well. Don't you think that's odd?'

'She's probably too upset. Or drunk. Got the telly turned up loud and wants the world to go away.' Thea remembered something similar in her own case, when her husband had died.

'Even so. Don't people *always* answer the door?'

'Of course they don't. There's no law says you have to. A person's home is his castle, or whatever it is. You can pull up the drawbridge any time you like.'

'Well, *I've* never done that.'

'Never mind. You tried. The man on the other side knows about me. It'll be fine. You must be wanting to get on.' She sagged after this burst of self-reliance and dignity, but stuck to the point. 'Honestly. You've been very kind.' She levered herself upright, and prepared to give up the comfort of the sofa. The role of invalid was already wearing horribly thin.

'Nosy, more like,' Cheryl countered. 'Seeing you in that police car – well, I did wonder . . .'

Thea's heart gave a startled thump of suspicion. This woman knew who she was! She knew that Thea Osborne, house-sitter, had a reputation for getting involved in nasty crimes. She had been intrigued and curious, not just about what might be going on in Stanton, but about all Thea's earlier adventures. The flu had diverted her from what she had really come to discover. She must be feeling very disappointed now. 'It wasn't anything interesting,' she said. 'Just my poor old car, which has never given me a moment's trouble.' She sighed. 'I expect I'll be hearing any time now what's going to happen next about that.' She stood up, with a faint intention of locating her handbag and telephone, in preparation for returning to normal efficiency.

As if in a kind of cosmic synchronicity, there was a knock at the front door, alerting both Blondie and Caspar, who barked in loud unison. 'I'll go,' said Cheryl, but Thea heaved herself up and followed her. She didn't like the way the woman was taking over, and she wanted to be sure her spaniel didn't get embroiled in any skirmishes. If the newcomer also had a dog, things might become complicated. She took a step towards the door, pleased at the return of steadiness.

'Wait a minute,' she said. 'Let me put the dogs in the kitchen.' She herded Blondie and Hepzie clumsily into the room and shut the door. 'Okay,' she said.

It was the man from the neighbouring house; the one Higgins had spoken to an hour or so earlier. Thea could see half of him, past Cheryl and her Great Caspar, and heard everything that was said. 'Oh!' he began. 'I was told . . . I didn't know you were here. What about the house-sitter? The one with flu?' Cheryl was holding her dog tightly and Thea saw the man take a step back. 'I thought I saw her with a spaniel . . .'

'That's right. I'm only here for a few more minutes. I don't know Mrs . . . the house-sitter very well at all.'

You've even forgotten my name, thought Thea.

'I see,' he said, plainly not seeing at all. 'So everything's all right then, is it?'

Thea moved forward. 'Do you know the woman on the other side?'

A rictus of disdain crossed his big face. He was a portly man, with a double chin and beefy hands. He wore a pale-grey waistcoat and tan-coloured jacket that looked expensive. 'Only as much as one knows a neighbour,' he replied pompously. 'We don't socialise.'

'Weren't you at the funeral do, then, yesterday?'

'I was at the church, and then I went to support Mrs Callendar, as all right-thinking people should have done. The fiasco next door was a social gaffe, to say the least.' He threw a look at Cheryl, as if expecting her to agree, before adding more quietly, 'In any case, what does the funeral have to do with anything?'

Cheryl gave her dog a wholly needless jerk, apparently

wanting to regain centre stage. 'She's not answering the door,' she said.

'Who? Natasha? I'm not surprised.' The man had plainly come out of duty because a police detective had asked him to. Further than that, he saw no reason to go. 'Well,' he concluded, looking at Thea, 'My name is Dennis Ireland, and I will be here at least until about ten tomorrow morning. In case of emergency, that is. I wouldn't want Philip and Gloria to accuse me of neglecting my obligations. I would have taken care of the animals and so forth, if it hadn't been for my promise to my family. I think they understood that.' He sounded almost forlorn to Thea, who thought he had a nice face. 'Do have a good Christmas,' he finished, with a quaint flick of a finger at an invisible hat.

'That's very good of you,' Thea rewarded him, from behind Cheryl. 'I am poorly, but not so bad I can't manage the dog and answer the phone. I'm bound to be better tomorrow. Cheryl was worried about me and called in, that's all. She's not staying.'

He had been on the brink of leaving, but he paused, still somewhat confused. 'You know each other?'

'No, no, not at all. The *dogs* do.' Thea laughed at herself. 'I mean, we bumped into each other yesterday morning, that's all. She's been very kind.' She sighed gently. Kindness was draining when you were on the receiving end of it. Thea sometimes suspected she handled it badly, and should make more effort to receive it gratefully, instead of resisting as she did. She knew there were claims that it was the chief of all the virtues, but she could never quite see it. The much less arguable case that its opposite was the greatest vice was not enough to convince her.

He departed and they heard the faint sound of his own door closing in the next house. Cheryl released her dog, which mooched aimlessly into the living room and flopped down on the floor. 'Don't get settled, my lad,' its mistress said. 'We're going soon.' She looked at Thea. 'If you need help, I advise you to opt for Natasha. That man is not what he seems.'

She was interrupted by a violent sound erupting from somewhere outside. Glass had broken. 'What was that?' asked Thea.

They both peered out of the window, Cheryl bending awkwardly over the sofa to do so. Thea, some inches shorter, had to actually kneel on it to get any kind of a view. There was nothing at all to see, except for a woman standing very still on the other side of the street. She was looking intently in their direction. 'What on earth *was* it?' Thea asked again.

'I can see glass,' reported Cheryl. 'A window must have broken, I think.'

'Where?'

'Next door. I'll go and see.' She was gone before Thea could climb off the sofa again. The Great Dane remained on the hearthrug which it had adopted with an injured air. Thea had a feeling the dog didn't really like its mistress very much. Her joints were complaining as she tried to follow Cheryl outside – knees especially.

Two more people had appeared by the time she got outside. They were all staring at some shards of glass on the ground beneath a large window at the front of the next house. 'It's been broken from the inside,' said a youth, who looked like a student home for the Christmas break. Thea could hear a TV or radio from inside the broken window.

'So somebody *is* in there,' said Cheryl, with a triumphant glance at Thea. 'Hello?' she called loudly. 'Are you all right?' She went closer, and put her face to the broken pane, peering through the hole. Then she screamed. A short, low-pitched sound of alarm; a kind of howl, in which Thea heard horror and disbelief and sheer astonishment.

'What?' said the youth and joined her, nudging her aside for a look. 'Fucking hell. Is that *blood*?'

Cheryl staggered away. 'Call the police,' she gasped. 'Quickly. Her attacker might still be in there.'

Thea blinked. 'Obviously somebody is. Why – what have you seen?'

The youth stepped away and spoke to Thea. 'It's Natasha Ainsworth, covered in blood. I think she's dead,' he said.

Chapter Six

'But who broke the window?' Thea asked the question for the third time, of nobody in particular. Chaos had quickly developed, with Dennis Ireland summoned back only minutes after he'd gone into his house, to help the student and another man break down the front door, in case there was still hope of saving the injured woman's life. People emerged from houses up and down the length of the main street, and asked the same questions over and over. Someone had been holding a mobile phone, inevitably, and had called 999. In the intervening fifteen minutes before an ambulance arrived, there was noise and confusion, with people wantonly trampling blood and glass in and out of the house, as they made clumsily noble attempts to revive the woman. 'No, don't,' Thea bleated vainly, as she realised what a mess they were making of what could be a crime scene. 'You shouldn't go in there. You shouldn't touch anything.'

'But she might not be dead,' Dennis Ireland paused to explain, with some indignation. 'The first priority is to save life.' Drama had rendered him even more pompous, it seemed.

Thea had not managed to catch a glimpse of the victim. It was of course feasible that she was alive, and should therefore be resuscitated if remotely possible. If there was no one else in the house, then she must have been the one who broke the window, and that required animation. But a second person might have done it and then made a hasty exit through the back of the house and over the garden wall.

The ambulance men added more trampling, taking what appeared to be an almost perverse satisfaction in covering themselves in the woman's thickening blood. When they emerged from the house to be confronted by the crowd, they were shaking their heads and rolling their eyes, expressing defeat and a belated admission that they had been dealing with a murder victim. They were paler than they had been when they went in. The police car that arrived at that moment was greeted with serious looks and muttered information that had a galvanising effect. Onlookers, some of whom had caught the words 'foul play' and 'knife wound' and repeated them loudly to others further back, were told to go away. Blue tape was strung across the doorway and Thea braced herself for the questions that must inevitably follow.

Except – why should they? She had nothing whatever to do with it. Cheryl, yes. Cheryl had banged on the door, peered through the broken window, and then fetched Dennis Ireland from his house. Cheryl had taken charge and authorised the demolition of the front door. It might even have been she who phoned the emergency services. All Thea had done was stand limply on the doorstep of the Shepherds' house and ineffectually try to warn people not to contaminate any evidence.

None of which would count for anything once DI Higgins or DS Gladwin got to hear about it. They would assume she was involved, if only as an unusually observant bystander. Or failing that, they would want to take her into their confidence, as a sounding board while they tried out various theories as to precisely what had taken place.

But I'm poorly, she whined to herself. Her headache had come back worse than ever, and her thoughts were sluggish as a result. Standing up became more and more difficult, not only because of the aching knees but the bouts of shivering did something to her balance. Besides, it already seemed self-evident that the person who had killed Natasha-the-girlfriend must have been Marian-the-wife. Far from being friends, as Higgins had surmised, they must have been arch enemies throughout. When Natasha threw the funeral party, Marian's rage and humiliation must have driven her to a frenzy, the result of which was a savage knife attack on her rival.

'But who broke the window?' asked Thea again, as she automatically went back into the house with Cheryl. The woman made no reply, but focused on her legs in dismay. 'I've got blood on my trousers, look. How horrible.'

'The whole thing was absolutely terrible,' said Thea, trying to summon the rightful levels of horror and outrage. 'Did you kneel by the body, then?'

'No, but I suppose I did get quite close. I knew her, of course. She was well liked. Quite young.' Her voice was fading, and Thea couldn't decide whether Cheryl was choking with shock or she herself was clouding over with flu.

The expected visit from a senior police detective did not take place. Somehow it was five o'clock, and dark. Cheryl had gone home, leaving instructions about keeping up fluid intake and not taking too many pills. She had settled Thea on the sofa with the television on, having fed the dogs and rats. More than that could not possibly be demanded. But instead of a promise to return next day with further succour, she dropped the bombshell that she was due to take a train to Exeter the following afternoon, where her sister had invited her to spend Christmas. This detail had been withheld until the final doorstep moment, and Thea experienced a pang of something like resentment. How soon she had allowed herself to become a helpless patient, she realised miserably. 'Well, thank you for all you've done,' she murmured. 'I hope the police will let you go as planned.'

'What? Of course they will. Why shouldn't they?'

'They'll want to get a proper statement from you about Natasha. I expect they'll do it in the morning.'

'I've already told them everything.' She stared at Thea aggressively. 'Why would they want me again? They never said anything.'

'I've probably got it wrong then.' She wasn't up to an argument about it. Besides, she couldn't say for certain what was in the official mind. She couldn't even say for certain that Natasha had been murdered. She might have deliberately slashed herself with broken glass, for all Thea knew. 'Thank you very much,' she managed, with a wan smile.

'I'll leave my details for you, shall I? Just in case.' Without waiting for a reply, she had found a notepad by the phone and written on it. 'Here,' she proffered the result.

Thea glanced at it, barely registering the address, having focused on the first name. *Cheryl Bagshawe. Old Mill House, Wood Stanway*. 'Oh – it's Cheryl with a C. Fancy that. I thought it must be an S.' Somehow it made a difference to her view of the woman. Cheryl was at least a real name, whilst Sheryl was not.

'You think I should pronounce it Cheryl?' said the woman, hardening the *ch*. 'Most people in this country do, I know. I think it's an awful name, either way, quite frankly.'

'I rather like it,' said Thea woozily. 'I was just confused about the spelling.'

Her visitor left Thea in the living room and finally departed with her dog. Thea watched them pass her window, a coat folded over the woman's arm, as if she felt too warm to wear it, and the dog's short lead grasped firmly in the other hand. Thea breathed a sigh of relief. The television was trying to impart the alarming news that the flu statistics were reaching new highs, with many millions of people affected. Whilst not an especially threatening strain of the virus, with reassuringly few deaths reported so far, it was debilitating, and the number of people failing to turn up for work was causing difficulties. If it hadn't been for the fact that it was Christmas, and therefore a slack time for most industries, the consequences for the GDP might have been a lot worse. Dozing fitfully, Thea took some solace from knowing that she was one of millions. There was official advice not to bother the doctor, who could do little but offer the standard advice to keep warm and stay away from crowds. The severe headache that was a feature of this particular virus was unpleasant but not dangerous. Aching joints, fever, and mild depression were all to be expected, and would pass within a few days. Anyone in a normal state of health would be very unlikely to suffer lasting damage. A forced cheerfulness on the part of the newsreader appended a laughing injunction to just lie back and make the most of it. Think of all those wonderful old films being shown on TV over Christmas, he said fatuously.

The day would have been distressing and exhausting even without being ill. The trouble with her car alone would have put a blight over everything. And Cheryl Whatnot had not exactly been an ideal companion for an afternoon. Bossy, argumentative, abrupt – any kindness had been obscured by her manner. What's more, Thea belatedly realised, Cheryl had given away virtually nothing about her own life. An ex-husband, a married son and a sister, scattered around England – that was all she'd revealed. What was her job? Who were her local friends, if any? What had impelled her to chase after Thea, anyway, having seen her in a police car? What was so alarming about that? Had it been simple concern, or something more sinister? Over the past few years, Thea had learnt that it was unwise to take anybody at face value. There were depths of past history and dark resentments that a newcomer couldn't hope to fathom on one brief encounter.

Because there really had been a murder in the house next door. The high level of police activity in the street and the house itself made that very obvious. Surely Higgins should have come to see her by this time? He would want to ask her whether she'd seen the victim alive, and if so when. All the usual questions would have to be asked and answered. But perhaps he felt he knew the answers already, from their encounter earlier in the day. She had not known who Natasha was, and had never even glimpsed her. All she had seen was the Callendar widow and her sons in the funeral cars, fleetingly, without knowing who was who. Natasha, presumably, had walked to the church and hijacked some of the mourners afterwards. The police already knew the basic facts of the two women in the man's life, from normal local gossip.

There had been blood; that much Thea knew. The people who broke into the house had it smeared on them when they reappeared, including Cheryl and Dennis, who had both patted worriedly at themselves. The ambulance men looked almost as pale as the neighbours, when they came out shaking their heads and muttering about massive blood loss. A severed artery, perhaps, gushing like a fountain with every struggling beat of the woman's heart. Drifting in and out of sleep, unsure of what was dream and what was real, Thea's imagination constructed several possible explanations as to what might have happened. It all seemed remote from her own immediate concerns. She was ill. Her body hurt. If she tried to stand for long, she folded up and landed on the floor. She couldn't face food. She hadn't got her car, and it was now only two more days until Christmas. Christmas Day loomed like a grinning monster, demanding a set of behaviours that it was almost impossible to avoid. You had to speak to all your loved ones; eat a lot of food;

drink a lot of alcohol; be nice to everybody; listen to carols and Bible stories on the radio and watch the same old movies on TV. It was all preordained. But Thea was ill, and was not expecting to obey a single one of the ordinances.

Despite the temptation to simply lie there on the sofa for the whole night, she did eventually drag herself upstairs, having made another Lemsip and let the dogs out for a final pee in the garden. Both animals were subdued, and when Blondie was shut into the kitchen for the night, she gave a single low protesting moan before flopping onto her bed. 'Sorry,' Thea told her. 'I'm doing my best. It won't be for long.'

Hepzie went upstairs with her, as always, and curled quietly at the foot of the bed, adapting herself to Thea's legs in the soft, warm way that endeared her to her mistress more than anything else. But Thea's feverish tossing and turning proved an impossible trial to the dog, so that after an hour or so, she jumped down and made a nest for herself on a sheepskin rug by the bed. Thea's dreams were horrible: threatening winged creatures that came right up to her face and then shrank to pinpricks, teasing and tormenting her in unpredictable waves. She was hot and threw the duvet aside. She was thirsty and reproached herself viciously for forgetting to provide herself with a bedside glass of water. She was at the back of the house, and all was dark and silent. She imagined a ghost next door, dripping dark blood and smashing endlessly at the window, in an eternally futile attempt to get help.

Eventually it was morning. For a minute, she thought it was Christmas already and her father would be coming any moment with her bulging stocking that had been filled downstairs overnight by Santa. All four children would have to wait patiently until their father fetched them from the fireside, and delivered them solemnly to their recipients. Nothing else throughout the year came close to the euphoric anticipation, the unique atmosphere of love and mystery and delight. The rest of the day would generally slide into a slow anticlimax, once all the presents were opened and the turkey demolished. The afternoon wreckage would stay in Thea's mind's eye for several weeks, from the age of about eight. The new toys became familiar and shabby, but that moment when the stocking was delivered never palled.

When she dragged herself out of bed, she could smell a sour sweat on her pyjamas that carried associations of old people and unwashed clothes. Her head was throbbing painfully, exacerbated by movement. Her eyes hurt when she turned on the bathroom light. 'I thought these things were always better in the morning,' she muttered. Hard as it was to admit, the fact was that she was significantly worse than the day before.

Who would come to help her? Panic washed through her with the stark truth that there was nobody. The Dennis man was going away, as was the Cheryl woman. Her mother was otherwise engaged. Her sisters were entirely occupied with their own concerns. Her daughter was frightened of rats. There was Damien, though. Her big brother, who lived not so very far away and had no children. Nobody would ever take him for a nursemaid, with his annoying proselytising, but he would come if asked. Until that moment, it had not for a second occurred to Thea to ask him.

His number was in her phone, but she could not properly see the buttons or the writing on the screen. Frowning fiercely, she forced it to do her bidding. There he was, in the list, D for Damien. She didn't think she had phoned him for at least the past three years. Not since Carl had died and there were ceaseless phone calls to and from everybody, in a crazy surge of emotional conversations, plans, and a simple need to maintain contact. The phone wanted to know for sure that it was her intention to make a call. She blindly pressed the same green button, wishing it would just get on with it.

'Peaceful Repose Funerals,' came a wholly unexpected voice. 'How can I help you?'

'What? Who's that?'

'Thea?' The voice came gentle and questioning. 'Is that you?'

'Drew! I was calling Damien, not you.'

'Both in the Ds,' he said lightly. 'Easily done. Are you all right?'

'Not at all, no. I've got flu. It's horrible. My head's killing me. I can't see properly.'

'Where are you? Not house-sitting again, I hope?'

'Stanton. Yes, I am.'

'But it's Christmas.'

'I know. You sent me a card, and I sent you one.'

'The flu's a disaster. Maggs has got it, and Stephanie looks rather hot this morning, so she's probably getting it. You'll have to go home. You can't work if you're ill.'

'It's not exactly work. There's only a dog and some rats. But I can't just leave them.'

'Well, at least there hasn't been any murder, then.' He laughed.

'Actually . . .'

'No! Don't tell me.'

'Next door. A woman. Yesterday. At least, it might have been an accident, or suicide. I don't know for sure. I had horrible dreams about it,' she remembered.

'Thea, you sound pretty awful. How long have you had it?'

'Um . . . Friday evening it started. It'll soon be gone. I'm sorry about poor Stephanie. I hope it doesn't spoil her Christmas.'

He made a sound that reminded her that this would be the first Slocombe Christmas without Karen, and likely to be somewhat flat accordingly. What would it be like, she wondered, trying to go through the usual traditions with two young children and no mother? 'Have you got them lots of presents?' she asked.

'Nothing special. Steph suggested we ignore it completely, as a sort of memorial to Karen, but

Timmy thought that was the worst idea he'd ever heard. He's right, really. Karen wouldn't take kindly to such self-denial. She always liked Christmas – made everything herself, of course. Pudding, pies, trifle. It's all bought stuff this year.'

'I got myself a few nice things at a supermarket on Thursday. I think that's where I caught the flu, actually. Now I can't face eating anything. It'll all get thrown away.'

He tutted and went quiet for a moment. 'Isn't there anybody with you? Surely you're not having Christmas there by yourself?'

'Don't you start. I'll be fine. I never meant to tell you about the flu. I haven't told Jessica or Jocelyn or anybody. Only Jeremy Higgins, and he's going to be busy with the business next door.'

'Remind me.'

'He's a DI. I don't think you ever met him. He shows up fairly often. He rescued me yesterday when I killed my car.'

'DI? Don't tell me . . . um . . . um . . . Detective Inspector! I knew really. Is your car dead, then?'

'I put diesel in it instead of petrol. I think they can fix it. It'll probably come back today.'

'It all sounds like a great deal of trouble, one way and another. What's the house like?'

'It's old and lovely. In the main street. The dog is gorgeous, but she's depressed. Missing her people, I suppose. And I'm neglecting her terribly. I would have

111

taken them up onto the Cotswold Way if I'd been all right. We had a Great Dane here yesterday as well.'

'Listen, Thea – I'll have to go. We were in the middle of breakfast. Den's coming soon, and babysitting while I go and see a man at the hospice. Funerals don't stop for Christmas, unfortunately.'

'Surely they do?'

'I meant *dying* doesn't stop.'

'How will you cope if Maggs is ill?'

'With great difficulty. It must have been like this in the Black Death – nobody around to do any of the vital work.'

'Except they all died. Nobody's dying of this flu, are they?'

'Some are, of course. But not many. Apparently it attacks people under fifty for preference. You have to admire these viruses,' he added whimsically. 'They really are very clever. I sometimes think they're the real rulers of the world, with proper societies and value systems, and long-term ambitions.'

'You sound nearly as delirious as me.'

'Are you delirious?' He sounded worried.

'A bit, in the night.'

'I should come and look after you. It's ages since I saw you. But . . . with Steph sickening, and Maggs . . . well, I don't see how I can.'

'Drew, I *promise* I phoned you by mistake. I absolutely intended to call Damien and tell him I was poorly. He's the only person doing nothing, as far as I know. He's a bit of a pain, admittedly, but he'd come if I asked him to.'

'I thought he was a thoroughgoing Christian? Doesn't that mean he'll be busy over Christmas?'

'Ah – well, that's the thing. He doesn't really belong to any proper church. They meet in each other's houses, and study the Bible and stuff like that. But they don't do the ritualistic song and dance. The idea is to live like real Christians – which would definitely include rushing to the rescue of a sister in distress. The trouble is, he isn't actually a terribly kind person, so he'd do it in a martyred sort of way, And he'd be all bossy and organising. But at least Blondie would get all her walks. If I told him that was the top job, he'd take it very seriously.'

'That sounds pretty awful.'

She sighed and said nothing for a moment. 'You've got to go,' she reminded him. 'You were going five minutes ago.'

'I'm thinking. Stanton's another village in the Cotswolds, right?'

'Right.'

'You know I've still got the house in Broad Campden. I was just thinking yesterday it was time I did something with it. It's a wicked waste just letting it sit there. But after Karen died, I sort of forgot all about it. I've had it nearly a year now.'

'It's not that long. It took six months or more for all the legal business to get done.'

'The house doesn't know that,' he joked. 'It's been gathering cobwebs and mice and wet rot for all these months. It'll fall down if I don't do something soon. I've already had letters about the garden from a neighbour. Apparently there's a giant hogweed by the shed.'

'Wow. I love giant hogweed.'

'So do I.' He spoke with a boyish wonder, which made her laugh. 'But most people regard it as the spawn of the devil.'

'So what are you saying? About the house?'

'I don't know. But let me get breakfast sorted, and the hospice visited, and I'll phone you back. Midday sometime, I expect. I'll have to find out how Maggs is before I decide anything.'

Her spirits leapt at the implications. Already her headache seemed to be fading. 'Okay,' she said. 'Nice to talk to you.'

'And you.'

She felt so much better after that conversation that she wondered whether the whole flu thing was psychosomatic after all. Had she been so full of self-pity at spending a solitary Christmas that she had made herself ill with it? Of course not, she decided – but perhaps there was an *element* of that, all the same. The pleasure at hearing Drew's voice had quelled the activities of the sneaky virus for a while, at the very least.

It was Sunday, December 23rd, she reminded herself.

Before long the church bells were sure to start ringing. Outside, the sky was brighter than the past few days. When she opened the back door to let the dogs out, the air was crisper. A perfect day for a walk on the wolds, if she'd been up to it. The shortest day had passed, and slowly the year would turn. It was a moment for pagan reflections about the reliability of the seasons and the timelessness that came with their predictable repetitions. A day for musing on the human condition and what it all meant. Drew would be good at that – and Damien would be hopeless. The undertaker trumped the fundamentalist Christian when it came to facing the eternal verities. Drew had freely stated that he didn't really believe in God, that he couldn't see a place for that whole layer of additional explanation and power that went with the idea of a deity. 'I prefer to think of everything just getting along by itself,' he said. 'No need for a higher intelligence controlling it all.'

Thea hadn't argued with him, but somewhere deep down she still wondered whether they might be missing something, and in due course would choose after all to embrace an extra dimension involving interactions between people that somehow weren't covered by Drew's scenario. She found she was rather looking forward to a future in which matters spiritual might take a larger role.

So she did not phone Damien after all. She forced herself to eat two Weetabix and drink a large mug of coffee. When the headache came back in full force, she took two more painkillers. They were half gone already, and there was only one sachet of Lemsip left. Only then did she remember her car, and how she was stranded in a village with no shop on a Sunday.

There were two police cars outside, and sounds of activity in the house next door. Plenty of scope for a whole team of SOCOs, she supposed. Who would be the senior investigating officer this time, she wondered? Most likely Sonia Gladwin, who would not want to give up Christmas with her twin sons and long-suffering husband. Thea had a confused picture of people like the detective superintendent and Drew Slocombe wading through a morass of obligations and distractions, determined to give their children the attention that other people's had. Her sister Jocelyn was married to a civil servant who took the full complement of bank holidays without a second thought. He would throw himself into games with the children and abandon all thought of the outside world. The fact that he had once meted out violence to his wife had tainted him, admittedly, but as a father he was irreproachable.

And Jeremy Higgins was another thwarted family man, she supposed. He had referred briefly to kids once or twice, and gave every sign of being ordinarily married. He would have to interview and question a range of witnesses and suspects in this killing.

She found she was having difficulty in paying attention to the events next door. She had never met the woman who had died, and found little space in her aching self to care about her. This was bad, a small voice insisted. It had clearly been distinctly horrible for the victim. There were factors that implied a painful, panicky and lonely death, to which Cheryl Bagshawe had almost been a witness. And Thea had shared the final moments at close quarters. She definitely ought to care.

It was suddenly half past ten and she had done nothing but let the dogs out and watch sporadically out of the window as dreamlike white-clad figures came and went. She should check the rats, poor things. They too were having an unusually restricted time, compared to the freedom their people generally gave them. Why had the Shepherds bothered to get a house-sitter, if not to ensure their animals had uninterrupted routines? The ferns could have lasted without water at this time of year. Blondie could have gone to kennels, and some local boy could have come in to feed the rats. It was an extravagance they might come to regret if they knew how feebly she was performing her duties. But at least she was a deterrent to burglars, she supposed – until she remembered the woman walking unimpeded through the back door on Friday evening.

She had not given Juliet and Rosa a thought for twenty-four hours or so, except to realise that the ransacked grave in Willersey had most likely been that of their relative. She had almost forgotten their names, in fact. They had comprised an odd interlude that she might almost have believed a figment of a fevered

117

imagination. There had been something dreamlike about them, anyway. They were like characters from a fairy tale. Perhaps they hadn't existed in the real world. What was *real* anyway?

'Don't start that now,' she muttered to herself. That way madness lay.

It was with inordinate relief that she heard the door knocker. Some white knight had come to save her sanity. And despite knowing it could not possibly be, she acknowledged a glowing hope that it might be Drew Slocombe.

Chapter Seven

It wasn't Drew, of course, but a thin young man wearing a heavy sheepskin coat and a fur hat with earflaps. 'Hello?' said Thea.

'Sorry to bother you, but I've been trying to get into next door and they won't let me. I want to know *exactly* what happened, you see.'

'Oh.' She had to accept that she didn't really see; nor did she care to. 'Well, I don't know how I can help.'

'You're her *neighbour*, for God's sake. You must have things you can tell me.'

'Actually, I'm not. I mean – I'm just a house-sitter. I only arrived on Friday. I don't know anybody. Or any*thing*.'

He stared at her intently. 'But you were here when it happened? Weren't you?'

It was cold on the doorstep, and he looked almost

as shivery and sick as Thea felt. 'You'd better come in,' she said grudgingly. 'If you don't mind my flu germs.'

He laughed at this. 'Not you as well. Don't worry – I've got it already. When did yours start?'

'Friday evening.'

'I'm two days ahead of you. You'll start to feel half human again by Christmas Day, then. I had to go to my father's funeral with a raging temperature and a murderous headache. It's a wonder I didn't get fatal complications.'

She took him into the living room, where Hepzie flung herself at his legs and Blondie cocked one ear in disappointment that he was not her master. He fondled the spaniel's long ears and then pushed her gently back to the floor. 'What a pretty dog,' he said.

Thea was reminded of Juliet, who had not only correctly identified the dog's breed, but had also told Thea she was pretty. 'Who are you?' she asked baldly.

'Sorry. The name's Ralph Callendar.'

'Thea Osborne,' she responded, without extending a hand for him to shake. Slowly her brain was making the link. 'I saw you on Friday. Were you the one in the second car?'

He nodded, with a grin. 'Banished, you see, in case my mother caught my flu. To be fair, she does have a compromised immune system, so it would be a bad idea for her to get it. She's had a fairly mild form of leukaemia for a couple of years now. She doesn't usually take it seriously, but my brother Edwin is paranoid on her behalf. My wife and kid came with me, on the assumption they were incubating the dreaded virus. As it turned out, they weren't.'

'He died in his bath,' she said, without thinking. 'I saw it in the paper.'

'Bloody silly thing to do,' he nodded. 'Everyone had told him it wasn't safe. He'd had that old radio for decades – the wiring was bound to be dodgy.'

'Your mother found him – is that right?'

'So she says. Can't see any reason to doubt her. There's only the two of them in the house in an evening. All the staff go home at seven.'

'Staff?'

'Just a cook and secretary, really. You don't count the cleaning woman as technically staff, do you? And the gardener's only part-time.'

'Your father must have been popular. It looked as if the entire village showed up at the church.'

'Don't you believe it. They just wanted to snoop. We're notorious, you know. And proud of it,' he laughed.

She squared her aching shoulders. 'So what do you want to ask me? I don't imagine I'll be of any help, but you may as well give it a try now you're here.'

'The woman next door – Natasha Ainsworth, she's called. I gather she's dead.' The last word shot out with unnatural emphasis, as if he was determined to confront it, however great the effort might be.

'So it seems. As far as I understand it, the funeral party was at her house on Friday.'

'Well, your understanding isn't altogether accurate,' he corrected her. 'Only about *half* the mourners went back there. The rest went to a very smart hotel for a late lunch provided by my mother. She sat at a table all by herself and didn't eat a thing.'

'*Two* parties?' Thea said wonderingly.

'We don't call them parties,' he reproved her. 'It was very far from a party atmosphere, I can tell you.'

'Sorry. But there were two – is that right?'

He gave a pained smile and nodded. 'Natasha always did stand up for her rights, as she saw them. You have to admire her in a way.'

'Somebody killed her. The police are going to focus on your mother and those around her, aren't they?'

He seemed suddenly to wilt and turn terribly pale. 'Can I sit down?' he gasped. Before she could reply he had flopped onto the sofa, narrowly missing Hepzie who had jumped into a cosy corner after her initial love-in with the visitor. She gave him a friendly nudge and rolled her big spaniel eyes at him. He automatically put a hand on her soft head. The only thing Thea knew so far about Ralph Callendar was that he was good with dogs, and thereby earned her favour.

She waited for him to recover his colour before asking, 'So that your boy in the car with you?'

'Mikey, yes. He's nine. We've got two more, actually. Girls, five and two.'

'And a dog?'

'Three dogs. One for each child. Corgis. Did you

say the police are going to think my *mother* murdered Natasha?' He stared at her as if really wanting to know.

She sat down herself before answering. 'Don't take any notice of what I say. I have no idea how things were between you. I never even glimpsed Natasha. It's only what I've heard.' She sighed, noticing that her lungs hurt when they were inflated. Nearly everything hurt, in a low-level I-do-feel-poorly sort of way. 'I'm not well enough to take much interest,' she added, hoping it hadn't emerged as a whine.

'It's an extremely stupid idea,' he went on, with more force. 'We all *liked* Natasha. She was a family friend for decades. We all grew up with her. She used to babysit me and my brothers. She's like part of the family. Not to mention the business. She's been indispensable in that department, as well.'

'Okay.' She tried to visualise how that could have been.

'How many brothers?' she asked, thinking of the funeral cortège she had witnessed.

'Two. I'm the youngest. The others are Edwin and Sebastian. Sebastian's been in disgrace, I'm afraid. He was caught cheating some of our customers, and they sent him to gaol for a bit.' He frowned briefly. 'Why am I telling you that?'

'Sorry. It's my fault. I always ask too many questions. I just like to get the picture. It makes me feel less defenceless,' she added, startling herself by the admission.

'I can see that, I guess. Well, Edwin's got a wife and two boys. Sebastian is still single. He always says he likes women too much to get married. He thinks that's an original joke. Basically, he's the troublesome one.'

'And your mother coped with your father's other woman, did she?'

'More or less. She freaked out a few times when he took Tash to local bashes instead of her. He did that rather often at one point. She managed to get him to be a bit more discreet.'

'But essentially he was a bigamist,' Thea summarised baldly, making no attempt to conceal her distaste. 'Getting away with it. How undignified for your poor mother.'

'My mother is a magistrate, a school governor and a campaigner against building on green fields, among many other things. Her dignity is very seldom in question.' His own dignity took pride of place in this defence of his mother, Thea noted. Try as she might, she could discover no precedent for such a set-up in her own experience. As she had realised before, her family was remarkably monogamous on all sides. Not so much as an unfaithful aunt or cousin could be found. She supposed it amounted to some kind of steadfast moral code passing down the generations, and almost never openly acknowledged, let alone questioned. Much of the credit went to her father, she believed.

'Good for her,' she said sincerely. 'So how has she taken your father's death?'

Ralph shivered. 'You don't mince your words, do you? Most people say *loss* or *passing*.'

'You said it yourself, about Natasha,' she reminded him. 'And besides, the language doesn't alter the reality.'

'It softens it, though. Don't you worry that people might think you're rather hard?'

She swallowed painfully. He had pressed a sensitive button, when she was least expecting it. 'Ouch!' she protested.

'Sorry. That was mean of me, when you've got flu. One does feel so defenceless, I know. As if a layer of skin is missing. I did have to make myself say it, but it didn't come easily.'

The onset of tears took her completely by surprise. Her face seemed to implode with a sort of crash, and a sob burst out quite beyond her power to control. 'Oh no,' he said. 'Oh, God. I didn't mean to . . . Honestly, what a mess it all is. Here's you, all on your own, with a dead woman next door and I turn up and tell you your character defects. Ignore me. I'm a monster. I don't know what I was thinking of.'

She rallied with a great effort. 'No, it's not you,' she sniffed. 'It's just the flu, like you said. I'm really quite all right.'

'You're not,' he corrected her. 'But then, which of us is? We just have to muddle through, don't we? I see it was idiotic of me to think you'd know anything about what happened to Natasha. I had no idea the people were away – not that I know them at all. They've left you to mind their dogs, of course. I get it.'

'Dog, singular. The spaniel's mine. She always comes with me.'

'She's lovely. They have such wonderful heads, don't they?' It was a skilful recovery, and very effective. By focusing on the dog, they both sidestepped the awkward moment. Ralph sniffed the air as if just noticing something. 'Smoker, are you? Have a fag if it'll make you feel better. Don't mind me.'

'No, I'm not. The Shepherds are. The house must smell of it, but I haven't really noticed.'

'I gave up a year ago. The smell still makes me happy.'

Thea smiled, but resisted any temptation to divert onto the topic of cigarettes. 'What was Natasha like?' she asked.

He answered thoughtfully, one word at a time. 'Good-looking. Fit. Late forties, I think. Clever. A great walker. We used to tease her and call her "Ms Footpath" because she was always mounting some sort of campaign to keep paths open, or protesting at diversions.'

'So people liked her?'

'Oh, yes.' He frowned. 'Most people did. She was outspoken, of course, saying what was on her mind even if it upset people. She always seemed to know best, which could be irritating.'

'Didn't anybody disapprove of her lifestyle? I mean – the thing with your father . . .'

'I think it just confused them. My mother never

wanted anybody's sympathy about it. She put a good face on it, insisting they weren't in competition.'

'But they were when it came to the funeral,' Thea suggested. 'That must have forced people to take sides.'

'Actually, not at all. The real family friends came to the meal at the hotel, and the rest had sandwiches at Natasha's. It all seemed to work out more or less harmoniously.'

'So you don't think that's why somebody killed her?'

He stared at her, with a half smile on his lips. 'Of course not.'

She nodded an unavoidable acceptance of his superior knowledge and offered to make him a drink.

'No, no,' he declined. 'I absolutely must go. I have a thousand things to do. Sarah's been a martyr to my sickness for much too long already. Plus having to go to a funeral was the final straw. It took us ages to find anyone to watch out for the girls. The woman who generally does it was at another funeral, believe it or not. People dropping like flies.'

'Don't tell me,' said Thea, thinking perhaps she'd fallen asleep and was in fact dreaming. 'It was the funeral of a woman called Eva who had cystic fibrosis. At least I don't imagine it's her cousin Juliet who's your childminder.' She laughed. 'That would take coincidence to a whole new high.'

'Close,' he said, with a seriously confused expression. 'Juliet's got a sister, Cordelia. She's not exactly a childminder, but she's fabulous with small children.'

'Same funeral, wrong sister,' said Thea. 'Still a ludicrous synchronicity.'

'Why?' He was already up and making slowly for the door. Thea wondered whether she should feel flattered that he evidently found it so difficult to leave. He checked himself before she could reply. 'No, don't answer that. Don't say another word. I'll come back another time. Except – oh, God, isn't Christmas a bloody nuisance? You can't get a morsel of sense out of anybody for at least a fortnight. We've got a whole load of stray relatives coming, not to mention about four sherry parties, carols, and I don't know what else.' He went to run a hand through his hair and discovered he was still sporting the furry hat. He rubbed it anyway, making Thea smile.

'It was nice to meet you,' she said. 'And I'm sorry about your father. It must have been a dreadful shock.'

He opened his mouth and closed it, putting a finger to his lips. Then, 'Bye,' he mouthed and was gone.

She had liked him for his sensitivity and politeness, as well as for helping her pass twenty minutes that might otherwise have hung heavy. She wondered whether they had given each other any help in terms of information about Natasha's murder – not that she had any right to expect it, she reminded herself. Perhaps after Christmas they'd meet again. He was definitely the nicest person she had met so far in Stanton.

Jeremy Higgins put in an appearance at eleven o'clock, looking rumpled and rueful. 'Can't stay long,' he said without preamble, when she opened the door to him. 'Just need to ask you what, if anything, you heard next door, during yesterday.'

'Absolutely nothing. But Cheryl heard voices when she went round there. I thought it might have been a telly or radio. Somebody must have turned it off at some point. Probably the paramedics.'

'Why did she go "round there"?' He made inverted commas in the air, raising one eyebrow.

'Um . . . to ask her if she'd keep an eye on me with my flu. There didn't seem to be anybody else, with the next-door man going away.'

'And how is the flu?'

'No better. Not much worse. Everything aches. But I'm assured it'll be gone in another day or so. I met Ralph Callendar this morning. He's had it as well.'

'How long was she gone? Mrs Bagshawe?'

'What? Oh – five minutes, maybe. Not very long.'

'Five minutes is a long time to stand knocking on a front door,' he corrected her.

'Less, then. I was a bit blurry, actually. I nearly fainted. I can't be sure of anything much.'

'Let's sit down a minute and I'll run you through it. Tell me if anything sounds wrong.' He was painfully matter-of-fact, and clearly assumed she would be the same. 'Miss Ainsworth was found dead at 2.50 p.m., having lost a large quantity of blood from a severed artery after an apparent attack with a sharp instrument. The attack took place in a room at the rear of the house, and the victim dragged herself into the front room and managed to throw a stone statue through the window onto the street. Before anybody could gain entry to the house, she was dead. It seems probable that she was attacked only minutes before she died.'

'Which artery was it? What was the weapon? Did you find it at the scene?'

He paused. 'I'm not supposed to say.'

'Fine. I just wondered if she could have done it to herself.'

'Very unlikely indeed, given the circumstances. And why would she try to get help if she was committing suicide?'

'Panic. Change of heart. Or she might have done it by accident.'

'We'll know more when the post-mortem's finished.'

'Are they doing it today?'

He nodded with a half smile. 'Starting any time now. It was a choice of today or Christmas Eve.'

'I don't think I'm going to be any use to you,' she said, with an unfamiliar sense of relief. She didn't *care* who had killed Natasha Ainsworth. Just at that moment she didn't care about anything very much.

'Did you see her at any point? Before or after she died?' Thea shook her head. 'She was a striking-looking woman,' he went on. 'Thick mane of white hair, even though she was not quite fifty. Very slim, deep-set eyes. You'd remember her if you saw her.'

'Well I didn't.'

'Who *have* you seen, since you got here?'

'Cheryl. Dennis Thingummy on the other side. Oh, and a person called Juliet Wilson, who barged in through the back door on my first day. I think she's got some sort of mental trouble. Her mother came to collect her. She comes to talk to Gloria and the pet rats quite often, I think.'

He lifted his tired head and stared at her. 'The mother's not called Rosa, is she? Are we talking about the Wilson women from Laverton?'

She nodded. 'I told you yesterday, in the car. You laughed at me. You said some rather hurtful things, actually.'

'Did I? I don't remember. Well, they've got nothing to do with all this. At least, I hope they haven't. We've had enough complications with those two, over the years.'

'Oh?'

Higgins gave no further elaboration, which left Thea assuming there had been complaints about Juliet's uninhibited roaming around the area and police helplessness to stop her.

Higgins continued with his questions. 'And that's it? There's nobody else you've bumped into?'

'Just Ralph. He was nice.'

'What did he want?'

'Information, I think. The way relatives generally do. They're desperate for it. I don't think the police understand how that works, actually. Making people wait so long for proper explanations.'

131

'Relative?' he frowned. 'He's not a relative.'

She thought it through. 'She babysat him when he was little. She's been like part of the family. I said his father was effectively a bigamist and he sort of defended him. He liked Natasha.'

'Or said he did,' Higgins remarked darkly. He in turn spent some seconds in thought. 'And Dennis Ireland? When did you see him?'

'He came to the door while Cheryl was here, after you asked him to watch out for me. He wasn't too happy to see Cheryl. She answered the door.'

'Why wasn't he? Surely she'd let him off the hook.'

'Maybe he wanted to be a good Samaritan and she thwarted him. He'd geared himself up to come and offer help and was disappointed when he saw he wasn't needed.'

'Where did he go after that?'

'Back to his house. We heard him shut the front door after himself. Somebody – Cheryl, I think – fetched him when Natasha was found. He must only have been inside for ten minutes at most. Quite a few other people showed up as well, once they realised something was going on. I don't know who any of them were.'

He sagged in frustration. 'The front and back doors were both locked. The whole scene was awash with blood that was well trodden about by all those helpful neighbours and paramedics. The murderer would almost certainly have blood on his – or her – clothes. Everybody liked the woman. And it's *Christmas*.'

'It must have been the wife. Mrs Callendar. She'd have found a key to the house in her husband's pocket and sneaked in and out when nobody was looking.'

Higgins shuddered. 'I bloody hope not. Marian Callendar's a pillar of the community, best mates with the commissioner, mother of three upstanding sons. Or two. The third one seems to be under a bit of a shadow.'

'All the more reason to dispose of the only part of her life that wasn't so respectable, then,' persisted Thea. 'The funeral gathering must have been the final straw. I might have killed her myself, if I'd been Marian.'

He pondered again, nodding slightly. 'Like Kevin said yesterday – the girlfriend getting one over on the wife. Right.' He gave her an enquiring look. 'Would that make a woman ballistic enough to kill?'

'Maybe if she's already off balance because of the husband dying like that.'

'Kev would say she probably did him in as well, chucking that radio in the bath. There's no evidence that she didn't.'

'You can't prove a negative,' said Thea absently.

'Sometimes you can,' he disagreed. 'But it's not easy.'

'What about the boy?' she said suddenly. 'Was he all right?'

'Boy . . . Which boy?'

'The one who looked through the window and saw all the blood. It must have been a big shock for him. He only looked about nineteen. A student, I imagine. Somebody's son, back for Christmas.'

Higgins scanned his memory. 'Not ringing any bells,' he said. 'How do you recognise a student, anyway? He might have been a local bank clerk.'

She thought about stereotypes for a moment. 'Wrong hair,' she concluded. 'And he had that listless sort of look that students have. You know?'

'Sounds more like an unemployed layabout.'

'He must have gone before you arrived, then. He did look very pale. I thought he might make a good witness. If I remember the timing right, he saw the inside of the room before anybody interfered with it.'

'Damn,' said Higgins with feeling.

'Do you want coffee?' she asked half-heartedly. Now she was comfortably back on the sofa, her body was begging her not to get up again.

'No, thanks. No time for that. I have to get going.'

'I haven't been very useful, have I?'

'You've made me think, as usual.'

'Is Gladwin the SIO?'

'Oh, yes. I dare say she'll call in on you sometime soon. Is that dog all right?' Blondie was somewhere at the back of the house, whining loudly. 'Sounds as if it wants to go out.'

Thea sighed. 'She hasn't done a poo for days – not that she eats very much. She's pining for her people, poor thing. I was hoping she'd wait a while yet, but I guess that's mean of me.'

'Stay there. I'll let her out. The back's secure, is it?'

'I locked it.'

'No, no. The *garden*. She can't get out and run off, can she?'

'Not according to the Shepherds. Thanks, Jeremy.' She used his first name unthinkingly, because Phil Hollis had always used it, and he felt like a friend. But he stiffened when he heard it and she realised she'd transgressed. He never called her Thea. Not like Gladwin, who saw no difficulty in blurring boundaries.

The DI went out to the kitchen, and the next thing Thea heard was a shout and a female cry. Blondie barked and the cry came again. *Juliet*, Thea identified with a powerful sinking feeling. Juliet must have been standing outside, trying to gain entry through the back door, and Blondie heard her.

'Come in here,' she heard Higgins order.

'Don't bully her!' she heard herself shout. Then she hauled herself upright and went to see for herself what was happening.

The back door was open and a muddle of people and dog were half in and half out. 'Juliet,' she said. 'Why are you here again?'

Higgins failed to suppress a groan. 'Hello, Miss Wilson,' he said. 'Remember me?'

Juliet gave him a nervous glance, quickly looking away again. 'Policeman,' she muttered.

'That's right. And you know perfectly well you ought not to be here like this. People don't like it.'

'They don't mind,' she disagreed lightly. 'They're my friends. I can trust them to look after me.' She met

135

Thea's eye. 'You shouted at me,' she accused. 'I didn't like that. I need to feel safe in this house, especially.'

Juliet's last visit felt like weeks ago to Thea, but it had been less than forty-eight hours. She habitually walked to Stanton from Laverton, it seemed – but where exactly *was* Laverton? As had happened so many times before, she felt badly disadvantaged by her ignorance of local geography. Cheryl from Stanway, the grave in Willersey, a cottage in Laverton – they must all be within a short distance, and she did know where Stanway was, but the lack of accurate knowledge felt disabling.

'I had to shout at you,' she said, rather wanting to shout again. 'I needed you to go. Why have you come back?'

Juliet widened her eyes and stood her ground. 'The rats,' she said. 'I always come and play with the rats. Gloria doesn't mind. She leaves the door unlocked for me. Now you've locked it,' she accused. 'That wasn't friendly.'

The idea leapt into Thea's head from nowhere. She glanced at Higgins, wondering whether he was sharing it.

Chapter Eight

It seemed he was. 'Were you here yesterday?' he asked. 'Do you know the lady next door?'

Thea noted the *lady*, a word you'd use when speaking to a child, not a grown woman. Juliet pouted and shuffled one foot. Blondie was pressed against her, looking more in need of protection than wanting to provide it. That was one unhappy dog, Thea thought guiltily.

'Can't remember,' said Juliet.

Higgins looked to Thea for help – which she made no attempt to provide. There had to be specific protocols for interviewing people with Juliet's type of difficulties. Murkily she heard the words *post-traumatic stress* and *attention deficit disorder* floating around her head, and perhaps applying to Juliet. With little personal experience of any sort of mental illness, she had acquired a very generalised grasp of what could go wrong via the normal run of reading and watching documentaries. Juliet appeared to be very nearly capable of ordinary life, but had an unsettling lack of inhibition. She apparently followed whims without due caution, and probably had a disablingly short attention span. There was no indication of potential violence. And yet Thea knew exactly what the detective inspector was thinking.

'Will you come with me to the police station?' he asked. 'Would that be all right, if I call for a policewoman to come with us?'

'What for?' demanded Juliet. 'You haven't found the flowers, have you?'

Thea watched him tussle with the temptation to agree to this idea. 'Not yet,' he admitted.

'I knew you hadn't. You never will, either.'

'Oh?'

'Because I took them. I don't know why, so don't ask. Perhaps I just thought they were too nice to sit rotting on a grave. I suppose you'll have to tell my mother.' She sighed. 'Am I going to be arrested?'

Higgins gave her a long thoughtful look. 'Technically, if you're one of the close relatives of the deceased, the flowers probably belong to you anyway,' he said.

Juliet's eyes widened, and then she laughed. 'So why do you want me to go to the police station?'

'Nothing to do with the flowers,' he said evasively. 'Something else . . . something more serious has happened.'

'You'll have to speak to her mother,' Thea interrupted.

'She's probably looking for her, anyway. Last time, she showed up here within about ten minutes.' Higgins turned on her angrily at the superfluous intervention, but Juliet answered the implied question quite calmly.

'She's out,' she said. 'Gone to get the turkey.'

Thea remembered that Juliet had a sister, who looked after Ralph Callendar's children. 'You know the Callendar family, don't you?' she blurted. 'And you've got a sister. What's her name?'

'Cordelia. She's married,' she said. 'She doesn't live with us.' Juliet was standing straight-backed, speaking with assurance, even a faint amusement. Thea wondered what Higgins made of her.

'Your mum likes Shakespeare, then,' she remarked. 'Juliet and Cordelia.'

'All right,' barked Higgins, evidently sensing a loss of control. 'That's enough chit-chat.'

The women gave him similar looks to those that both dogs threw at him. Four females were permitting him a dominance that he was momentarily at a loss to capitalise on. 'We have to get on,' he said with a hint of apology. 'I'll call the WPC and we'll be off.'

'What about her mother?' Thea repeated.

'That's for us to worry about. You just concentrate on getting over that flu, okay?'

She made no objection to being patronised, given the circumstances, but it didn't go unnoticed. She was unable to resist a final word. 'What about my car? I still haven't got it back.'

Higgins almost lost it. He clung to politeness by a gossamer thread. 'I'm afraid it's no longer one of my primary concerns,' he grated. 'Given what happened yesterday. It's Sunday. If they didn't get it done yesterday, then it'll have to wait until tomorrow. You don't need it, do you? Haven't the people texted you, like they said they would?'

She was well and truly outmanoeuvred, remembering that Higgins had clearly told her she was to keep an eye on her phone and deal with the garage direct. But she held her ground. 'I don't need it immediately, no. But I would like to know where it is.'

'Have you checked for a text?' He met her eye unwaveringly.

'Well . . . no. It's all been so busy. But you're right, I ought to have done. I forgot. Sorry.' No sense in antagonising him, she decided. He hadn't done anything wrong. He merely represented many of the frustrations and confusions of recent days.

She watched him take Juliet out to one of the police cars cluttering the lovely old street of stone houses, and returned to the sofa to think. The spaniel jumped into her lap and snuggled down. Was it possible that Juliet had killed Natasha Ainsworth? Logistically, it seemed all too easy to imagine. If Juliet was in the habit of letting herself into the Shepherds' house, then perhaps she did it all along the row. Gardens and alleyways, low walls and open archways were all highly accessible to an uninhibited visitor, who was apparently regarded as harmless and readily tolerated. For all Thea knew, Juliet did casual gardening work, or dusting, or dog-walking for half the residents of the village. Reaching for the map lying on the window sill behind her, she checked the position of Laverton, where Juliet lived. There was a direct footpath connecting the two settlements, barely half a mile in length. It would be an easy stroll for anyone with the use of their legs.

And yet the images that filled her mind were from an earlier era, where a vulnerable young woman roamed at will down rural lanes and in and out of people's homes. These days, there would be a plethora of official concerns; oversensitive householders with triple locks on all their doors; unrealistic fears for children and complaints on every side. The people of Stanton, just like the people of every Cotswold village she had seen, remained close to home, almost invisible to a visitor. They might be glimpsed trimming a hedge on a Saturday afternoon, or weeding a flower bed, but they did not mill about in the street or stand chatting on each other's doorsteps. Somebody like Juliet would be regarded with intense suspicion, simply because she failed to abide by the innumerable unspoken rules.

But on the other hand, Thea argued with herself, there had been Cheryl Bagshawe and her huge dog. *She* strolled along the roads and footpaths, apparently with ample free time. She acted on impulse, walking a mile or more to discover why Thea had been in a police car. People would accept her, because she didn't just walk into their houses without invitation, but she *was* a bit weird, all the same. Her accounts of herself were minimal, but even then they seemed to contain certain contradictions. For a start, where exactly did she live? The pad with her address on was out in the hall, and Thea tried to visualise it. Stanway was definitely part of it, but Thea couldn't think of any dwellings there, other than the great Stanway House, and a short row of old cottages across the road from it, which most likely accommodated staff who worked there. Cheryl was definitely not a farmer, either. Another scrutiny of the map gave little clue as to the answer. As far as Thea could see, there was no habitation between Stanway and Stanton. It was all open fields and the cricket ground. Much of the area probably comprised parkland belonging to Stanway House and was thereby preserved from development for centuries to come. Perhaps Cheryl had simply been trying to impress by claiming to live in Stanway. The word had definitely been on the bit of paper she had given to Thea, containing her name and address. Perhaps there was such local status to the address, that she used it to boost her own image. Perhaps that fitted with a person who would own a Great Dane, Thea thought, before reproaching herself for the unfairness. For all she knew, the dog had belonged to the errant husband, who had abandoned it along with his wife. Perhaps she had been left it by a dead parent. In any case, it was a perfectly nice animal.

She found herself wishing that Gladwin would put

in an appearance. The detective superintendent had a refreshing originality to her: a female take on the best way to solve murders that fitted well with Thea's own approach. Apparently chaotic, with a tendency to sidestep rules and procedures, Gladwin seldom panicked or even made very much fuss. Quite how she behaved with other police officers was opaque to Thea, who generally saw her on her own. Her guess was that they found her confusing at times, even alarming, but that essentially they trusted her.

But Gladwin, like Drew, had children and work and determination to do the right thing by them both – leaving little or no space for Thea and her solitary flu-ridden state. Self-pity nudged at her, as she felt her feverish brow form beads of sweat. She was weak and useless and even poor Blondie had definite cause for complaint. As for the rats, they were unfairly imprisoned because their temporary minder couldn't face the thought of having them run free, even for a few minutes. When it came to the point, she wasn't entirely sure she could reach out and pick up a full-sized rat. It might bite her. She might drop it and lose it. A dog might get it – *her* dog, specifically. Dogs did kill rats, after all. That was a fact of nature. Even Blondie might forget herself under certain circumstances.

The world had shrunk around her, she realised. She had no car, and even if she had, she was too ill to go out anywhere. The village outside the door felt simultaneously claustrophobic and uncaring. Its people would be shopping, wrapping parcels, keeping excited children amused. Its streets had become picturesquely Dickensian with the mullioned windows, thatched roofs and coach entrances. Many of the mullions had artfully sprayed fake snow in the corners, and coloured lights behind them, echoing a thousand Christmas card images. Even the fact of a very nasty murder in their midst could not seriously disrupt the festivities. Whatever the residents might have thought of Natasha Ainsworth and her shameless affair with Douglas Callendar, they were unlikely to permit her death to impinge on them for at least the next few days. Did they all know, without needing to discuss it, that Marian Callendar had done the deed? Or even poor Juliet? Or one of Douglas's sons? Frustrated at being obliged to make wild guesses on the basis of virtually no hard information, Thea irritably forced her thoughts onto another track.

But none of the tracks she could think of were any more agreeable. Jessica would soon be arriving at Jocelyn's – she couldn't remember exactly when – and everything would be busy and noisy and warm and excessive. Food and wine and toys and games would keep the house reverberating with laughter and animation. The images made Thea's head ache more fiercely, even as she conceded that she was jealous.

Thoughts of Drew were even more unsatisfactory. He wanted to be with her, as much as she wanted to be with him. It felt like sheer bad planning that they'd ended up forcibly apart. Nobody would object to them spending Christmas together, if only they had managed it. Maggs, initially very hostile, had finally admitted that she thought Thea would be good for her boss, and that she would not make difficulties if anything were to develop. The children would inevitably compare her to their mother, probably to her disadvantage, but she had no serious worries that her presence would upset them. She had no intention of becoming their stepmother, in any case. The only obstacles were logistical, which seemed ridiculous. If the will was there, then they should be able to override such difficulties with a bit of careful thought. She had almost forgotten the Broad Campden property, until Drew mentioned it on the phone. It was obviously more than he could cope with at the moment, but the opportunity it represented could not be ignored. Even if he made a move to give it some attention, it was hardly going to happen the day before Christmas.

She spent an hour flopped on the sofa, letting her thoughts roam over a succession of depressing topics, before her natural resistance to inactivity asserted itself. Even though she was ill, she could still do *something* – although she didn't quite know what. Let the dogs out, perhaps. Change the rats' drinking water. Run the vacuum cleaner around the living room. She stood up slowly, noting the swimming sensation and the rubbery feel to her legs. She probably ought to eat something, she told herself. Since the virus took hold, she'd consumed virtually no solid food. Could that be compounding the alarming weakness she felt? Was she up to scrambling some eggs? Or should she settle for bread and Marmite? A childhood memory surfaced, in which her father would cut very thin slices of white bread for the children when they were ill, and spread them with Marmite. Somehow he managed to make them taste utterly wonderful.

Eggs would be more nourishing, she decided, and embarked on the task of preparing them, startled to see that it was almost one o'clock. The events of the day swam in and out of focus – several people had been in the house since she got up. The first one, Ralph Callendar, seemed a very distant memory now. What had he wanted? Had he been pretending to be nice and caring about her flu, when all along he was a murderer? The idea seemed laughable. So did any notion of Juliet being a killer. She'd have given herself away instantly, splashed with bloodstains or still holding the weapon. Unless, of course, her appalled mother had quickly concealed all such traces and persuaded her daughter to say nothing at all about Natasha, or where she was on Saturday afternoon. And what about Dennis Ireland, who now became a sinister figure with his expensive waistcoat and faintly odd reaction to seeing Cheryl in the Shepherds' house? He might quite easily have done the deed himself. Perhaps he had been madly in love with the woman, and been rejected when he tried to replace Callendar in her affections? Perhaps he so profoundly disapproved of her liaison with the married man that he had flipped when she gave the funeral party so publicly.

The eggs were somewhat overcooked, but they went down fairly easily. She drank some cold milk with them, imagining herself as an Edwardian child doing Nanny's bidding and taking wholesome food that would boost her energy. It was a new discovery that being ill returned a person to childhood, even when there was nobody there to nurse you. You became your own nurse, recapturing old injunctions that went back through generations, even if you hadn't personally experienced them before. 'Feed a cold and starve a fever' had been echoing in her head for days. So had the slightly crazy controversy as to whether a person with a high temperature should be kept warm, or stripped of all bedcovers and encouraged to cool down. It was not an argument Thea had ever really engaged with, but she recalled Carl, her husband, insisting that nature knew best, and when the body got hot, it was for a reason, and so the sensible course was to go with it and pile on the blankets. It had seemed to work on the occasions when Jessica was poorly.

She did feel marginally better after eating the eggs. She addressed the two dogs – who had watched every mouthful – in a more cheerful tone. 'Let's go outside, then, shall we?' She opened the back door and led them into the garden. Hepzie was unenthusiastic, sniffing under the dry red stalks of a dogwood bush. Blondie went down to her far corner and raised her head for a long careful listen to whatever might be happening in the village beyond. All Thea could hear was car engines, faint voices and a plane overhead. This was not proper exercise by any standards. The garden wasn't large and neither dog showed any inclination to romp. But it was December, midwinter, and no animal could expect long sessions of enjoyment in the open air. Sheep would be glumly gathered behind hedges, rabbits would be hunkering in their burrows. Hedgehogs went to sleep for months on end. 'It's the best you can hope for, just now,' she told her charges. 'Sorry. But at least you can stay out here for a bit.'

Then Blondie's sharp ears angled forward and she barked one short note. Thea had heard nothing, but with due attention she caught the sound of raised voices in the street the other side of the house. One was female and sounded urgent. 'What's going on?' she wondered aloud.

She left the dogs and went back through the house to look out of the living room window. An altercation was taking place barely three feet away, between a middle-aged woman and a younger man. Thea recognised the woman by her dark glasses and long chin – it was Marian Callendar, last seen in the funeral limousine on Friday afternoon. The man was most likely one of her sons who had been in the same car, Thea guessed, although she couldn't identify him from the glimpse she'd had of him. 'Don't try to stop me,' the woman said shrilly. 'It's none of your business.'

'It most certainly is,' he argued, and grabbed at her arm.

If the mullioned window had been double-glazed, it would have been harder to hear what they said. As it was, there was no difficulty. Furthermore, the woman caught sight of the eavesdropper and paused in her struggles. 'Seen enough?' she shouted, right into Thea's face. It was the sort of thing people said in *Eastenders*, but this was a smartly dressed woman, widow of a wealthy businessman, with a pure BBC accent. Thea grimaced her embarrassment and withdrew into the room.

'No! Come out here,' the woman ordered. 'Let's have a proper look at you.'

Mrs Callendar was also a magistrate, Thea remembered, accustomed to giving orders to delinquent youths and befuddled drunkards. On shaking legs she obeyed the order, slowly pulling the front door open and stepping into the street. In Stanton there were few proper pavements, and this house had the scantiest of boundaries between itself and the thoroughfare. No kerbs or yellow lines, simply a semicircular flower bed in winter dormancy, under the window. Passing traffic had to be trusted not to drive over it.

'Where's Gloria Shepherd?' demanded the woman. 'Who are you?'

'She's away. I'm house-sitting for her.'

'Name?'

'Thea Osborne.'

Behind her, both dogs had come to the door. Blondie now emerged and went directly to Marian Callendar, giving her pseudo-snarl that was really a smile. The woman squawked exaggeratedly and backed away. 'Hold that dog! It's going to bite me.'

Any respect or sympathy Thea might have had for her instantly evaporated. People who behaved stupidly with dogs had always been on her list of candidates for the firing squad. She told herself it was fine to be intolerant of intolerance and clung to her position unless an individual could give rock-solid justification for theirs. 'She's not going to bite you, you fool,' she snapped. 'Blondie, darling, come here.' The Alsatian did her bidding with a canine shrug, that said *I was only being friendly*. Thea smiled understandingly and patted the big white head. The poor dog must have spent its whole life being misunderstood. The behaviour classes that Cheryl Bagshawe had mentioned had almost certainly not been at all necessary.

'Mother, can we go now?' said the man, who had hovered uncertainly to one side. Thea diagnosed him as another dog-unfriendly nuisance.

'We're not going until somebody lets me into this house.' She pointed at Natasha Ainsworth's erstwhile home. 'There are things of mine in there that I want to reclaim.'

Thea knew she had a chance to retreat. She could gather up the dogs and firmly shut herself back into the house she was meant to be looking after. But the scene she had been dragged into was far too interesting for that. And the chilly air seemed to be clearing her head slightly. She looked to the man for the next move. He obliged with a valiant effort. 'You can't. You, of all people, must know that. It's a sealed crime scene. See the tape? You know what that means. What the hell's the matter with you?' he finished in exasperation.

Thea wondered why nobody else had emerged from nearby houses to see what the noise was about. Probably they were all watching from their windows, remaining in the shadows rather more successfully than Thea had done. She focused on what the woman had said. Who did she think would let her into the house? There was no sign of any police people, who were the only ones likely to have such authority. 'There's nobody here to let you in,' she said aloud.

'Haven't *you* got a key? Being next door, I'd think you would.'

'Not as far as I know. And this man's right. It's a crime scene. Nobody can go past that tape.'

'"This man" is my son, Edwin. He's been treating me like a lunatic ever since . . . well, you don't want to know all our business. It's nothing to do with you.'

Rudeness from another person always gave Thea a little thrill, which she had recently worked out was because she was occasionally inclined that way herself. Discovering that other people could commit the same sort of indiscretion came as a kind of reassurance.

'You're quite right,' she nodded. 'Although, you *did* bring me out here.'

'Only because you were snooping at us through the net curtains.'

'I heard shouting. It was only natural to come and see what was going on. Especially as there was a violent murder here only yesterday.'

Marian Callendar subsided so completely it was like watching a balloon burst. One minute it was all round and colourful and buoyant, the next it was a limp rag, and you never quite caught the moment of transition. 'Murder,' she repeated with a shudder. 'Such an awful word.'

She *was* a lunatic, Thea decided, with a glance at the son. He met her eye impassively, as if afraid to give anything away. But his mother was also a pillar of the community, a school governor and suffering from leukaemia. She did also have some excuse for erratic behaviour, given the events of the past week or two. Thea could find nothing to say that would be safe, so she clamped her lips shut, and wrapped her arms around herself. She was out in the cold without a coat. Medical advice had been to stay in the warm; she had every reason to leave the Callendars to their own messy lives. But she did want to see what happened next.

'Mother, we have to go,' bleated Edwin. 'Half the village are going to be out here soon, wondering what the noise is about. There's nothing of yours at Natasha's, anyway. I can't think why you ever had such an idea.'

152

'Yes there is,' hissed the woman. 'What would you know about it? For a start, she had half my CDs. He kept "borrowing" them without asking, and then listening to them with her. Stupid man.'

'For God's sake – he's *dead*. Have a bit of respect.'

'I know he is. And I want my music back. I put up with a lot from your father, but I don't see why I should let some house clearance people take what's mine. What's so crazy about that? Just tell me—' She whirled round to look at Thea. 'Tell me what's wrong with that, will you?'

'Nothing,' stammered Thea. 'Sounds reasonable to me. Except you still won't be allowed in there, even with a good reason.'

The dark glasses had been an impediment from the start. Unable to see the woman's eyes made it impossible to fully assess her mental state. Except, of course, the very fact of shades in December suggested something awry. Presumably they were intended to hide signs of weeping from the public gaze, but even if she had been crying at some point during the day, she certainly wasn't doing so now. Or could it be something medical, like oversensitivity to light, Thea wondered. Something associated with the leukaemia? There had been a time when she might have asked outright, but her new resolve to be less confrontational and inquisitive was still holding good.

Edwin was giving her a grateful look, which she found slightly pathetic. This was brother to Ralph, son of the man who died in his bath. Neither of them betrayed much in the way of grief for their father – but Thea knew from her own experience that feelings could be concealed all too easily. Beneath the competence and composure a morass of acute suffering could be lurking. The British way was to keep calm and carry on, even when your lifelong partner died suddenly and left you floundering. Drew often talked of his admiration for the way bereaved people behaved in this society, the quiet, dignified stoicism making his job a lot easier than in some places around the world.

'I'm sorry about your father,' she said to Edwin, out of the blue. She could not pretend to herself that this was a simple statement of condolence. She knew it was intended to prompt some sort of disclosure, some further information that she had no right to. 'It must have been a terrible shock.'

He nodded briefly and returned his attention to his mother. *Okay*, Thea told herself. *Just leave it alone, will you?* She took a step towards the open door of the house. It would be dark in another hour or two. She would try to find something watchable on TV and think about something trivial. She might phone Jessica and see whether she was at Jocelyn's yet. She would tell the story of her car and conceal the fact of her flu.

But social interaction had not yet finished, rather to her annoyance. Before she could get inside and close the door, another person appeared. Dennis Ireland had all too obviously been listening to the exchanges in the street and now came out of his own house, with a half smile. 'Hello again,' he said, nodding vaguely at her. 'Everything all right, is it?'

'I thought you were going away,' Thea frowned. 'Isn't that what you said?'

'Change of plan.' He made a little face of self-reproach. 'Hadn't taken my good sister's priorities fully into account, and jumped the gun. Families, eh!' He twinkled at the two Callendars, who were standing close together a few inches from the police tape across Natasha Ainsworth's house.

'Did you hear what we were saying?' Marian challenged him. 'Who are you, anyway?'

'I heard raised voices, that's all. It's a quiet street, as you can see. Incidents such as we've had this weekend are severely upsetting. Everyone's nervous. To be honest, I'm rather glad to be delaying my departure, under the circumstances. One never knows what predations might take place in one's absence, you see.' He glanced at Thea as if expecting endorsement of his words. 'Besides, the local constabulary have asked me to keep an eye on this young lady, who never bargained for such goings-on, I'm sure.'

Thea winced inwardly. Here was at least one Cotswolds resident who had no idea of her reputation, then. Neither, come to that, did the Callendars appear to know anything about her. Perhaps she was much less famous than she'd come to suspect.

'Does your sister live with you?' she asked, needing as

always to understand as much as she could of people's domestic arrangements.

'Heaven forbid!' he cried, with much more drama than necessary. 'No, she's in Lower Swell – which is still too close for comfort. There's more than a touch of the Gargery woman about our Elspeth, let me tell you. Just as Sebastian Callendar is a dead ringer for Steerforth. Different book, of course.'

Something had happened to the man, Thea was beginning to realise, through the haze of her flu. Either he'd been sampling the Christmas sherry, or had received some good news. He was much more buoyant than the last time she'd seen him. Most likely it was the reprieve his sister had given him. 'So are you here for Christmas, then?'

'Ah – no. Sadly not. It seems I stand little chance of escape, although I continue to hope for a miracle. We have another sister, you see, in Edgware, who insists on the ritual gathering of the clan every year. Nine of us, at least. It's torture.' He laughed grimly. 'There are twin grandchildren who will be three by now. A desperate age, I'm sure you'll agree.'

Nobody took him up on this. His prattle was rapidly being perceived as crass and inappropriate. Marian Callendar evidently came to this conclusion at the same moment as Thea did. 'A woman has been killed here,' she said starchily. 'Show some respect.'

Her son gasped audibly at this turnaround. Thea almost laughed. 'Come on, Mother,' said Edwin, taking

156

hold of her arm. 'This is ludicrous. We can ask the police to arrange for you to collect your things in a day or two. Nothing's going to happen to a few CDs, is it? We'll go back and sort out some more of Dad's paperwork. Ralph might come over to lend a hand. There's plenty to do.'

Marian looked at Dennis. 'The Gargery woman,' she said slowly. 'You mean the one in *Great Expectations*?'

The man nodded. 'Same sinewy forearms.'

'I always thought Natasha was like the Dartle woman. Same martyred air of injury.'

'You can't beat Dickens for capturing a character, can you? They stay in your mind for life.'

'They do,' she agreed. There was a shared sigh, as the two people retreated from reality for a few moments, into a world of Victorian fiction where everything turned out right in the end.

Chapter Nine

The sense of being stuck in a Dickens novel persisted as Thea finally shut herself back inside the Shepherds' house. Out in the village there were flickering lights in some of the windows, and winter birds were collecting on the trees behind the houses, forming sinister black clusters. She pulled the curtains across, knowing it wouldn't be long before the daylight fully faded. The dogs were restless, pottering up and down the hall, their nails clicking on the tiles.

Her flu was becoming a familiar companion; the headache a background constant that made thinking difficult. She felt heavy and tired and shivery. The people outside had diverted her for twenty minutes or so, their oddness increasing as she listened to them. Perhaps her own condition had exaggerated this. Perhaps she had only imagined some of the things they said, some of the faces they made. She didn't know who 'the Dartle woman' was, and only very faintly remembered the one from *Great Expectations*. It was rude of people to exchange literary references like that. People in Stanton were proving to be quite rude, she concluded. Even Cheryl and her impossible dog had been pretty direct on first acquaintance.

She should phone Jessica. It would take some energy and concentration to find the phone, press the right keys, make rational conversation. First she had to locate her bag, which occupied a few minutes. It was upstairs in the bedroom, and coming back down the stairs proved painful for her knees. They refused to bend properly, and hurt when forced. But it was eventually accomplished and her daughter responded quickly. 'Hi, Mum!' she chirped. 'How's things?'

'Not bad,' came the careful reply. 'One or two glitches.'

'Oh?'

'My car, mainly. I put the wrong fuel in it and it died on me. I don't know when I'll get it back.' Uttering these words engendered a sharp pang of anxiety, which she found shockingly disabling. What if it was another three or four days before she was mobile? She would run out of milk and bread before then.

'You idiot. How will you manage? Is there a shop in wherever-it-is? It's *Christmas*, for heaven's sake.'

'I'll survive. I brought lots of stuff with me. There's dog food here, and tins and things.'

'Mum? You sound very weird. You're not drunk, are you?'

'Of course not. What a thing to suggest!' But she did feel giddy and confused, unsure of exactly which words would emerge from her mouth next. 'Are you at Jocelyn's now?' she managed to ask.

'Not yet. We decided I should go down tomorrow morning. I suppose I could call in on you, actually. It must be pretty much on the way. Why didn't we think of that before?'

The temptation added to her feebleness. Jess could bring supplies, sympathy, suggestions. She might even sort out the car people for her. But she would also make a great fuss about the flu and the murder and the rats. 'You forget the rats,' she said.

'I could cope for an hour or so, if I didn't have to go into the same room. I could buy some provisions for you. Or has somebody else offered to help?'

'Not really. It's all a bit chaotic here at the moment.'

'Oh?' Jessica repeated ominously. 'In what way?'

'A woman was killed yesterday. Next door. It's rather a complicated story.'

'It usually is. How involved are you?'

'Not at all. I never even saw her. I've seen Jeremy Higgins . . .'

'Who?'

'He's the detective inspector who was so kind over the thing in Lower Slaughter. He's investigating this one, with Gladwin.'

Jessica had uttered a little mew of distress at the mention of Lower Slaughter. It had become an intensely personal catastrophe for the whole family, following very closely on the death of Thea's father, and was seldom mentioned as a result. 'No wonder you sound so strange,' said the girl.

'I know. But it's a nice house, in a very pretty little village, and I've got all I need, really. You don't want to waste time doing a detour tomorrow. The traffic's going to be horrible.'

'Okay, then,' agreed Jessica, far too readily. 'I expect they'll fix the car for you by tomorrow, anyway. They'll want to get things clear before Christmas, won't they? And it doesn't take long to drain the engine and get it back to normal. When did it happen?'

Thea had to concentrate hard to answer that. 'Yesterday morning. Higgins brought me home.'

'Home,' repeated Jessica softly. 'You think of it as home, after two days, do you?'

'Of course not. I just . . .' She couldn't think what to say. Home was a cold, empty little cottage in Witney, where she and Carl had been an ordinary happy couple for twenty years before calamity befell them. 'Home is where my dog is,' she finished, with a quick little laugh. The truth of it stabbed her viciously. The dog was already almost halfway through its life. What sort of a dependency had she let herself get into when her only anchor was a slightly scruffy spaniel?

'Right,' said Jessica, with a hint of impatience.

162

'As Granny would say,' she added with a little laugh. Self-pity was taboo throughout the family, largely thanks to Thea's mother having had a tendency that way while her children were growing up. Whatever they said, she would make little effort to take a more tolerant view. But since her own widowhood, she had improved considerably, much to everyone's surprise. 'So I'll stick to Plan A, then, unless you call me tomorrow with a change of heart. I'm leaving at eight, so you'll have to make it early.'

'That's fine, Jess. Have a lovely time at Jocelyn's. At least the weather's not too bad.'

'Rain, they say, for the rest of the week.'

'Really?' The prospect was far more lowering than it ought to have been. 'That's a pity.'

'Well, I expect you'll keep yourself occupied, as always. I suppose you have to walk the dog?'

'Dogs, plural. Yes.' Two days now and the wretched animals had barely stepped outside. But she wasn't going to admit that. 'I don't suppose it'll rain the whole time.'

'No. Okay, then. See you sometime in the New Year.' And she rang off.

Thea was left with a swirling mass of unpleasant emotions. She had concealed her state of health for no very noble reasons, probably hoping subconsciously that Jessica would somehow divine the truth without being told. She had had a glimpse of herself as a stubbornly isolated martyr, when she could quite easily have been part of a lively, noisy family celebration. Although not with flu, she reminded herself. Jocelyn would not have welcomed her presence if there was a risk she'd infect five children and their parents. She had casually mentioned a murder, with no hint of the tragedy and wrongness that went along with a violent death. Yet again she assessed herself harshly, unable to deny the less attractive elements of her character. She couldn't even give the long-suffering dogs a decent time. Well, as a penance, she would definitely release the rats that evening, for their customary run. That was the very least she could do.

Blondie was whining at the front door, she noticed, and probably had been for a few minutes. 'What do you want?' Thea asked the dog.

The reply was unmistakable. *I want to go out for a walk*, said the pricked ears and steady gaze at the invisible street outside.

'But I'm *poorly*,' Thea told her. 'And it's cold out there.' But it wasn't, really. And hadn't she just spent several minutes outside without a coat? What a waste that had been, when she might have been giving the dogs some fresh air. Her own animal was watching her closely, head cocked sideways. It was beyond anyone's power to resist. 'Oh, all right, then. Just a little way. And don't *pull*.' She wasn't sure she had the strength to restrain them if they both decided to take control.

When she reached for the leads hanging on a hook next to the coats in the hallway, both dogs went crazy with excitement. She had not seen Blondie anywhere near as animated since she arrived. She turned in small circles and wagged her heavy tail. 'Wait,' Thea ordered. 'I've got to get my coat on this time. I need to keep warm.' She looked at the hooks for a moment, unable to locate her garment. A blue woollen coat with big buttons was next to it, which confused her. *When did I rearrange them?* she asked herself, remembering that her own jacket had been sharing a hook with a brown coat. The skirmishing continued as the Alsatian was attached to her lead and let out through the front door. Hepzie was permitted to stay free, given the paucity of traffic and her disinclination to run off, as a general rule. 'Steady!' Thea shouted.

What happened next was utterly, horrifyingly unexpected. Hepzie was jumping at Thea's legs, while Blondie started to head along the street, towards the higher ground at the end. The larger dog gave a snarl as Hepzie landed awkwardly, bumping against her. Just what the snarl expressed in dog language would be forever a mystery, but the spaniel took great exception to it, and totally gratuitously began to snarl in response. Furthermore, she opened her jaws and clamped them shut on Blondie's pointed left ear. Then she shook and pulled as if she had a rat in her mouth.

Thea was slow to grasp what had happened. Blondie screamed a long blood-curdling protest, full of pain and shock. Hepzie just shook and pulled some more, creating a gash from which bright blood spurted onto the thick white coat. 'Stop it!' Thea screamed and kicked hard at her own dog. 'Let go, you bloody fool.'

When nothing changed, she called 'Help!' as loudly as she could. Blondie's screams were considerably louder, and surely more likely to bring rescue. Inside all those houses, just feet away, there were strong men who did not have flu, and who could prise open a spaniel's soft jaws with ease. Nobody came. Not even Dennis Ireland emerged from his front door, yet again summoned by noises in the street. A car came into view around the gentle bend, and Thea waved frantically at its occupant, while still kicking at Hepzie, and watching blood splatter everywhere.

'Good God, Thea – is that you?' came a familiar voice. Before she could answer, strong hands had grabbed the spaniel by the throat, squeezing her until she let go of the ear. 'Let go, you little beast,' she ordered. 'What the hell are you thinking of?'

'Gladwin,' breathed Thea, before tottering backwards and slumping against the wall of the house. 'Thank heaven!'

The detective superintendent lifted Hepzie bodily into the air and thrust her at her mistress. 'Here. Hold her,' she ordered. Thea obeyed clumsily, clasping the wriggling dog to her chest in arms that felt quite unequal to the task. The shock of what Hepzie had done was numbing her brain. With no previous hint of anything resembling aggression, Thea would have trusted her spaniel with a newborn baby, without a second thought. Or a litter of blind kittens. Though perhaps not with a rat. The idea that she would attack a dog five times her own size, for no reason at all, would have been dismissed as ludicrous less than ten minutes previously.

Blondie was whimpering miserably, shaking her bleeding head, sinking down onto her stomach like a collapsed sheep. Gladwin peered closely at the torn ear. 'It's not so very bad,' she judged. 'The blood looks worse on the white coat. She's lovely, isn't she.'

'She's a wimp,' said Thea.

'Alsatians often are. I expect she was taken by surprise. What's her name?'

'Blondie. She's been pining for her people ever since I got here. She seems to have a reputation locally for biting, but I don't think she deserves it. She does a sort of smile that looks like a snarl.'

Gladwin crooned over the wounded dog, soothing bits of nonsense that seemed to have some effect. Thea remained propped against the wall, clutching her wicked pet. 'I can't imagine why she did it. They were terribly excited about going for a walk, and then something just flipped.'

'It's very common. I've seen it lots of times. We had Irish setters when I was young, and they did it. Best of friends one minute and snapping and biting the next. And I was called to an incident just like this, some years ago, in a park. A Jack Russell tore an Alsatian's ear right off, and all he did was cry.'

'Oh, well, a Jack Russell,' said Thea. 'What do you expect? But Hepzie's a *spaniel*.'

'True. But they're both bitches, and that'll do it. Has Blondie been spayed?'

'I have no idea. How could I tell?'

Gladwin moved to the white dog's rear end, and unceremoniously lifted her tail. 'Ah! That'll explain it. She's coming onto heat, look. Hepzie won't have liked the hormonal vibes, for some reason.'

Thea leant closer for a look at the Alsatian's genitalia. 'It looks a bit swollen,' she admitted.

'Right. I imagine she's not just pining, but feeling a bit queasy. I swear dogs get period pains, the same as people do.'

'So does she need a vet? For the ear?'

'I'm afraid so. It'll have to have a few stitches. First we'll stop the bleeding. Can we go in?'

Stumblingly, Thea led the way. This, she told herself, was what she was being paid for – to summon help if her charges got into trouble. But it was definitely not part of her remit for her own dog to inflict that trouble. The shame and embarrassment made her hotter than the flu had done.

Gladwin efficiently mopped the gashed ear, having located Dettol and a sponge under the kitchen sink. The hair all around the wound was wet and dirty with blood. The good ear drooped in sympathy, the dark eyes wide with reproach and self-pity. 'Poor Blondie,' sighed Thea. 'She's going to be scarred for life.'

'It won't show for long, if they sew it up properly.'

She gently fingered a flap of flesh that had almost separated from the rest of the ear. 'But we ought to be quick.'

'I haven't got a car,' Thea remembered. 'I can't take her. And where's the nearest vet, anyway?'

'Stow, I suppose. Isn't there a number somewhere? Haven't the people left a list?'

'Oh, yes. Everything's written down.' Thea rooted in the drawer beneath the phone where she had put Philip's instructions for safe keeping. 'Here it is. Will they come out, do you think?'

'Not a chance. I'll take you.'

'Oh.' Outside it was close to dusk, and very uninviting. 'Actually, I'm not very well. I've got flu.'

'So I gather. Higgins told me about it. But I don't think you've got a choice, have you? I absolutely must be somewhere at four-thirty, which gives us just over an hour. I can't risk being late, so I'm going to have to drop you at the vet and leave you to get a taxi back. Shouldn't be too difficult.'

'But . . .' *I've got flu*, she wanted to whine. But she knew she would get scant sympathy. Gladwin had doubtless worked through innumerable viruses and injuries without complaint herself, and expected no less from other women. She probably believed, as Thea more or less did too, that the best treatment for illness was to ignore it.

'Leave your dog in the house. Get your bag and phone. I'll put Blondie in the car while you do that.

We'll be off in exactly one minute.' The briskness brooked no argument. Thea found the necessary objects, gave Hepzie a stern command to stay where she was, and slammed the front door behind her. Only then did she wonder whether she had a key to get in again.

'Key!' she flustered. 'I don't think I've got the key.'

'Coat pocket?'

By some miracle, it was there, and not alone. There was a jingling collection on a brass ring. Front, back and garden shed padlock could all be accessed, after all. 'Phew!' said Thea.

In the car, Blondie panted and whined on the back seat with Thea while Gladwin sped through the darkening lanes. Thea's mind remained uncharacteristically blank. 'You should phone ahead to say we're coming,' Gladwin said.

'I can't. I forgot to bring that sheet of paper.'

'Here it is.' Gladwin produced it from her jacket pocket. 'You're really not firing on all cylinders today, are you?'

'I've got a horrible headache and all my joints hurt. Plus I've got a temperature. I keep going all hot and cold. It's not easy to think, with all that going on.'

'Just tell them you're bringing in a dog with a torn ear. There's someone living over the surgery, I expect. We'll be fifteen minutes.'

Thea manipulated her phone, her thumb seeming much too big for the delicate little keys. A person answered, the tale was told and promises made. It took very little time.

'The murder,' Gladwin said, the moment the phone call was finished. 'In the next house to yours.'

'What about it?'

'Any ideas? Any observations? Higgins thinks you're our most promising witness so far.'

Thea's mind resisted this appeal quite strenuously. 'How can I think about that now?' She stroked the injured dog remorsefully and crooned reassurances.

'Easily, if you try. You're doing all you can for the dog – with my help, I might remind you. All I'm asking is that you repay me with any snippets you think we should be aware of.'

Thea made an effort to comply, but nothing came to mind beyond the events of an hour or two earlier. 'Did Higgins question Juliet?'

'I expect so. She's not very relevant.'

'He thinks it was her.'

'What do *you* think?'

'If it was, her mother would know about it. She'd have washed the blood off her and told her to stay quiet. Any mother would.'

'She's not a child, you know. It wasn't Juliet Wilson. At least, it's highly unlikely. She was seen in Laverton by three different people during Saturday afternoon. She'd have needed to move incredibly fast.'

'Higgins seemed to know about her.'

'Oh yes. All you have to do is key "Stanton" into

171

the database and she pops up. For about twenty years now, she's been regularly reported as lost, trespassing, causing a nuisance, in need of protection, doing all kinds of things the locals think are worrying.'

'So what's her problem?'

'She was never quite right, apparently. But there was an incident when she was in her teens, something deeply traumatic that she's never got over. Caused a lot of very nasty feeling at the time, accusations flying. I must say her church have been brilliant. Everyone rallies round as much as they can. It's a staunchly Methodist family.'

Almost too much information, Thea felt, when the central issue concerned the Callendars and Miss Natasha Ainsworth. She acknowledged Gladwin's generosity in sharing so much, before going back to the main point.

'I saw the wife, Mrs Callendar, today. She came to Stanton and tried to get into Natasha's house to collect some CDs. She seemed a bit mad to me.'

Gladwin slowed the car and gave Thea a startled look. 'You're joking! *CDs?* That really does sound crazy. Was she by herself?'

'No, one of her sons was with her. Edwin. And I met Ralph this morning as well. They all keeping turning up on my doorstep,' she finished crossly. 'And I really wish they wouldn't.'

'She's obviously the one we've got our eye on. We're looking into the death of her husband a lot more closely now, needless to say.'

172

'I hope he was buried and not cremated, then.'

'What? Oh, no need for that. He definitely died from electrocution while in the bath. The question is, did someone chuck that defective radio in with him, or did it just fall in?'

'How can you ever know?'

'Good question.'

'It must be tempting to see it as a straightforward case of the jealous wife killing her husband and his lover, then? Except she's a magistrate and a school governor and a matriarch with three fine sons.'

'Two fine sons and a black sheep, actually.'

'Oh? I saw them all on Friday, going to the funeral. They all looked okay.' She tried to remember what Ralph had said about his brothers that morning, but it only came back when Gladwin explained.

'The middle one has served time in prison for fraud. He only got out a month ago. I suppose they could hardly shun him at the funeral of his father, but I don't think they've treated him like a prodigal son, exactly.'

'Now I remember. He's a womaniser, as well. Dennis Ireland says he's like Steerforth, I think that was the name. But talking of shunning, they shunned Ralph because he's had flu, and his mother was scared to catch it. She's got leukaemia, so her immunity's rubbish.'

'What? Who told you that?'

She paused. 'Ralph. He said she had poor immunity, because she'd had a mild form of leukaemia for two years. Why – isn't it true?'

'First I've heard of it. But then we don't generally investigate a person's medical records, unless there's a good reason. She's still working. It can't be very bad.'

'Maybe she's in remission or something. But surely she'd have to tell the court people about it? If she's that worried about catching things, she'd make sure nobody sneezed on her during a hearing.'

'So who else have you met since you got here? Any other likely murderers?'

'Only Dennis Ireland. He was lurking about yesterday afternoon. You'll have a statement from him, probably. He was amongst the people who broke in and found Natasha. There could have been a feud between them, and he waited until the Shepherds were out of the way before attacking her.'

'And a woman called Bagshawe, right? She was in the house with you when it happened.'

'Cheryl, yes. With a Great Dane.' Thea shuddered. 'Thank goodness Hepzie didn't tear his ear off as well. I wouldn't want to get on the wrong side of Cheryl. She's fairly formidable.'

'Who is she? Where does she live?'

'You'll have her in your system – she made a statement yesterday, as well. She's going away today – probably gone by now. I know virtually nothing about her, but she said she lives in Stanway. That seemed a bit odd to me, actually, because there are hardly any houses in Stanway, are there? She wrote it down for me somewhere, but I don't remember where I put it.'

'Um . . .' Gladwin had lived in the Cotswolds for less than two years, and could be forgiven for gaps in her knowledge about some of the villages. 'Stanway House,' she hazarded. 'With that big orange gate affair. Cottages. Farms. Is the Great Dane woman a farmer?'

'I think not.'

'She probably lives in Wood Stanway, then. There are several houses down there.'

Thea thought about it. 'There's a place called Wood Stanway? I had no idea.'

'There is, and if she's in the system, we'll have her address. I've been focusing mainly on the family so far. They have every reason to dislike Ms Ainsworth, under the circumstances. Except—'

'Don't tell me – none of them will admit to anything of the sort. She was a beloved old family friend, and it was fine with them if their dad had a thing with her.'

'More or less. Hard to believe, of course.'

Thea veered off the subject 'Do you know a Dickens character called Dartle?'

Gladwin showed no discomposure at this, but answered quite readily, 'Rosa Dartle? In *David Copperfield*? Same as Steerforth – what's all this Dickens stuff about, Thea?'

'It seems to be a sort of game the locals like to play. What was Rosa Dartle like?'

'Oh, heavens. Now you're asking. Let me think. She sat by the fireplace, and had a nasty scar down her face. Steerforth did it when he was a boy, and she made a big thing of forgiving him. Except that really she made him suffer agonies of guilt for it, all his life. That's amazing – I had no idea I knew so much. Mind you, I always did love *David Copperfield*.'

'I must confess I've never read it. She sounds rather nasty.'

'I still don't get what she might have to do with anything?'

'Dennis Ireland said Natasha Ainsworth was like her. And his sister is like the Gargery woman in *Great Expectations*. And Sebastian Callendar is Steerforth. I think Dennis was mostly just showing off. I thought it was a bit rude, quite honestly.'

'If Natasha was like Rosa Dartle, does that mean that somebody did her a great injury, years ago, and that person has now killed her, just to get her off his back? Was the Ireland man trying to say that Sebastian Callendar did it?'

'I have no idea,' snapped Thea. 'No good asking me.'

'I'm not. I'm just thinking aloud.'

'It would make sense for it to be one of the sons,' said Thea with a rush of confidence. 'That would fit the Rosa thing perfectly. They knew Natasha when they were little. Did Steerforth murder Rosa Dartle, by any chance?'

'I don't think so. He seduced Little Em'ly and she emigrated to Australia. He was quite a bad 'un. What does Dennis Ireland know about it, anyway?'

'Rosa . . .' Thea repeated. 'Juliet Wilson's mother is called Rosa. What a coincidence!'

Beside her, Blondie squeaked in a clear protest at being ignored. Thea turned to pacify her. 'Not long now, old girl. Does it hurt?'

'Is it bleeding again?' asked Gladwin. 'I don't really want blood on the seats, although it wouldn't be the first time.'

'It doesn't seem to be. She's shaking it, though. What if she starts scratching at it?'

'You'll have to stop her. Don't be so useless, Thea. It's not like you.'

'I haven't had to deal with a dog this size before. She's bound to be stronger than me if it comes to a disagreement.'

'We'll be there in a minute, so stop fussing.'

They were approaching the complicated junction just before Stow, and Thea began to worry about what happened next. 'Are you sure I'll get a taxi? Will they take Blondie as well?'

'The vet might keep her in.'

'Surely not! It's Christmas Eve tomorrow. They wouldn't do that. And how would I collect her again, without a car? Oh God.' She slumped in the seat, and put both hands to her head. 'My head hurts,' she whimpered.

'So does Blondie's, I expect.' She zigzagged through the traffic lights, and in another minute was pulling up outside a building that she evidently already knew. 'They're good in here. We've used them a few times.'

'Personally or professionally?'

'Both. There was a very nasty business with a horse, just a few weeks ago . . .'

'Don't tell me,' begged Thea.

Gladwin laughed and turned off the engine. 'I'll help you get her out of the car and then you're on your own. Call me tomorrow and tell me how you got on.'

'Thanks, Sonia,' said Thea miserably. 'I'm sorry to be such a nuisance.'

'Not at all. You've given me some very helpful insights, as usual.' She had driven away before Thea could say anything. She could not imagine what the woman meant.

Chapter Ten

The vet deftly cleaned and stitched the Alsatian's torn ear, using a local anaesthetic and a sedative. The dog behaved impeccably throughout. 'Give her half an hour to get back on her feet and then you can go,' Thea was told.

'I'll have to call a taxi,' she said apologetically. 'Do you know one who'd take me and the dog?'

The young man pursed his lips, as if this was by no means a reasonable request. 'First we have to do the paperwork,' he said. 'How do you want to pay?'

Payment had not occurred to Thea until then. If this was the vet that the Shepherds routinely used, perhaps they had an account and the cost could be dealt with when they came home. But Thea knew that she herself would have to find the money sooner or later. By any standards the injury had been her fault, and she would have to shoulder all the responsibility. 'How much is it?' she asked.

The man sighed. 'I'll have to put it all through the computer. We need to go back to basics – your name and address, and so forth. Normally the secretary would do it, of course.'

'But she's not here,' Thea stated the obvious.

Between them they satisfied the computer's craving for irrelevant information, and a final sum was displayed at the bottom of a lengthy column of services, extras and tax. It was almost two hundred pounds. 'Thank goodness you don't want to keep her in overnight,' said Thea with a gulp. 'I'll have to use a credit card.'

'I'll want to see her again at the end of the week,' said the man. 'And let me know meantime if there are any problems. She ought to wear a collar to stop her scratching it. Have you got one?'

'You mean those awful plastic cone things? No, of course I haven't.'

'I'll get one, then,' he said with an air of martyrdom. 'You can have it on loan. Bring it back when you come next time.'

Not once had he remarked on how ill she was looking, or expressed any concern for her being alone at Christmas with an injured dog. She knew she was pale and clammy and could scarcely drag herself about. But nobody cared. Even Gladwin had been hurtfully lacking in sympathy. The prospect of struggling back to Stanton with Blondie was taking on the quality of a trek across the Himalayas. 'Taxi?' she reminded the vet.

'I have no idea,' he said unhelpfully.

'Come on,' she pleaded. 'There must be a card somewhere – everybody has cards for minicabs pinned up. Your customers must have to use them sometimes.'

He shrugged, and then – finally – he really looked at her. 'Where is it again? Where do you have to go?'

'Stanton. It's not very far.'

'You're in luck, then. I've got to go to Broadway this evening. Oh, and there's something I should drop in at a farm in Wood Stanway. I'll give you a lift. You don't look awfully well.'

'No, I'm not. Thank you.' She almost wept on him. 'Things always seem so much worse when it's dark, don't they?'

It wasn't yet five o'clock, but outside it was definitely night already. She stroked Blondie's thick white coat and found that she was actually weeping. The dog was so well behaved, so beautiful and misunderstood, that sadness washed uncompromisingly through her. Why was it, she wondered fiercely, that almost every dog she met gave cause for worry, guilt or grief? Did she displace onto animals emotions that rightfully belonged to human beings? She suspected that was the judgement of a lot of people around her. She ought to be shocked and outraged by the killing of Natasha Ainsworth, instead of mooning uselessly over a damaged pet. She wiped her eyes with her hand and hoped the vet hadn't noticed. 'We'll just wait quietly for a bit, shall we?' she asked. 'Until she's ready to go?'

He nodded. 'I have to go back upstairs and get ready. But you can't stay in here.' He looked round at shelves of drugs, hypodermics, scalpels, and other dangerous veterinary materials and winced. 'It's not allowed. You'll have to go into the waiting room. I'm afraid it's a bit cold.'

'What about Blondie?' The room had no soft surfaces on which a dog might comfortably lie.

'Take her with you. You can keep each other warm.'

She forced a smile. He was doing his best, having obviously drawn the short straw and been dubbed the emergency vet for the Christmas period. Although, if he lived over the surgery, this must be a regular obligation, she presumed. He struck her as single, on the basis of very little evidence. Still in his twenties, with bad skin and poor people skills, she couldn't see that he'd readily find a girlfriend. But what did she know about him? He was nifty with a suturing needle and did possess a warm heart somewhere, it seemed.

Then it turned out that he had no way of taking her credit card payment. 'The stuff's all locked down for the night,' he said. 'And I'm not sure how to use it, anyway. We'll have to trust you.'

Thea just nodded, thinking vaguely that her finances would be in great disarray for the next few weeks, with this and the bill for her car. It did not seem to matter in the least.

* * *

The vet drove a big estate car, with the rear section full of plastic boxes, rubber garments and long boots. Blondie was helped onto the back seat where she slumped dazedly and again Thea squashed in beside her. The dog was yet to have the unpleasant plastic collar fitted. Privately, Thea had already resolved not to use it if it could be avoided. She couldn't imagine how any creature could sleep wearing such a horrid thing. Surely she wouldn't scratch at her ear once she realised the painful consequences.

At the crossroads by the statue of St George they turned left, where a sign said 'Didbrook Wood Stanway'. Thea had automatically assumed that it led to a place called Didbrook Wood, and perhaps a smaller part of Stanway.

'Oh – it's Wood Stanway,' she realised aloud. 'I never knew there was a separate village of that name.'

'It's very small. A couple of farms and six or seven houses. The road peters out and just turns into a farm track.'

She peered ahead down the dark lane, seeing no sign of habitation. They took a left fork, and the vet drew up beside a gateway beyond which she could make out a big Dutch barn with its curved roof. 'I'll be three minutes maximum,' he said. 'It's just some antibiotics they need for lambing. It all starts at the end of the week.'

'No rush,' she said comfortably.

They were parked near a triangular patch of grass

in which was planted a post with indistinct footpath signs. Faint light from the farmhouse windows made it visible. Just as Thea was imagining life inside the scattered houses, all doors closed firmly against the early onset of darkness, a figure hurried towards her. She assumed it was coming to speak to her – perhaps suspicious of a strange car, or even recognising it and wanting a word with the vet.

But instead, the person stopped at the post, and began to attach a white sheet of paper to it. Awkwardly, with a torch gripped under one elbow, she tied string around the upright, both at the head and the foot of the notice. As the beam wavered erratically, Thea caught enough detail to recognise Cheryl Bagshawe. Her conversation with Gladwin came back to her, with this confirmation that the woman really did live in Wood Stanway, as suggested. Cheryl and her Great Dane lived here, in a tiny hamlet that nobody knew about. Even walkers on whatever footpath it might be would probably not register where they were unless they kept a very firm eye on a map.

She shrank down in the seat, hoping to go unseen. The attaching of the notice was quickly completed, and Cheryl disappeared the way she had come. The vet appeared half a minute later, and got quickly into the car.

'Have you got a torch?' Thea asked him.

'Yes, but I don't need it. It's not so dark as all that.'

'Where is it?'

'Probably under your feet. I tend to keep it down there, so I can grab it quickly.'

She fumbled on the floor of the car and found a substantial Maglite against the hump running down the middle of the floor. 'Can you wait just a minute?' she asked. 'I want to see what that notice says.' She was out of the car before he could respond, shining the light on Cheryl's notice.

The main part was printed in large bold capitals, and occupied five lines. CONTRARY TO PREVIOUS INFORMATION, IT IS NOW DEFINITELY CONFIRMED THAT THERE WILL BE A PERMANENT DIVERSION TO THIS PATH IN OPERATION FROM JANUARY 1ST. Below was a map and grid references to indicate the route of the diversion.

'How boring,' muttered Thea, and got back into the car.

The road from Stanway to Stanton, between the huge old trees, with no lights showing on either side, seemed distinctly sinister. There was a mist, for good measure. 'Rain tomorrow,' said the vet. 'And all over Christmas.'

'Oh dear. That'll ruin the atmosphere, won't it?' She felt inane, inarticulate. Her head was pounding, and she could think of nothing whatever to look forward to. Just a long, miserable winter ahead, once she had survived another week at Stanton. What did she care if it rained? What difference would it make?

'Stanton's where that woman got killed yesterday, isn't it?'

'Right. In the house next to where I am, actually. I never met her, though. It looks like a family thing. At least . . .' She wasn't equal to the task of explaining the unorthodox arrangements of the Callendars. It wasn't her business, anyway.

'Family? I thought she didn't have any family.'

'Oh. You know who she was, then?'

'Sort of. My mother's in some club that she was in.'

'A book club?' Thea hazarded.

'No, no. It's a fundraising outfit for sick horses.'

'Is your mother a vet?'

'Actually, yes – sort of. She's in research, now. All very leading-edge stuff. She knew Callendar quite well. His company sponsors some of her work.'

Thea knew that if her mind had been functioning properly, she would grasp all these connections and make a pattern out of them. Something medical to do with Callendar snagged at her. 'What exactly did Mr Callendar do?' she asked.

'He ran a business that transports urgent medical supplies for animals. Semen for horses, as well. And blood for transfusions. There are a whole lot of new developments in animal medicine. They're talking about organ transplants, last I heard.' He spoke carelessly, as if the subject was only marginally interesting. 'Not my sort of line at all,' he added. 'Horses are my least favourite of all the things I deal with. Reaction against my mother, I expect. She's obsessed with them – same as Natasha was.'

186

Thea was relieved to have her niggling curiosity satisfied. 'I saw it in the paper. Callendar Logistics. I wish they'd stop using that word.'

'It's "Solutions" that gets me,' he laughed. 'I suppose the people who first thought them up felt so pleased with themselves. They ought to get royalties every time a new business uses one or other of them.'

'This is me,' said Thea suddenly. They had almost passed the Shepherds' house, in their belatedly absorbing conversation. 'Thanks ever so much.'

'I'll help you get the dog out. She'll be woozy for the rest of the evening. Don't forget the collar.'

'Do we have to? They seem such cruel things. How is she supposed to sleep wearing the horrible thing?'

'I know they're awful, but I'm required to recommend it. You can probably leave it for tonight, with her being so zonked with the painkillers, and see how she is tomorrow. You'll have to keep a close eye on her and definitely put it on if she scratches at the ear.'

'Thanks. That's what I thought.'

Between them they got the dog out of the car and into the house. Hepzie came flying to greet them, as always, and Thea froze in panic at the prospect of a renewed attack on the Alsatian. But the spaniel completely ignored Blondie and simply bounced around her mistress's legs, as well as giving a quick scrabble at the newcomer's trousers.

'Is this the aggressor?' he asked.

'I'm afraid so. I don't know what came over her.

187

Gladwin said Blondie's coming into season, which must be something to do with it.'

'Hormones,' he nodded. 'You'll have to keep them separate from now on.'

Thea groaned at the idea of all the careful closing of doors and individual meals and walks for the next week or more. 'I suppose I'll have to watch out for unwanted suitors as well.'

'She won't be very interesting for a few more days. Didn't her people warn you?'

'Not a word.'

'I think they're planning to breed from her,' he said with a frown. 'I remember something about it a few months ago. How long are they away?'

'Another week.'

'They'll catch her in time, then. The ear will have mended by the time she's ready for mating. She is a lovely specimen, I must say.'

'Much nicer than any horse,' Thea agreed.

The vet laughed. 'Wash your mouth out. That's a scandalous thing to say around here.'

He was gone, with a backward glance of concern, both for Thea and the Alsatian. She closed the door on him and turned reluctantly into the dark house. All that awaited her were hungry rats, tedious yuletide television and a restless feverish night.

But there were still hours of evening ahead, before she could crawl up to bed. Ill she might be, but lying under

188

a duvet with nobody to bring her soothing drinks and tempting morsels was not an appealing option. She had enjoyed her father's sympathetic ministrations as a child, but even then it had been unfashionable to stay in bed all day. Sick children of her generation were lucky to be allowed quiet days huddled on the family sofa. Working mothers meant the whole business was complicated and stressful. The sufferer was liable to be shipped off to neighbours or grandmothers, or left in the charge of a resentful teenager recruited from some distant branch of the family. Thea's schoolfellows had plenty of anecdotes along those lines. But her own mother had been at home, more than happy to consign the patient to its bedroom and run up and down the stairs with necessities that included books, puzzles, and conversation. When her husband came home, Mrs Johnstone had handed the job over to him, like a nurse at the end of her shift.

Perhaps it was this bout of nostalgia that made Thea feel steadily worse as the minutes rolled by. She ached all over, and was very shivery. 'It's the ague,' she muttered to herself, closing her eyes. 'I've got the ague.' The word enlarged in her mind, shouting itself at her, losing all sense. Andrew Aguecheek materialised, thin and dim-witted, dressed like a harlequin and jabbing a finger at her. She quickly opened her eyes again, and reached for the warm consolation of her dog.

Dog! What had she done with poor Blondie? It was Hepzie pressed close against her on the sofa, not the big white animal. Had she put it in the kitchen and shut the door? Wasn't that awfully unkind? But what else could she do? Swop them over? That would be more just, in the circumstances. Hepzie had done a very bad thing, after all. But it would require more effort than she could summon up. 'At least we're all alive,' she muttered, genuinely grateful for this basic fact.

People had come to her aid throughout the day, so there was no need to panic. If she really needed help, rescue would be available from somebody somewhere. *Yes – but who?* asked her inner voice. Somebody, that's who. Just beyond her door were unknown Samaritans who would feed the dogs and water the plants and boil a kettle for another Lemsip, and generally keep things going for another day or two. Just because Jessica was impossible and Drew unthinkable did not mean she was entirely abandoned. There was Gladwin and that vet, and Cheryl and even the Wilson mother and daughter – they were all quite liable to manifest themselves before she could even call them.

But the person who did manifest herself was not on that list at all, and was almost the last one Thea would ever have expected.

Chapter Eleven

The effort of answering the door was prodigious and she almost gave it up. The knocker sounded again as she dragged herself down the hallway. There was no glass in the door, so she had no clue as to who might be on the other side. 'I'm coming,' she croaked. Even her lungs seemed to be involved in the overall weakness that was afflicting her.

A familiar woman stood there, minus hat and glasses, but with the same coat as before. 'Mrs Callendar,' said Thea. 'Again.'

She had lost track of events from the past twelve hours. It felt as if Marian Callendar had been on the same spot only a short time ago – until she remembered the dog fight and the trip to the vet which had taken place since.

'Let me in,' ordered the woman, and began to push

into the house without invitation. Thea clung to the door for support. 'I need your help,' the new widow added.

There was a reason why she ought not to comply. Something about immunity, or the lack of it. The Ralph person had told her something. Her muddled head strove sluggishly to recapture the information. Leukaemia! That was it, or so she had concluded. His mother had leukaemia or something very like it and should stay away from infection. 'I've got flu,' she said. 'Quite badly.'

'So what?'

'You . . . you might catch it.'

'I won't. I've been vaccinated. Listen, dear – just let me in and get out of the way, all right? I'll be in and out before you can shake a horsewhip.'

Thea searched the woman's hands in vain for such an item. Just a turn of phrase, then. 'No,' she protested. 'Not without an explanation. I'm responsible for this house. What are you going to do?' Recollection of Marian Callendar's erratic behaviour earlier in the day gave rise to a delirious jumble of fears. She might set fire to the house, or break a window, or upset poor Blondie.

'I'm going to go out of your back door for five minutes, then come in again. That's all. Nothing for you to worry about.'

Even with flu, Thea had no difficulty in understanding the implications. 'You can't,' she said flatly. 'They'll have locked it all up.'

'They won't know where the spare key to the back is. They won't have expected anybody to slip in that way. Why would they? And I only want to collect one or two things.'

'CDs,' nodded Thea.

'That's right.' The patronising little smile told Thea that the CD story was spurious; a convenient cover for something more sinister. And she imagined the police would certainly have anticipated the risk of someone breaking in through the back. Quite what they might do about it was a different question.

'Did you kill her?' she asked, point-blank. 'You must be the chief suspect.'

'Of course I didn't. Tash was an old friend. I'm going to miss her desperately. And what's more, that house now technically belongs to me. Douglas bought it for Natasha, fifteen years ago, but it was never in her name. I get to inherit it now they're both gone.'

She should know the law, Thea supposed, being a magistrate. All the same, it didn't sound altogether right to her. 'Did she pay rent for it?' she asked. Her brain was clearing as she plunged into her habitual analysis of the story. She felt a little spasm of excitement at finally being included in the heart of this Stanton mystery.

'Enough to cover the maintenance costs, that's all.'

'All the same, I doubt if the police would regard that as justification for breaking in. Doesn't your son know you've come back here?'

'Edwin? He just dumped me back at the manor and

rushed off somewhere. I'm all on my own in that bloody great barn – except for the horses, of course.'

Again, Thea's lurking delirium painted a picture of Marian Callendar snuggled up in a barn against the flank of a great shire horse. She smiled to herself. At this rate, she was going to come to rather enjoy being so feverish.

'Do you have any idea who did kill Natasha?' she asked boldly.

'Why in the world would I tell you, even if I did?'

'Good question,' mumbled Thea. They had progressed awkwardly down the hall and into the kitchen, where the back door seemed to glow as a point of conflict. If the older woman chose to exert even the slightest force, there was no way Thea could prevent her from doing what she liked. 'It's probably somebody I haven't met, anyway. Probably I'll never even know when they're finally caught. I'll be onto another job and won't even see the news when it comes.'

Marian ignored her and made for the back door. Blondie was in her basket in a corner of the kitchen, head resting on the padded edge, sharp nose overhanging. 'Mind the dog,' said Thea. 'She's not very well.'

'Don't tell me she's got your flu.' The accompanying laugh was not pleasant. 'That dog has always been a pain in the posterior.'

'Why? She's a lovely animal. As soft as anything. Why don't people like her?'

'She barks too much. She runs off and chases sheep.

She's come within a whisker of getting herself shot, more than once.' She squinted down at Blondie. 'What happened to her?'

Thea flushed. 'My spaniel tore her ear.'

'Who stitched it up?'

'The vet in Stow.'

'Toby Harris? Son of our good friend Barbara?'

'Probably. Young, fair. He didn't tell me his name. But he said his mother knew Natasha.'

'That's him. God knows why he took up vet work, when he's so useless with horses. At least he ought to have gone to some city where it's all cats and hamsters. Half the work here is equine.'

'You've got horses, have you?'

'Just a few.' The irony suggested a large herd of the beasts. 'Though I imagine I'll have to downsize now, without Natasha. She ran the business side, you see.'

Thea did not see at all. But at least she had managed to delay the woman's illegal entry into the house next door. The urgency of this task had acquired a whole extra dimension, fuelled by Edwin Callendar's obvious efforts to prevent it earlier on. Although Mrs Callendar was now much less volatile than before, much quieter and more reasonable, her central purpose remained as irrational and unthinkable as it had been from the start. It was increasingly obvious that she wanted to remove evidence, pervert the course of justice, cover up the identity of a murderer. This was not a good thing to do. Even in the depths of her fluey fever, Thea knew this.

195

'You must know I'm friendly with the police. I've known Sonia Gladwin since she first moved down here. And DI Higgins. And—'

'Detective Superintendent Phil Hollis,' Marian supplied. 'Yes, I know. So what? I'm friendly with the police myself.'

'Don't you think I'll tell them that you broke into the scene of a crime and removed something important?'

'I think that by the time you do that, it won't matter any more. Besides, I'm just collecting some things that are mine anyway. I won't touch anything else. I didn't kill anybody. It's a small detail in the larger picture. Nobody's going to lose any sleep over it.'

'What sort of things?'

'Just a few bits that I need. I told you – CDs, mainly.'

Thea hovered between anger at the vagueness and a weary resignation. 'Well . . .' she began.

'Look – it's none of your business. All you have to do is go back to your sickbed and leave me to do what I have to. You won't get into trouble. You're not aiding and abetting a murderer. I've got an alibi for Saturday that completely clears me – as if that was necessary. Stop being so prissy about it,' she finished in exasperation. 'I should have been on my way home again by now. Just get out of the way, will you?'

The loss of patience was unnerving. Blondie lifted her head and whined at the raised voice. Thea shared her pain, putting a hand to her own head in sympathy. 'You're upsetting the dog,' she said. 'Stop shouting.'

'I wasn't shouting. But I'm not going to be thwarted again, so have some sense. Stop asking questions, will you. The less you know, the better. It's sensitive business data, that's all.'

'Don't you think the police will already have found it, in that case? They'll have copied everything from Natasha's computer by now.'

'Maybe,' shrugged Marian, in an unconvincing show of unconcern. 'But I want to see for myself.'

In spite of everything, Thea felt a dawning sympathy for the woman. Police investigations frequently unearthed evidence of dealings and doings that had no direct link to the murder, but which led to other lines of enquiry and unwelcome revelations. Not until it was too late did they accept that their discoveries had been mere red herrings in the murder enquiry. Too late to cover them up again and let sleeping dogs lie.

'Do you promise it has nothing to do with her murder?' she asked.

'Since I really don't know who killed her or why, that's not easy to do. Life's not that simple, is it? Things connect. People conceal their real motives. Natasha was involved in things I knew nothing about. She might have hurt or offended someone years ago, and they're only now taking revenge. Or they might be worried about something she was going to do, and had to stop her.'

Thea's head was pounding. She sank into a kitchen chair and leant forward over the table as if her spine had turned to soft rubber. New suspicions were gathering cloudily – the middle Callendar son was surely in the mix somewhere, for one thing. Convicted of fraud, someone had said. Had Natasha known something that might further incriminate him? 'I can't stop you,' she moaned. 'Even though I know it's wrong, what you're doing.'

'It's not wrong.' Marian spoke sharply. 'It's for the greater good. It's a small misdemeanour that will save a far greater injury. And that's all I intend to tell you.' She was through the kitchen door in a flash, leaving it open for cold air to get in. There was a wall between the two gardens, three or four feet high, made of Cotswold stone. No doubt Natasha had a shed where she kept a key to the back door, or an upturned flowerpot – some obvious hiding place that Marian had always known about. The woman's competence was daunting. Even her earlier loss of control and humiliating removal by her son had not entirely concealed the solid core of confidence and determination.

She came back within ten minutes – a spell that had felt extremely long to Thea. She closed the door, nodded without a word and was away through the front before Thea could properly focus on her.

But she had seen what the woman was holding.

Chapter Twelve

Marian Callendar had promised her that the object she wanted from Natasha's house had no bearing on the woman's murder. But then she would say that, wouldn't she? She would hope that Thea simply left it all alone and looked the other way – a foolish hope, given that Thea had already told her how intimate she was with senior members of the police force. Except, of course, that Marian herself was also likely to be intimate with the same people, given that she was a magistrate. She would carry professional clout and have no difficulty in persuading them that all her actions were entirely justified. And Marian was right if she thought Thea was too ill and achey to care much anyway.

Even so, the question of Marian's motivation niggled at Thea. Natasha Ainsworth had worked for Callendar Logistics. She was friendly with a veterinary researcher and a family who owned a substantial number of horses. Douglas Callendar and his Callendar Logistics had sponsored some sort of medical research that involved animals, according to the young vet from Stow. It all seemed to fit together, as well as being a very obvious activity for people living in the Cotswolds. There were racing stables and stud farms scattered all over the area. Stanton itself had a riding school on its northern edge. Horses were an inescapable side effect of the affluence and social climbing that characterised much of the region. Thea had no problem with horses, other than a low-level irritation she shared with almost every other car driver. She could imagine it was a delight to ride all day across the tops of the wolds, the views and the easy rhythm a balm in a busy business life. With history her main interest, the fact of horses and their central place in human activity through the ages could not be ignored. Their decline into useless appendages fit only for expensive leisure pursuits or exploitative gambling was a melancholy evolution. The moment people could no longer afford to ride or place bets at the races, horses would be destroyed in their thousands and perhaps never be part of the landscape again. One more unforeseen consequence of economic catastrophe, in a long list. Unless, of course, the opposite happened, and horses were once again employed for transport and haulage when the oil ran out.

Not normally inclined to fantasies about Armageddon, Thea's flu seemed to be pushing her in that direction. It was said to be depressing, she recalled, and this evening of the day before Christmas Eve seemed to offer plenty to feel gloomy about. People were dying, it was going to rain, Drew was being run ragged by all the demands on him, her car was in some nameless garage and Hepzibah had torn Blondie's ear. The last in itself would be enough to bring worry and trouble down on her. If she had been well, she would certainly have tracked down her car by this time and made efforts to retrieve it.

Out in the village there would be celebrations and excitement. Nobody, as far as she could tell, was especially prostrated by the killing of Natasha Ainsworth. On the discovery of her body there had been shock, even horror, but nobody she had seen looked to be personally affected. And yet many of them had been at her house the day before she died. Some people had chosen to toast the passing of Douglas Callendar with his mistress, his paramour, rather than with his wife. There had to have been more significance to this than mere geographical convenience. There had been twenty people or more – a substantial proportion of the population of Stanton – accepting Natasha's sandwiches and sherry and tacitly condoning her relationship with the deceased. Had one of them crept back next day and stabbed the wretched woman to death?

Despite the physical violence, Thea found herself visualising the killer as female in her overactive imaginings. Dennis Ireland was the predominant man on her list of possible candidates, and he had struck her as lacking the necessary rage or resentment for the deed. As did Ralph and Edwin Callendar. In contrast, she had met a number of angry, unusual, unpredictable women. Rosa Wilson, Cheryl Bagshawe, Marian Callendar, Juliet Wilson, the vet's mother and the Callendar sons' wives all crowded into her mind clutching sharp knives and raging at the faceless Natasha. And if Natasha Ainsworth had been capable of seducing one woman's husband, she might well do so again. There could be Stanton wives working themselves up into such frenzies of suspicious jealousy that the only recourse had been to kill the woman before she could snatch their own Rupert or Henry, Justin or Adam.

As she tried to shake her head free from such unwholesome meditations, Thea experienced a small revelation. It came in a flash, and seemed both blindingly obvious and completely new. House-sitting was boring. Sitting in somebody's house while they enjoyed exotic holidays or fulfilled complicated obligations elsewhere was almost the dullest occupation there could be. All you could do was explore the neighbourhood and interfere in the lives of the surrounding people. She had done this time and again – although there had also been occasions when the neighbours had forced themselves onto her attention. Her reputation as a harbinger of calamity was only justified by a long series of contingencies that all turned out to have logical explanations. It was her persistent habit of getting involved that marked her out as special. And that had effectively been due to her relationship with the police. Having found a body during her very first commission, she did not, as most would have done, settle back into the house and keep her head down. She roamed the village talking to people. She befriended them and made deductions about them. Her dead husband's brother was a senior police officer – a fact that had shown her that the police were human beings, approachable, fallible, and very often extremely grateful for her assistance. It had somehow enabled her to unreservedly enter into a relationship with Detective Superintendent Phil Hollis, and treat him as she would any other man. Here her conscience gave her its familiar stab, at the memory of how badly she had actually treated Phil. She had developed a habit of rationalisation that took over every time she thought of him. She had been punishing him for not being Carl. She had felt constrained to show him her darkest side. She had been in the grip of turbulent hormones, so common in a woman's forties. She had panicked at the increasing intimacy and instinctively acted to repel any further closeness. Or all of the above, she thought glumly.

The thing about having a fever and a headache and heavy clumsy limbs was that your thoughts ran away with you. The suffering brain created pictures out of nothing, enhancing and illuminating the thoughts with fantastic illustrations. There was no stopping them, if you couldn't jump up and take the dogs for a long winter walk. If you didn't trust yourself to let the frustrated rats out for a run, because you weren't sure you could catch them again. You saw the world through a mist, with the usual clear boundaries between yourself and everything else oddly blurred. You might reach out for a rat and discover you were clutching your own other hand.

'I'm worse!' she realised, speaking out loud. She looked around the room, unaware of the time and only dimly mindful of the place. She was stiff and cold. There was a noise outside. She listened carefully to it, and finally concluded that it was rain. Somebody had told her it would rain for Christmas. How horrible! She couldn't recall a Christmas Day where it had rained. Rain was for Good Friday and Royal Occasions. And Wimbledon.

'Stop it!' she muttered. There was movement against her legs and she reached down to encounter long soft hair. Her spaniel was stirring, at the sound of her voice. Her wicked treacherous spaniel who had done a very terrible thing and was unpleasantly tainted as a result. 'Oh, Hepzie,' she sighed. 'We are in trouble, aren't we.'

The dog slowly wagged its tail and turned its big soulful eyes onto her face. In the kitchen there was a lonely abandoned Alsatian with a painful ear. It ought to be the other way around. Poor Blondie was hormonal and pining for her people. She would have been better off in kennels, or left in the house by herself with somebody dropping in to feed and walk her twice a day.

Other troubles began to crowd in on her. She had allowed Marian Callendar to use the house as a way into next door. She had almost killed her car. She had distracted Gladwin from her rightful work. She sank weakly into the cushions of the sofa and wondered whether anything would ever be right again.

She managed to get up to bed, having laboriously checked that everything was off in the kitchen and fed the rats. Blondie refused to go out into the wet garden and Thea lacked the strength to drag her. If she peed on the floor in the night, so be it. Who could blame her? Hepzie followed her up the stairs and onto the bed, as always.

'It's only flu, not the Black Death,' Thea said. 'And it's always worse in the evening. I'm not going to die.' But she could not avoid an impression that dying might be rather like this. A jumbled forgetting of reality, a sinking into self-pitying befuddlement. An inability to separate the important from the trivial. And above all, a stark loneliness, so that in reaching out you encountered nothing more substantial than a small spaniel or your own cold hand.

The night seemed an eternity, fuelled with anxious dreams about Jessica and Jocelyn and the nameless student who had been outside the house next door when the murder victim was found. He sailed around like a cartoon ghost, expanding and contracting and weeping red tears. There was something urgent about him, some imperative task that Thea was supposed to perform. A voice shouted a list of names from somewhere invisible. She knew, through much of this, that it was all a dream, and yet she believed it was real and relevant at the same time. When she struggled awake at intervals, she could not be sure whether this was a real awakening, or merely another level of dream-ridden sleep. Outside it was raining loudly enough to penetrate the single glazing and Thea's fever and add a sinister background music to the apparitions conjured by her fevered mind.

At last it was morning. The sky outside was grey and thick-looking, but at least there was light. A new sound reached her, but it was minutes before she identified it as Blondie howling down in the kitchen.

'Oh, no!' she groaned, and forced herself out of bed and down the stairs to investigate.

There was blood on the dog's bedding and a large puddle of urine on the floor. The injured ear was bleeding and ragged-looking. 'Oh God, you stupid animal – you've pulled some of the stitches out.' The self-reproach flowed through her in a bitter tide. She should have attached the plastic collar, as instructed. How would she ever face the vet again and admit her omission? How could she even get Blondie back to Stow for his attentions? The dog lay miserably in its bed and avoided her gaze. Feeling guilty about the puddle, Thea supposed, as well as suffering from a painful ear.

Her own illness forgotten, she knelt down to inspect the wound more closely. The vet had shaved away some of the hair, leaving a swollen-looking area at the base of the ear, marked with ugly black stitches. There was dry blood scabbing over, making it hard to see exactly what had happened. 'I'll have to bathe it,' she said. 'Stay there.'

She found Dettol under the sink, and added it to warm water. A small hand towel would do for swabbing. The dog squealed once, when she touched the bruising, but lay still after that. Miraculously, it appeared that all the stitches were still intact. The blood came from the one closest to Blondie's head, where the lips of the gash had separated. 'Another stitch ought to have been put in there,' she muttered critically, while at the same time enormously relieved to find the damage less than first thought. 'Now, my girl – you're having that collar, like it or not.'

Attaching the clumsy thing was no easy task. It had to be threaded around the dog's own collar, and adjusted to fit, leaving no space for a scratching paw. The lovely Alsatian looked like a clown, and clearly felt ridiculous. 'Now I'll have to mop up that puddle,' she told herself. The fact of having something to do made her feel considerably more human than she had expected to. She was doing the work she was paid to do, acting responsibly and functioning more or less normally. She had let Hepzie out into the garden, holding onto her as they traversed the kitchen, and closing the door on her. She was now scratching to come back in. 'Wait a minute,' Thea shouted.

The mopping finished, she relented and readmitted

the spaniel, who came in looking as if she'd been for a long underwater swim. 'Blimey, Heps – it's not that bad, is it? I thought the rain had stopped.'

She peered out at the back garden, and saw that she'd been quite wrong. Water was dripping from all the bare branches and accumulating in any depressions in the ground. It splashed off the stone wall surrounding the Shepherds' ground, and filled the containers that were scattered around. A metal bucket was already brimming over. The water butt that had been cleverly attached to a downpipe from the house roof must have reached capacity hours ago.

Thea firmly closed the door and went to see how things were at the front. Without a proper pavement, with associated gutter, it occurred to her that there were no real barriers to prevent water running off the road and under the front doors, all along the street. Some sort of defence must have been devised, she supposed, over the years, but the position of the village at the foot of an escarpment must make it vulnerable to run-off. Water would cascade down the hill, and quickly find itself in the village street with nowhere to go.

Peering out of the window, she could not immediately see any cause for concern. A car passed by, making a swishing sound on the wet tarmac, but nothing worse than that. There must be drains and gullies usefully positioned to deal with whatever the heavens threw down. Gloucestershire had suffered badly a few years earlier, when rivers overflowed their banks – but Stanton was not on a river, and this was only one night of rain, after all. Annoying and isolating it might be, but there was no need for panic. Ever since Lower Slaughter, and the indirect consequences of a rainy evening, she had associated such weather with disaster.

Next door still had police tape around the entrance, but no sign of any personnel. The SOCO people seemed to have concluded their searches, departing at some point the previous day. Perhaps they had bundled up carpets, computer and clothes, taken all their pictures and samples and decided they had enough to be going on with. So far as they knew, the house would remain untouched until they chose to come back for more investigating.

A dilemma was niggling at the back of her mind, and the more she thought about it, the less complicated it became. She would have to tell Gladwin about Marian Callendar's invasion of the sealed house. She owed no loyalty to the woman, after all. It had been a disgraceful thing to do, by any standards. How could she possibly expect Thea to stay quiet about it, when by doing so she would be obstructing the course of justice? Perhaps if Gladwin hadn't been a friend she might have left it, pleading illness or forgetfulness or Christmas as an excuse, if the truth ever emerged. As it was, she could not contemplate the shocked expression of betrayal on Gladwin's face if she ever found out.

Thinking it was still early, she decided to leave it for a while. Only when the reproduction grandmother clock in the hallway began to chime did she revise her idea of the passage of time. Idly she counted the first eight notes, expecting it to stop there. When it did two more, she trotted out to stare at it, and check it against another clock in the living room. Her watch was still upstairs beside the bed. The kitchen only offered a small digital read-out on the cooker, which was hard to see. 'Ten o'clock!' she gasped. 'It can't be.'

Ten o'clock was halfway through the morning. It made her feel breathless with a whole lot of urgencies. Her car. The rats. The police. Blondie. *Christmas*, for heaven's sake. She should compose messages for her family, to be sent in various forms depending on who it was. And Drew. She wanted to make a special effort with Drew, hoping for a chance to give him a careful expression of her hopes and concerns involving him and her. For the past weeks, she had kept Christmas as the moment for a proper conversation with him; the moment when his own obligations would be most apparent to them both, and the future possibilities for their friendship could be identified. With the looming new year the prospect of solitude and singleness was at its most acutely unappealing. People killed themselves in those final days of the year because Christmas had forced them to see how lonely they were, how unloved and insignificant. There was no risk of her or Drew doing anything so extreme – but they were still quite likely to make resolutions concerning each other. Too much time was being wasted, for no good reason.

Much of this was perfectly clear in Thea's mind. But there was a lot more that remained confused. Drew's children had to take priority, as did his business. He earned shockingly little money from his alternative funerals, taking handouts from relatives and top-ups from the state in order to buy shoes for the kids and meat for his freezer.

But it was ten o'clock already and she had to put her day in order. The flu was in abeyance, fortunately, and two large mugs of tea seemed to send it off even further. She would call Gladwin first and get that out of the way. Resentment against Marian Callendar was forming a tightness in her breast as she realised that without her, the whole business of the murder could have stayed firmly out of mind. It was a distraction too far, an annoyance she could well do without. If her own unwholesome curiosity had motivated her on previous occasions, this time it was almost entirely absent. She was being dragged reluctantly into it, simply by being in the neighbouring house when it happened. Anybody would agree that she had been deposited in the middle of something in all innocence. Something that had probably started with the death of Douglas Callendar nearly two weeks earlier, and which had nothing whatever to do with Thea Osborne.

So she made the call to Gladwin's mobile, the number of which was in her own phone's memory. It was answered swiftly, in a voice that conveyed a sort of brisk patience, that Thea found reassuring. As if the

211

detective was saying *I will listen to you, on condition that what you have to say is important and relevant.*

There was no preamble. No 'How's the dog?' or 'Is your flu any better?' Instead, Gladwin simply said, 'Thea. What can I do for you?'

Normally quite fluent, Thea stammered out the first few words. 'Mrs Callendar, the widow, came here again. She pushed her way in. I couldn't stop her. She's very forceful . . .'

'What did she do?'

'She went next door,' said Thea flatly. 'Round the back. Over the garden wall.'

'She went *in*? How?'

'I don't know. I suppose she knew where Natasha kept a key.'

'To the back door?' Gladwin sounded sceptical.

'Why not? She was gone ten minutes or so. She came back carrying something. She said she'd gone for CDs, but that wasn't what she had in her hand.'

'So . . . ?'

'It was a sort of metal flask with a label on it.'

Gladwin was silent for some moments. 'We emptied her fridge and checked the contents of her freezer. We looked in the bathroom cabinet. Nothing like that anywhere. I've seen the whole of the inventory.'

'It looked like something medical, I think. I mean – what else would it be? She's not going to go to all that trouble for a thermos to put soup in, is she? She told me it was *CDs* she wanted, which was totally untrue.'

The barefaced dishonesty of it was a shock. She wanted Gladwin to understand how she felt, and was not entirely disappointed.

'But she let you see it. Wasn't that odd? Wouldn't she know you'd tell the police?'

'Maybe she didn't care. She seems to think she's above the law, pretty much. She said it had nothing to do with your investigation. She just wanted to rescue something that was hers. But she *did* say it was CDs. And it wasn't.'

'Hmm.' Gladwin sounded worried. 'She could deny the whole thing, of course. Her word against yours.'

Thea had no reply to that. It was oddly offensive to be put into that position. Was it possible that Marian Callendar had thought this through already and knew exactly how it would turn out? She could insist that Thea had imagined the whole thing, and in her fluey condition, people might well believe Marian rather than her.

'Not your problem,' said Gladwin. 'Don't worry. Now listen – Jeremy says you have to do something about your car. They need your permission, I think. You have to call them today, if you want it back before the end of the week.'

'Who? Who do I call?'

'The AA, I suppose. They must have sent you a text. That's what they always do these days.'

Panic set in without warning. She had no reference number for the incident, no idea where the car had

213

been taken. She had spinelessly let Higgins take over, without asking any sensible questions. No doubt he would have brought her up to date on Saturday if he hadn't been distracted by the murder. She could hardly blame him. Even if there was a text, that would only be the start of it. She had the unappealing prospect of being endlessly transferred and put on hold through far-away call centres. 'Bloody hell,' she said.

Gladwin was not sympathetic. 'Come on, Thea, it's not that difficult, is it?'

'You don't know the full story. It's going to take me all day.'

'I doubt that. But I advise you to crack on with it. There'll be charges for the space it's taking up, otherwise.'

'Surely not! It isn't a horse. They won't have to feed it.'

Gladwin laughed. 'That's true. In any case, I'd have thought you'd be desperate for it. Don't you feel trapped there without it?'

'I would if I wasn't so poorly. And if it wasn't raining. As it is, I have no desire at all to go out. It's bad enough taking the dogs for a pee in the garden.'

Again, sympathy was minimal. 'Well, nobody's forcing you, I guess. You must have known it'd be pretty bleak spending Christmas in a strange village.'

'You'd think so,' agreed Thea, aware that *bleak* didn't even come close.

'Well, I expect I'll be seeing you before long. Me or

214

Jeremy or one of the team. You're sure to come in useful one way or another. After what you've just told me, we'll have to come back and check for what's missing, and secure the back door somehow. That Callendar woman has a cheek, I must say.'

The reaction struck Thea as rather belated. 'Absolutely,' she confirmed. 'That's what I'm trying to tell you. She was arrogant and bossy and thinks herself above the law.'

'Yes, you said that already. I can't believe she really does think that. If so, somebody made a serious mistake in selecting her as a magistrate.'

'She's still the most obvious suspect for the murder, isn't she?' Thea knew such remarks were close to the edge of what she was allowed to say. Despite Gladwin's frank admission of her usefulness, there were limits to how involved she was ever permitted to be.

'There are laws about slander, character assassination, false witness and so forth,' Gladwin warned her.

'I suppose there are,' Thea sighed. Then she remembered how Higgins had withheld the details of exactly how Natasha had died. An artery had been breached, resulting in a lot of blood – that was all she knew. 'But whoever did it must have got blood on them, according to Jeremy,' she persisted. 'That must help.'

'The pathologist and SOCOs rather knocked that one on the head. The blood flow wasn't too drastic to begin with, but seems to have increased after she dragged herself into the front room. There's no certainty that the killer would be bloodstained. Nearly all the blood went onto the living room floor, where people knelt and walked in it.'

'Oh. That's a pity. What about the weapon? Did you find it?'

'No. A sharp knife with a point is all we know about it.'

'But the fact that you can't find it proves that this is a murder. Is that right?'

'Yes, Thea Osborne, it is. Now I'll have to go. You sort out that car, okay?'

'Yes, ma'am,' said Thea.

She fully intended to obey the order, and had even picked up her phone and started to rummage in her bag for the card on which the AA's number was printed. But before she could lay hands on it, she noticed a certain droopiness in one of the precious potted palms in the living room. Nothing had been watered since Friday, and now it was Monday. Gloria had been very clear about the needs of her indoor greenery. Not only did they need water, their leaves had to be wiped and sprayed with a fine mist of foliage nutrients. It was a central element in her tasks, and to neglect it would be almost as bad as letting the dog get its ear half torn off.

She was *not* irresponsible, she insisted to herself. Admittedly, there had been times when she felt she knew better than the homeowners just what their animals and possessions required. And she had once or twice totally failed to keep said animals and possessions safe. Death and destruction had taken place here and there. But on the whole she had done as asked, and handed the property back more or less intact. Jobs that had looked simple sometimes turned out to have hidden complexities. The people themselves had not always been entirely honest with her. In some cases there turned out to be quite sinister reasons for employing a house-sitter in the first place.

Dealing with the plants proved to be quite a pleasant chore. There were cheese plants, ferns, a rubber plant and numerous other things, in the living room, hall and on the landing halfway up the stairs. They inhabited handsome planters, some of which looked to be valuable antiques. There were few ornaments or pictures in the house – decoration relied almost entirely on the plants. The hall seemed rather dark for maximum plant health, until she worked out that they were all shade-loving things – ferns in particular. The aerosol containing the spray was surprisingly good fun to operate, and she persuaded herself that the leaves perked up within seconds, after her ministrations.

Next, to prove conclusively that she was continuing to function, she went to refresh the rats' food dish and give them some more bedding. Gloria had suggested mucking them out halfway through her stay, unless they got smelly before that. 'People are far too obsessed with keeping their animals clean,' she had said, rather to Thea's relief. 'If you change their nest every day, they never get to feel it's home, I always think.' In any event, the rats had plenty of space in the cage, without having to sit on top of their lavatory. All three of them cuddled up together made quite a big furry heap. One head was raised and a beady eye inspected her, as she carefully poured some more corn into their bowl. 'I *will* let you out one evening soon,' she promised guiltily. 'As soon as I summon up the nerve.' After what had happened to Blondie, her confidence had slumped to zero when it came to the rats.

The window onto the back garden revealed a cessation of the rain, when Thea went to look. It remained a wet world, but there were no longer constant splashings in the puddles and pounding on the roof. Perhaps she ought to take Blondie out for a little walk, in her idiotic collar. The exercise would be beneficial and might make her feel more normal.

'Not you,' she told Hepzie sternly, and shut the spaniel in the living room.

Blondie took some persuading, and once outside simply plodded miserably across the soaking grass without showing the slightest interest in anything. Her head hung down, as did her tail, and she kept her belly close to the ground. The collar kept catching on the grass and every time it did so, the dog stopped walking and simply stood patiently like a horse pulled up by the reins. Thea tried to encourage her, but the dripping trees were making her wet and it was colder than she had expected. After a few futile minutes, in which the

218

dog showed no inclination to relieve itself or indulge in any meaningful exercise, Hepzie could be heard barking in the house. It was her bark that announced company, but Thea had not heard the door knocker. 'Okay, then,' she gave in to the Alsatian. 'We can go back now, and see what's happening.'

Hepzie was yapping excitedly inside the living room door, and Thea almost forgot to confine Blondie to the kitchen before letting her own dog out. She had no way of telling whether someone was at the front door, but Hepzie seemed convinced. She flew at the door and started whining. 'I hope this isn't a false alarm,' said Thea, and opened it slowly.

On the step outside stood two people: a man and a small boy.

'Hello,' said Drew with his familiar wide smile. 'I brought Timmy for a Christmas visit.'

Chapter Thirteen

'It was Maggs's idea,' he went on, with a disarming lack of diplomacy. 'She said Timmy was getting short changed just because he wasn't poorly. She's got Steph in bed with her, and Den's running up and down with tempting morsels for them, while Tim and I came out for a drive in the rain.'

'But how did you know where I was?'

'Easy. Don't forget what a good detective I am.'

'The police tape, of course,' said Timmy. 'Across the house next door. Something bad happened there, didn't it, Daddy?'

'It seems so, son. Can we come in?' He cocked his head at Thea and she felt herself filling up with relief and delight and amusement and . . .

'Oh, it is nice to see you,' she sighed. 'You'll never know how wonderful it is.'

He met her eyes with a long open gaze of frank agreement with her sentiments. Then he glanced down at the child and laughed. 'First, we want to see the rats,' he announced. 'Tim's always had a thing about rats, ever since Samuel Whiskers. Most kids find him rather scary, but not our Timothy.'

'I used to have dreams about him.' Thea blinked at the sudden memory. 'I hadn't given that a thought for nearly forty years. Dear me, now I feel really old.' She probably *looked* quite old as well, and decidedly unattractive. She didn't remember brushing her hair that morning, and felt frowsty after the restless hot-and-cold night. No way could she have faced a shower or a bath, but had simply dabbed herself here and there with a flannel. It hadn't occurred to her that it would matter.

The visitors waited to be escorted into the rats' room, which was slowly accomplished as Thea told the sorry tale of Blondie's troubles. 'You do have bad luck with dogs, don't you,' said Drew, with a hint of reproach.

Thea sighed. 'I suspect I'm not strict enough with them. They take advantage of me.'

Timmy insisted on having a rat out of its cage to play. Drew promised to take full responsibility for what happened to it, and Thea knew when she was overruled. She watched the child delightedly handle the sinuous rodent, letting it climb onto his shoulder and down his arm. It looked like instant mutual adoration. 'Now he's happy,' said Drew. 'He'll bore me and Stephanie rigid with rat stories for weeks now.'

'Do you want coffee? Come and meet poor Blondie.' They left Timmy with the rats and moved into the kitchen. Drew admired the house, with its solid square rooms and flamboyant plants. 'It's typical Cotswolds,' said Thea.

'How did they do it?' he marvelled. 'The proportions and colours are always so perfect and timeless. It'll all still be here in a thousand years.'

'The new houses aren't so nice. The yellow's too bright, and the construction sometimes seems quite flimsy, compared to these older ones. They don't have the same *soul*.'

'New things are generally rather soulless. Give them time,' he said easily. 'Things have to happen in them to add that extra dimension.'

'I know. But I'd hate to have to be the first person to make a mark. Wouldn't that be horrible?'

'I imagine some people would feel quite the opposite. The idea that somebody might already have died – or even been born – in their house makes them very uneasy.'

'How ridiculous,' said Thea.

He knelt down by Blondie's bed and gently inspected the ear. Until that moment Thea had quite forgotten that he had been a nurse before he was an undertaker. 'She's been scratching it,' he said accusingly.

'I know. I hadn't the heart to make her wear that awful collar in the night.'

'She doesn't seem to mind it. She's very beautiful, isn't she?' He stroked the white coat, which was looking a lot less glossy and dazzling than it had done two days ago. The dog heaved a long sigh. 'She seems very unhappy, though.'

'She's got a lot to be sad about. Her people have abandoned her, she's coming into season, and her ear hurts.'

'They've left her with you when she's in season?' He frowned his disapproval.

'They didn't know. It's only just started. I think they're planning to breed from her. Imagine a whole litter of little Blondies. They'll be worth a fortune.'

'You wouldn't think the market would be very strong, the way things are. People are abandoning their dogs in droves, from what I hear.'

Thea shuddered. 'Don't get me started on that,' she begged.

'It looks sore,' he judged. 'Did they give you any painkillers for her?'

She shook her head. 'I can swab it with Dettol, that's all.'

'I expect she's had antibiotics,' he murmured to himself. 'It's not a very clever bit of stitching. There's a gap.'

'I saw that. I thought she might have pulled it out with scratching.'

'No. It was never there. It's been bleeding.'

'Yes, I know.' She was tiring of his observations about the dog. 'But she seems to like you.'

'She just wants lots of love and reassurance, like any patient.' He went on stroking long sweeps down Blondie's back. 'Don't you, lovely girl?'

'I've never seen you like this with a dog. I thought you didn't much like them.'

'I like this one.'

Thea experienced a humiliating wave of jealousy at his attentions to the dog and wanted to give herself a sharp smack. 'I'll do the coffee,' she said. 'And we should make sure Timmy's okay. He might let the other rats out or lose the one he's playing with. Has he ever handled them before?'

'Hamsters and a ferret once or twice. He's got a little friend whose father's a gamekeeper. They do a lot of outdoorsy country stuff together.'

She tried in vain to visualise the life down there in Somerset, for a young motherless boy with an undertaker for a father. 'Sounds very . . .' she couldn't think of the word. Wholesome? Not quite, when gamekeepers were tainted with the trappings of privilege and mindless killing of defenceless birds.

'It is,' he smiled. 'Very.'

She busied herself with the coffee for a minute, while he went on stroking the Alsatian.

'So tell me about the murder,' he invited. 'You do realise that's the reason I've come all this way, don't you?'

It might well be true, she supposed, or half true, at least. Looking at his face, she thought he seemed strained, the witty banter an automatic veneer over something far darker and sadder. When she first met him, he had confessed to a tendency to interfere more than was wise in matters of crime and justice. He had his own experiences of violent death and cunning criminals. She hoped the Stanton situation had simply given him an excuse to visit, when he had already wanted to. He struck her as being in need of diversion, desperate for a break in a routine that was imbued with grief for his wife and responsibility for his children. She smiled weakly and did her best to convey everything she knew about Natasha Ainsworth.

He interrupted frequently, with sharp questions that made Thea feel soft-headed. He made her describe all the people she'd met – the Callendar mother and her sons, Cheryl Bagshawe, the Wilsons and Dennis Ireland. He was particularly interested in Dennis Ireland. 'At first inspection, my money's on him,' he said. 'Means, motive and opportunity.'

'What motive?' Had she missed something?

'Oh, something about being neighbours, some old feud,' he said airily.

'They weren't neighbours. This house is between them.'

'That counts as neighbours. You don't have to be right next door.'

'Don't you? I thought you did.' She became aware

that her head was aching again, as badly as ever. The realisation came with a wave of disappointment. She had hoped she was getting better, and had believed that Drew's mere presence would work as a cure.

'You're not well, are you? I should have asked sooner. You seemed okay at first, but now . . .'

'It started just after I got here. This is the third day, I think. It hasn't been so bad, really. Just achey and feverish.'

'Stephanie was quite bad at first. Ever so sorry for herself. But it looks as if Tim and I have escaped it, for some reason.'

But what about me? she wanted to whimper. 'That's lucky,' she said.

'Listen – why don't you go and have a hot bath, and then go back to bed for a bit? I can answer the phone or even go and fetch some milk or something. I don't imagine you want to go out, do you?'

'I can't, even if I want to. I haven't got my car. I'm supposed to be doing something about that this morning. The AA took it away and now I don't know where it is.'

He looked alarmed at this, but set the matter aside for a while, urging her to rest, instead.

'I'd feel ridiculous,' she protested. 'How can I lie up there like Lady Muck, leaving you to twiddle your thumbs down here? That's no treat for Timmy. He'll soon get tired of the rats.'

As if to confirm her fears, there was a loud squeal

from the back room as she spoke. She and Drew both rushed to investigate. Timmy was holding the rat high over his head, as Hepzie made determined jumps at it. Thea grabbed the dog and Drew gathered both boy and rodent to him. 'I opened the door and the dog ran in,' gulped Timmy. 'I didn't know.'

'We forgot to tell you,' said Thea. 'It wasn't your fault.' She shook the spaniel savagely. 'You damn dog – what's the matter with you?' she shouted. The idea that another Shepherd pet might have been injured or killed by her own animal made her quite faint.

'She's just doing what comes naturally,' said Drew mildly. 'It's up to us to keep them apart.'

'I don't think she's ever killed anything in her life – I don't know what's come over her.'

Drew evidently felt he'd had his say on the matter. 'No harm done,' he pointed out. 'I want my coffee. Drink, Tim?'

The little boy was pressed against his father, cradling the threatened rat and softly crooning to it. 'She wants to go home now,' he said. 'She was *very* scared.'

'So was I,' said Thea with feeling. The subtle implication of reproach that seemed to follow her around the house was beginning to irritate. She passed her annoyance directly to her dog. 'Hepzibah Osborne – you are in big trouble, do you know that?'

'Is there somewhere you can confine her?' asked Drew. 'At least while we're here.'

'The bedroom, I suppose. But she'll yap. If I had my

car, I could put her out there for a while. That'd teach her.'

They put the rat back in its cage, and shut the door with exaggerated care. 'She can stay in the living room while we're in the kitchen with Blondie,' said Thea. The earlier suggestion of having a hot bath and crawling back to bed began to gain allure. Normal life was so turbulent, so unpredictable and demanding. But it seemed that Drew had changed his mind in the other direction. 'We could go out somewhere for lunch,' he suggested. 'And take the dog.' He looked at her critically. 'It might do you good, if you wrap up warm.'

'It's Christmas Eve,' she reminded him.

'So?'

'I don't know.' *People will think we're a family* was one of many instinctive objections. 'It'll be chaos out there. Office parties,' she added wildly.

He laughed cheerfully. 'Maybe they'll let us join in, then.'

This was a man who had been widowed less than six months earlier, an impoverished father of two with every reason to be bowed down with worry and grief. He shouldn't be laughing so merrily. It made her very happy that he was. 'All right, then. You win,' she capitulated. 'Give me ten minutes to make myself respectable.'

'I expected you to be in a dressing gown, actually,' he said. 'You were up and dressed at eleven o'clock, which is quite impressive in the circumstances.'

'Pooh!' she said, which made Timmy smile.

They left the house just before midday, and climbed into Drew's car. 'So where are we going?' he asked.

'Um . . .' Her mind went blank. 'I can only think of The Mount, and we could walk there. It's at the end of this street.'

His hand hovered over the ignition key. 'Is that where you'd like to go, then?'

The decision was ridiculously difficult. 'I had intended to give it a try while I was here. And it is up a steep hill that I don't think I've got the strength for. We could drive there, I suppose. It might rain again and we'd get wet if we walked.' It went against all her instincts to drive a quarter of a mile, but she *was* ill, she reminded herself. 'I don't expect you were planning to have a lot to drink, were you?'

'Pints and pints,' he joked.

'All right, then. Let's go there. It's that way.' She pointed ahead and they set off.

The pub's two car parks were each half full. They left the dog in the car and stood for a moment, getting their bearings. 'I hope I'm not infectious,' Thea worried. 'I could pass flu to the whole village. By the look of it most of them are here already.'

'You're probably okay now. And it's everywhere by this time, anyway. Anyone in the habit of going to the pub will have been exposed to the virus long since.'

'You're always so reassuring,' she told him. 'It must be your chief quality, I think.'

'Comes with the job, I guess,' he said modestly.

'Speaking of which – have you closed down for Christmas, then? What if somebody dies and you're not there? Maggs isn't going to go and collect any bodies, is she? Not if she's ill.'

'Remove,' he corrected her automatically. 'Not collect. And yes, we're closed for Christmas. Not even answering the phone. If anybody really wants to use us, they'll have to wait a bit. It's not such a risk, really. We might lose someone from a nursing home, but it's unlikely.'

'And how's business in general?'

'Middling. We've done a hundred and four burials this year, which is pretty good. It puts me below the poverty line, but that doesn't seem to mean much these days. You get used to not buying stuff, and there's loads of people worse off than us. Karen's parents have been very generous.'

'Aren't they coming for Christmas?'

'No. The old man doesn't travel.' Drew had stopped in his tracks to gaze at the view from the car park. The village of Stanton was spread out below them, blurred by the low cloud, like an abstract painting of greys and browns. The wet roofs pointed in jumbled directions, with numerous winter trees around and amongst them. Beyond was a dimly discernible stretch of farmland on rising ground. 'We came that way, didn't we?' he asked uncertainly.

'Probably not. That's west. You came from the south.'

'It was far from straightforward,' he said ruefully. 'We got very confused around Cheltenham.'

'Everybody does.'

'Now who's being reassuring?' he laughed. 'But seriously – that view's like something from a fairy tale. Look at those roofs!'

'It'd be better in the summer. But they are nicely chaotic, I agree. Not a whisker of symmetry. That's the Cotswolds for you – never a straight line to be seen.'

Timmy was squinting in the same general direction, trying to grasp what the appeal might be. 'There are *lots* of straight lines,' he objected. 'The tops of the roofs are all straight.'

'Very true,' Drew conceded. 'But that's pretty much it. Most places build all their houses in a nice tidy row, but not here.'

'Winchcombe,' Thea sighed. 'Winchcombe's amazing in that respect. It ought to be a World Heritage Site, or whatever they call it. And nobody even knows about it.'

'It's your own special secret,' said Drew, in the same voice he'd used for his child. 'Oh.' He suddenly focused on a silver-grey car with text on its door, on the far side of the parking area. 'That says Callendar Logistics, look. Must be something to do with the man who drowned in his bath.'

'His wife's probably here,' Thea concluded with a shiver of apprehension. 'What a pain.'

'I'll protect you,' said Drew stoutly. 'Now come on. It's chilly out here.'

The pub was lavishly decorated inside, with a warm aroma of mulled wine and burning logs to add to the atmosphere of festivity. The two bars were festooned with dried hops, entwined with shiny streamers and coloured lights. The noise level was moderately high, with a medley of Christmas carols playing in the background. People were mainly standing in groups near the bars, leaving enough empty seats for Drew to choose a table near the window that looked over the same view he had just been admiring and settle the three of them around it.

'Pricey,' he gasped, on inspecting the menu.

'I'll pay,' said Thea. 'You're my guests.'

Drew's objections were half-hearted, but he selected the cheapest items he could find. 'Saving ourselves for tomorrow,' he said. 'Do we order at the bar or will somebody come?'

'You have to go to the bar, I expect.' She eyed the menu without enthusiasm. Food still held little appeal for her. 'Have you got a turkey?' she asked Drew.

'Big chicken, actually. And mince pies. Even if Stephanie had been on top form, we'd never have got through a whole turkey. And chicken's actually tastier, let's face it. None of us like Christmas pud, either. Steph and Maggs made the pies last week.'

'You don't all get together, then? You and Maggs and her husband. What's his name?'

'Den. We haven't ever established much of a routine. Den's mother and stepfather usually go to them, and sometimes Maggs's parents as well, so they do their own thing. It's all collapsed this year because of the flu. Nothing definite's been planned, although Maggs did invite me and the kids to go round there for the main meal, a few weeks ago. I had to rush out yesterday and find a chicken, when I realised that wasn't going to happen.'

'Is Den working?'

'He is, actually. He's finally bitten the bullet and got a job at Bristol airport. Security. It wasn't what he wanted, really, but it pays well. He hates having to wear a uniform, and it's a fair bit of driving every day, but in spite of himself he finds it interesting.'

'Absolutely fascinating, I should think.'

'There's a huge amount of nonsense, of course. Maggs never stops making fun of it all. She thinks it's institutionalised paranoia, and no self-respecting terrorist would ever dream of attacking poor old Bristol.'

'She's probably right.'

'He likes the people – the general travelling public. So many crazy stories about lost kids and broken cameras and harassed tour guides cracking up and screaming at some daft American asking too many stupid questions.'

'Oh!' Thea interrupted him with a small yelp of surprise. She was sitting with her back to the window and could see most of the people in the two adjacent bars.

'What?'

'That's Cheryl Bagshawe over there. With the man in the furry hat. She's the one with the Great Dane. She told me she was going to be away. What's she doing here?'

'And who's the man?' asked Drew in a low voice.

'Ralph Callendar, son of the man who died. I think he said he was the youngest one of the three. The one who made me cry. He must have come in the car outside.' Too late, she remembered that she had omitted the crying from her account of events over the weekend.

'The swine! Shall I go and punch him?'

She giggled. 'Don't be silly. He didn't mean to. He was being nice – sort of.' She frowned. 'But I didn't think Cheryl knew the Callendars well enough to fraternise. She doesn't live in Stanton.'

'I imagine everybody knows the Callendars, one way or another, from what you've said. Big employer, big house, wife a magistrate, girlfriend a murder victim. I feel as if I know them myself.'

'She hasn't seen me. She *definitely* said she was going away.'

'Maybe she's having one last drink for the road. Maybe the person she was going with has got flu? What's the big deal?'

'I don't know. It's just a bit unsettling, that's all.' Gradually it dawned on her that she was taking the discrepancy personally, suspecting that Cheryl had lied in order to avoid any further involvement with the

flu-ridden Thea. That was a lunatic idea, she told herself
crossly. What possible obligation could the woman feel
to devote herself to tending a sick house-sitter she'd only
just met? Why would she bother to lie to get out of it?

'I see,' said Drew, uncertainly. 'I think.'

'I'm hungry,' said Timmy in a matter-of-fact voice.
'And thirsty.'

'Drinks – yes,' said Drew purposefully. 'What are we
all having? We can't just sit here, can we?'

Thea ordered a chunky winter soup and a fruit juice,
and Drew went off to place the order and start a tab.
She was relieved that he hadn't put up much of a fight
about paying, even though her own credit rating wasn't
particularly healthy. 'Well, this is quite an adventure,
isn't it?' she said to the child across the table. 'I don't
suppose you get out like this very often, just you,
without your sister.'

Timmy considered carefully. 'No,' he agreed. 'But I
think Daddy wanted to come, and he had to bring me
with him, because nobody else would have me.'

'I can't believe that. It'll be fun for him, just having
you two men together.'

'Yeah,' he said politely and without conviction.
The gap where his mother should have been was
achingly apparent. Other children might be taken
out by their father for all kinds of reasons, under all
kinds of circumstances, and some might even have
absent mothers, living far away with new partners. But
very few indeed had such totally permanently absent

mothers as Timmy and Stephanie did. The tragedy of it was plain on the little boy's face, even after so many months. He might join in with jokes and eat with a hearty appetite, but the truth of his bereavement never quite left his eyes.

'It's nice that you like rats,' was all she could think of to say. 'You can play with them again when we go back, if you want. My dog can stay in Daddy's car, to be on the safe side.'

'Thanks,' he said. 'The rats are really cool. And can I stroke the other dog? The white one?' He had hardly glimpsed Blondie, in her corner of the kitchen, but she had evidently made an impression.

'Course you can. She'll like that.'

'There's a lady . . .' he said, looking past Thea with interest.

She turned, expecting to see Cheryl Bagshawe approaching. Instead, she found herself face to face with Rosa Wilson, mother of Juliet and Cordelia. And Rosa was plainly not happy.

'What have you been saying about my Juliet to the police?' the woman said, without any polite preamble. 'They came round asking questions first thing yesterday, as if we were a family of criminals. I wasn't there, which made it a lot worse. From what Juliet told me, it's a wonder she wasn't marched off to the station and questioned there. All thanks to you. You'd think they'd have known better with her history.' She shook her head as if in disbelief at the lack of police sensitivity. 'They never get it right – you know that? Never have the least idea how a person might be feeling.'

'Um . . .' Thea looked at Timmy, partly for rescue and partly out of concern that this unprovoked censure would upset him. Rosa was unsettling chiefly because she managed to present herself both as victim and aggressor at the same time. She had iron-grey hair curling around her face and down her neck. Her cheeks were flushed and one eye was bloodshot, which gave her an aura of wildness, even dissipation. On their previous encounter, she had seemed much less forceful – rather disorganised, if anything, but essentially normal. Thea floundered for a reply to accusations that were manifestly unjust. Juliet had materialised in front of DI Higgins, behaving sufficiently oddly for him to have little choice but to investigate further. 'It really had nothing to do with me,' she defended. Timmy simply sat there, glancing from face to face and then out of the window.

'Don't give me that,' Rosa hissed, coming closer. 'You must have told them something about Friday, because they knew all about it.'

Thea rubbed her head. 'I can't remember,' she admitted. 'But I hope they didn't upset her.'

Rosa shook her head. 'She's past being upset, after everything she's been through. This sort of thing just sends her further into herself – which is worse.'

'What is her trouble, exactly?' Thea found herself

asking, doubtless with the same indelicacy that Rosa had found in the police. 'Is she bipolar or something?'

'I hardly think that's any of your business. What sort of question is that, anyway? Have you the slightest idea what you're talking about?'

'Not much. But I like her. She's got character and obviously isn't stupid.' Where the hell was Drew when she needed him? She did not want to continue this conversation. But she saw the older woman soften. 'So you see,' she insisted, 'it isn't really my fault that I got involved. I can't help it if people turn up in the house without invitation, twice.'

'All right,' Rosa accepted. 'But let me tell you, it's not just me with an axe to grind. They're all talking about you over there.' She tipped her head towards the far side of the room where Thea had already seen Cheryl and Ralph. None of the others in the loose group was familiar to her. She hoped Rosa was exaggerating.

'Nothing I can do about that, is there?' she said. 'I promise you I'm not very interesting.'

'All right,' said Rosa again, with a glance at Timmy as if seeing him for the first time. 'Is he yours?'

'No.'

'Well, I can't answer your questions here. Let me just say that Juliet was viciously attacked as a girl, and had a breakdown as a result. She's never entirely recovered.'

.And then Drew came back at last, eyeing Rosa with frank interest. 'Hello,' he said, and deposited three glasses on the table.

Thea gave her head a little shake, instead of making any attempt at introductions. Timmy grabbed his drink as if dying of thirst. 'The food will be half an hour,' said Drew. 'They're terribly busy.'

'No problem,' said Thea resignedly. The prospect of sitting in full view of people who were already discussing her was not very appetising, but she couldn't see much alternative. 'At least we've got somewhere to sit.'

Rosa grasped that she was being cold-shouldered, and marched away without a backward look. 'Who was that?' asked Drew.

'She was cross,' said Timmy. 'Cross with Thea.'

'Uh-oh. What've you done, then?'

'Shopped her daughter to the police, the way she sees it. She got it all wrong. I think I pacified her a bit, luckily.' She spoke softly, but the noise level in the bar was more than enough to ensure that nobody could overhear. 'If she's annoyed, I dread to think how Marian Callendar must be feeling. I *really* dropped her in it.'

'And that's her son over there – right? Should we expect him to come over for a shout as well?'

'Probably.'

'And they'll all be wondering who I am.' He seemed to relish the idea.

'You'd think they'd have better things to do on Christmas Eve, wouldn't you? What about last-minute shopping and peeling chestnuts and taking the kids for walks in the woods? Don't people do that stuff any more?'

'Not the shopping. Not the men, anyway. Nor the chestnuts. And the woods are dripping wet today. There's nothing left but a good old-fashioned pub lunch. And it's a very nice pub, with the view and everything.'

'Oh, Drew,' she sighed.

'What's the matter?'

'It's all so much *trouble*. And I forgot to call about my car – again. That's your fault. It's probably too late now. How will I manage for three more days without it?'

He reacted with impressive concern. 'Oh gosh, yes. That's a serious problem, isn't it. Did you say you have no idea where it is? Who *does* know, then?'

She explained again and Drew paid close attention. 'I'm surprised the AA took it without you to authorise it. Did Higgins give them your mobile number?'

'They already had it, from when I first phoned them.'

'Have you checked for messages?'

'Um . . . sort of. I mean, I switched it on sometime yesterday and it didn't warble at me like it does when there's a message.'

'Let's see. Where is it?'

She rummaged in her bag, where the neglected gadget habitually lived. However much other people

241

might become addicted to their phones, Thea had never acquired the same dependency. She could see its usefulness in a general sort of way, but at heart she quite disliked the thing. Having found it, she handed it to Drew. He took it warily. 'What is it?'

'A BlackBerry. You must have seen it before. I've had it a year already. Jessica gave it me last Christmas. I expect it's more or less obsolete by now.'

'Where does it keep text messages? How do you turn it on?'

Thea looked at Timmy and raised her eyebrows at him. 'Maybe your son can do it,' she suggested.

Drew laughed. 'No, no. He's as bad as me. We're both stuck in the Stone Age.'

Thea snatched the phone back and tapped some buttons. 'Oh look!' she chirped. 'There are *four* messages. Silly me.' She read them silently for a minute. 'Jessica, my mother and the AA – twice.'

'What do they say?'

'"Your car, collected on December 22nd in your absence, is at Walker's Garage, awaiting your instructions." And a phone number. That's the first one. The second one says "Please contact them urgently." How refreshingly straightforward.'

'You'd better call them right away. We can drive over after lunch and collect it, then.'

'Do you think they'll have fixed it?'

'Ah. Maybe not. Not until they're sure somebody's going to pay them.'

242

'Precisely. What a fool I am not to have seen this sooner. They sent it on Saturday.'

'You were poorly,' said Drew forgivingly.

'I'll have to phone anyway, to ask them where they are. Do you think they'll be there?'

He shook his head to express complete ignorance on the matter.

It seemed dauntingly complicated to her, even with Drew's theoretical assistance. 'Have you got a pen?' she asked him. 'I'll have to write this number down.'

He found a small ballpoint of the type sent free by charities and handed it over. Before she could locate a piece of paper, there was a tap on her shoulder. 'Another lady,' remarked Timmy, with waning interest. The last few minutes had been dull for him and he had been kicking the bar of his chair and mumbling to himself.

'I thought I should come and see how you are,' said Cheryl Bagshawe. 'You must be wondering what I'm doing here.'

'Not really. It's none of my business.' She caught Drew's eye, hoping for a flash of approval. Instead he just seemed amused. 'And I'm a bit better, thanks.'

'At least you seem to have found someone to look after you,' Cheryl went on. 'That's a relief.'

'Thanks.' She knew she should introduce Drew, but some perverse spirit prevented her. His identity was none of Cheryl's business come to that.

'Is he here for Christmas?'

'No.'

Cheryl gave up and changed the subject. 'I saw Rosa shouting at you just now. What's the matter with her?'

'You know her?' Thea frowned thoughtfully. 'And you know Ralph Callendar. So why weren't you at his father's funeral?' And what was that business the previous evening with the footpath sign, she wondered? Ought she to mention it, or would that be another intrusion into private matters?

'I didn't know the old man well enough. I don't move in their circles. It's a small village, though. Everyone knows everyone.'

'You did seem to know a bit about Natasha as well as Dennis Ireland,' Thea remarked.

'So what? What's your point?'

'I'm just trying to get things straight in my mind. It's a habit I have. At the very least, it saves me from making a gaffe. If people are sworn enemies, for example, things can get awkward for someone who doesn't realise.'

'No sworn enemies in Stanton,' laughed Cheryl. 'As far as I know,' she added quickly.

There was no need to observe that enmity in some form had surely led to the murder of Natasha Ainsworth. Cheryl had the grace to blush slightly as she caught the thought. 'Anyway, I've got to go. I left Caspar at home, and he chews things if I leave him for long.'

'Have a nice Christmas,' said Thea. 'I hope you don't get the flu.'

'I won't. I'm never ill. I seem to be immune to virtually everything.'

'I thought I was,' said Thea sourly. 'You can never be completely sure.'

They watched as she threaded her way to the door, and gave a general wave to the occupants of the bar – none of whom responded, as far as Thea could see.

'Who was that?' Drew wanted to know.

'Cheryl Bagshawe, owner of the Great Dane.'

'The one who's not supposed to be here,' he nodded. 'I overheard her talking to that man, when I went to order the food. Something about a delivery being delayed. What does she do for a living?'

'No idea. The subject never arose. She wasn't at work on Friday afternoon. I vaguely assumed she ran some sort of local business – on the basis of nothing, really.'

'Seems a bit horsey to me.'

'Really? That would link her to the Callendars, then. And Natasha Ainsworth. Except I'm still totally hazy as to just what they all do. The only person to tell me anything concrete was the vet.'

'You need to sit down and talk the whole thing through with me. We'll do it after lunch.'

'How boring for poor Timmy,' she objected. 'And honestly, I don't really want to. I just want to stay quietly in the house for the rest of the week, and keep Blondie warm and safe. She can't go out much anyway, now she's in season.'

'I insist,' said Drew firmly. 'It's what we do, in case you hadn't noticed. Timmy can play with the rats again. And don't forget your *car*.'

'Oh damn. I did forget my car – again. It's all seems such a hassle.'

'This isn't like you. A little thing like calling a garage and sorting them out wouldn't normally bother you.'

'I've got *flu*,' she reminded him. 'It makes my head hurt, and everything's fuzzy and strange. I have hallucinations in the night.'

Timmy looked up from his drink, which he had just about finished. 'Stephanie has those,' he said.

'Hallucinations? Is that what she calls them?'

He nodded. 'She says there's a big church window with people in it, who come alive, and they're all red and purple and they get hugely big and fly at her.' He grinned.

'That sounds like hallucinations to me,' Thea agreed. 'Mine are pretty much like that as well.'

'They grabbed onto the word when I used it a few days ago,' Drew explained. 'They sing it to each other. You know how kids are with a new word.'

She didn't. Her own child, with no sibling with whom to play word games, had been more interested in drawing and construction kits than books or comics. Carl had taken her on nature rambles and bought her a microscope with which to examine leaves and bugs. Her unexpected choice of the police as a career had startled and upset him. He died still believing that she would change her mind at the last minute. 'It's a good word,' she said.

'And a most pleasing coincidence that you just used it,' he said.

She understood, in a vague way, that the little boy would find a kind of confirmation in hearing the word used by someone outside the family. She even remembered something from her own childhood where a man in a shop had used a phrase that she had only ever heard from her father. Suddenly the world had seemed a friendlier place as a result.

Drew looked at his watch. 'Only five more minutes till the food comes,' he said. 'That went quickly. More drink, anybody?'

'Yes, please,' said Timmy, lifting his glass in a comically adult fashion. 'That was nice.' He had asked for a Coke, rather to Thea's disapproval.

Drew caught her look. 'Bad for his teeth, I know. But you can take these things too far, don't you think?'

She shrugged. 'It's entirely up to you.' But she could hear Carl's distant expressions of horror. Their child had never been allowed such an unwholesome drink at such a young age. Another hallucination, she told herself. Drew wasn't Carl, and it was a very bad idea to make comparisons. Was it working the other way as well, she suddenly wondered? Did Drew compare her with Karen? The much more recent death surely suggested that he must do.

'Karen would never have allowed it,' he said, reading

her thoughts. 'She had very strict ideas about food. I'm afraid standards have slipped terribly in the past few months.'

He didn't look as if it bothered him too much, she thought. 'We do what we can,' she said carefully. 'Looks to me as if you're making a pretty good job of it.'

'Thanks. They're a lot tougher than I realised, which is a relief. Aren't you?' He cocked his head at Timmy, giving the child a close scrutiny.

'Aren't I what?'

'Tough.'

'Mm.'

'He talks to himself a lot, which can seem a bit unnerving sometimes. Apparently it's fairly common with boys of his age. He says he's just acting Pokemon games to himself.'

'Sounds pretty harmless to me.'

'The teachers don't like it. They gave it some stupid label, that I can never remember. The word *inappropriate* features somewhere.'

'Yuk!'

'Exactly.'

'I'll stop when I'm eight,' said Timmy confidently.

'That's fine, then. Less than two years to go.'

Thea felt a wash of sadness at the conditioning that every child had to go through at the hands of adults. What would an entirely natural little boy be like, she wondered. Was there such a thing, anyway? And if so, was it likely to be an appealing creature?

The food came almost exactly as scheduled, and they lapsed into silence for the first few mouthfuls. Tim had scampi and chips, while Drew had opted for lasagne. Thea herself spooned small quantities of soup into her mouth, finding the lumps hard to swallow. 'I still don't feel much like eating,' she admitted.

'So I see. Stephanie's the same. I've been making tempting soups for her, but she isn't at all keen. I hope Den's having better luck with her today.'

Around them, the pub noise seemed to be getting louder. New people arrived, filling all the available space. Thea sat back and looked at all the faces. Universally white, well dressed, manifesting good fellowship and self-satisfaction, they represented the cream of the Cotswolds in all its comfortable affluence. Rosa Wilson stood out as a misfit, with her unkempt hair and defiant air. She had struck Thea as a woman battered by life, accustomed to struggling to get by, burdened by her unpredictable daughter. Anger was evidently a central part of her character – much more visible now than on their previous encounter. Her voice could be heard now, its rich tones no different from those of the other people around her, but her intonation sharp, almost explosive. She gave barking laughs now and then, deep in her throat. She was talking to a couple, who seemed content to stay quiet and listen.

Ralph Callendar was still there, holding a chunky

pint glass with a handle and deep in conversation with another man. He had given no sign of recognising Thea since she and Drew had arrived. Surely he must have seen her, she thought. Was he being delicate, remembering how she had cried on him on Saturday? Or did he have too many other matters to attend to, to bother with an emotional house-sitter?

'I still haven't called about my car,' she said suddenly.

'It's too noisy to do it in here. We'll do it as soon as we've finished, and I'll drive you to the place, wherever it is.'

'Thanks.' She sighed. 'It's probably too late now. But what the hell? If I have to wait till Thursday, it won't be too disastrous, I suppose, if you can take me to a shop for some milk. I've got plenty of food.'

'Especially as you're not eating,' he commented, eyeing her unfinished soup.

'Right.' She thought of the random items of food she had bought in the supermarket, the previous week, and how unlikely it was that she would eat them all. Like every other household in the country, she would be discarding perfectly edible material into a bin at some point over the next few days. 'It's all a terrible waste, isn't it,' she said.

'What? What's a waste?'

'Food. All the Christmas stuff people buy and never eat.'

'That's one thing we do get right in our house. We never throw anything away, do we, Tim?'

250

The boy shook his head. 'The pigs get it,' he said.

'Pigs?'

'We keep a highly illegal pigswill bin for a friend,' confessed Drew. 'Peelings and stale bread and that sort of thing. Karen used it for compost, but I'm afraid the garden is very neglected these days.'

'Do you get pork in return?'

'Of course. It's a very neat system.'

'I've finished,' Timmy announced. 'Can we go now?'

'Might as well,' Drew agreed.

'We've been here an hour and a half, nearly,' Thea realised in wonder. 'That's amazing.'

'Time flies when you're having fun,' said Drew. It ought to have sounded fatuous, but he said it so genuinely that it was endearing. 'And nobody else seems in any hurry to go home.' It was true – Ralph Callendar, Rosa Wilson and all their friends were still cheerfully drinking and chatting, as if on holiday. They probably *were* on holiday, Thea realised, apart from Rosa, who looked considerably less relaxed than everybody around her.

They filed out without meeting any obstruction or interruption, and followed the pathway back to the car park. 'It's gone,' said Thea, staring at the space where the silver-grey car had been.

'What?'

'The Callendar car isn't there. But Ralph is still in the pub. So who took it?'

'Does it matter?'

'It might. I thought you wanted to be a detective. Isn't this significant?'

'I don't know. Anybody in that pub could have been on the staff of Callendar Logistics. Probably a travelling salesman with a company car.'

'Could be,' she said doubtfully. 'I'm not even sure that Ralph works for his father, now I think about it.'

'So – no more distractions. Call that garage and let's go and rescue your car.'

'Yes, sir,' she said.

Chapter Fourteen

The garage was open until two, which left forty minutes to find it, discuss payment for the work they had trustingly done, and collect Thea's car. 'Plenty of time,' said Drew. 'We don't need to go home until five or so.'

'Christmas Eve,' Thea remembered all over again. 'Stockings, mince pies for Santa, lights on the tree. Have you got it all covered?'

Drew winced and gave Timmy a sideways look. 'Sort of,' he whispered.

The vision of the two of them spending solitary evenings seventy miles apart on such a night brought a wave of depression that left her weak. Surely there was a way in which they could surmount all obstacles and be together? Should she just pack up and leave the Stanton House for twenty-four hours and hang the consequences?

But Drew might not want that. The ghost of his wife must still be very much in evidence, on this first Christmas without her. The bereaved little family would have their own ways of getting through it, with Stephanie's flu perhaps a useful distraction, compelling them to modify the usual traditions for other reasons than the loss of their wife and mother.

Was it primarily this shared fact of widowhood that had brought her and Drew together in the first place, she wondered? And was it too neat a connection for them to ever establish a healthy relationship?

'Navigate,' he ordered her. 'I have no idea where anywhere is.'

'That's not true. You could find Broad Campden, for a start.'

'Not from here I couldn't.'

'Well, we have to go in that direction. Do you want to look at your property while we're there? It's only another three or four miles.'

'Tempting,' he said thoughtfully. 'It might help me decide what to do with it. But only if there's time.'

The country lanes were cheerless in the wan afternoon light. The huge naked trees on the road to Stanway seemed to loom ominously over them, staking a prior claim to the land and its business. 'Trees are such a major factor around here,' Thea said. 'You can't ignore them. I remember Phil saying that in Temple Guiting. They've seen all the petty goings-on of the people through umpteen generations. Some of the estates have enormous old specimens that go back centuries.'

'What's that?' Drew asked a minute or two later, as the gatehouse of Stanway came into view on his left. He paused for a better look.

'Stanway House. And church, look. All very historic. Jacobean.'

'Some other time,' Drew said regretfully. He drove on, and a few seconds later stopped again to gaze up at the imposing war memorial at the junction with the main road. 'Blimey! Whatever next?'

'It's George and the dragon, which is a bit strange for a war memorial, don't you think?'

'Look, Tim. How about that, eh?'

'Nmm,' said the child without interest. He had been mumbling to himself on the back seat, apparently content to be ignored. Thea guessed that he would normally be bickering with his older sister, and the solitude came as something of a respite.

'Left here,' she said. 'We'll have to bustle. It's half past one already.'

'"Have to bustle,"' Drew repeated happily. 'My mother always used to say that.'

'You never talk about your mother,' she noted. 'Don't you ever see her? What about your father?'

'I haven't seen them for years. They're in New Zealand. They emigrated when I was twenty-five. I tried not to take it personally.'

'Gosh! Don't they ever come back for a visit?'

'Hardly ever. It's a long way. They're busy running a business. They make boats.'

'I'm amazed we haven't covered this before. How old are they?'

'Dad's sixty-one and Mum's sixty-three. They're good for another thirty years by the sound of it.'

'Left again up there,' she said suddenly. 'I think. This is where I got a bit lost on Saturday morning.' *Where all the trouble started*, she thought with a hint of melodrama. The man at the garage had given unusually careful instructions, which she had written down. Now, with a map on her lap, she was confident of getting it right, even though her head was aching again and she felt the same heaviness in her limbs as the day before. She was directing Drew along a country road some distance before the one she had taken two days earlier, finding it to be a shorter way. It ran through woodland, towards Snowshill, and came out onto the A44 slightly north of Blockley. As far as she could tell, it would be their quickest way.

Although the rain had stopped, visibility was still poor. Grey mist swirled between the dripping hedgerows, and thick cloud obscured what little daylight might have been available. It was a gloomy day by any reckoning. From what Thea had gleaned, the next day was predicted to be very much the same. 'What about Karen's parents? Don't they visit sometimes?'

Drew did not reply. Instead he gave a surprised yelp

and stamped on the brake pedal, only seconds after making the turning off the larger road.

'What?' demanded Thea, who could see nothing to alarm anybody.

'I saw a woman in those woods.' He stared hard at a shadowy patch of trees to the right. 'I'm sure I did.'

There were dense woods on both sides of the road, creating a tunnel fit for a fairy tale. No gateways or tracks led from roadway to woodland; and nowhere near enough width to park a car without causing an obstruction. Thea sighed. 'And you want to go and investigate.'

'I should. She looked distraught. She might do herself a mischief.'

'Charnal Plantation,' Thea read from the big map on her knees. 'I think that must be it. It's not very big,' she added inconsequentially.

'There are no houses in sight,' he said, with equal lack of logic.

'But there are footpaths all over the place. She must have been a walker. Maybe she was having a pee, and was horrified that you'd seen her.'

'Did you say "charnal"?'

'That's right.'

'You know what that means, don't you? It's the old word for slaughter – where they killed the animals. Isn't that spooky?'

'You're wrong, Drew. You're thinking of shambles. A charnal house was where they kept bodies, either because it was too frosty to dig a grave, or for other odd religious reasons. This place spells it with an a, instead of an e, which is interesting.'

'I forgot your were so hot on history. Embarrassing for an undertaker to confuse shambles with charnel,' he sighed. 'Can you see where the actual charnel house was?'

She peered at the map in the poor light. 'Not really. There's a farm not far away and a keeper's house. The whole area is actually quite well inhabited. Drew – she'll be fine. We'll miss the garage if we go and investigate. Honestly, I don't think it can have been anything. You stopped within about twenty yards – we'd be able to see her if she was really there.'

'Did you see a ghost, Daddy?' Tim asked, as if such an idea was only mildly interesting.

Drew was reversing the car to a point dangerously close to the junction. 'She was wearing dark clothes. I could just see a face, and an outline. But she was very near. As I turned the corner, there she was, in the woods. Over there.' He was obviously worried, torn by the dilemma.

'So she can climb out into the road quite easily. That pub on the bend is only half a mile away. Did she look hurt? As if she couldn't walk?'

'I don't know.'

'Well, we can't stay here. We'll get hit if somebody comes behind us.'

'Where *is* she?' he wondered.

'Listen,' she said with an effort. 'If she wanted help, she'd be waving at us, making sure we could see her. Instead, it looks as if she deliberately disappeared into the trees, to hide from us. She doesn't *want* to be rescued, Drew. Not everybody does.'

He turned a look on her, full of pain and chagrin. A look that said she had pressed a button that hurt. A rueful thread of self-knowledge that kinked a corner of his mouth merged with some memory of past trauma or mistake. 'Ouch,' he said.

'Gosh – what did I say?'

'I think you know.' He put the car into gear and drove on, slowly. He had not switched off the engine during the minute or two since he'd seen the apparition.

'Only in the vaguest way. I'm not criticising you. After all, you're rescuing me at this very moment, and I'm extremely grateful.' She paused, as a flicker of self-knowledge gripped her in turn. 'And I'm being entirely selfish, aren't I? I want you to put my needs before everything else.'

'Hush,' he said tightly. 'Tim's probably right – it was just a ghost.'

'It's the right weather for it. And the right season, I suppose. There's a link between Christmas and ghosts, isn't there?'

'If Dickens can be believed.'

'Funny how often Dickens gets a mention these days. I'm beginning to think Stanton's populated by characters from his books.'

'Well, my ghost wasn't a woman in white – she was definitely dark grey.'

'That's not Dickens, anyway. The woman in white was that other chap – Wilkie Collins. I've never read it.'

'Nor me.'

Harmony was almost restored, she realised with relief. Drew's painful reaction had apparently faded. Their pace increased, and she navigated successfully all the way to a car repair shop on a small estate on the outskirts of Blockley. They arrived eight minutes before two.

'I'll have to follow you back,' Drew said, when Thea was finally in the driving seat of her restored vehicle, with her spaniel on the passenger seat. 'I can't possibly remember the way.'

'I'm not entirely sure that I can,' she admitted.

'Course you can. The navigator always remembers every turn.'

It was true, she supposed, and the route was not actually so complicated, once visualised as a map. 'Okay, then. You'll have time for some tea and biscuits before you go home.'

She set off carefully, conscious of an increase in traffic as people got home early from the last day of work, or rushed off to the shops at the last minute, or journeyed back and forth between relatives. She disliked driving in convoy, as a rule, but once across the main road and back into the smaller lanes, she could

260

see few potential hazards. Except for Drew's ghostly woman in the woods, of course.

Charnal Plantation ran alongside the road for almost a mile, giving an impression of a considerable expanse of forest, especially the final quarter-mile when it stretched across to the other side of the road as well. The day was rapidly closing in, and a thin drizzle was starting up again. Nobody in their senses would be wandering amongst the trees in these conditions. Nonetheless, Thea kept a sharp eye out for a sighting.

When it came, it was with utter disbelief that she identified the figure standing on the wet grass verge, wearing a long grey coat. It was Juliet Wilson.

Automatically, Thea stopped the car, and heard Drew do the same, a few yards behind her. She got out, and went around her car to the woman. 'Juliet? Are you all right?' she said. 'What are you doing out here?'

Drew had joined her, looking bemused. He had set the hazard lights flashing on his car, and the yellow beams created an incongruous element in the monochrome setting.

Juliet gave a short laugh. 'A rescue party!' she crowed. 'Sent by my devoted mother, I suppose.'

'Who is she?' Drew asked in an undertone. 'Do you know her?'

Thea performed a proper introduction. 'Juliet, this is my friend Drew. He's visiting me this afternoon, with his little boy. Drew, this is Juliet Wilson. We saw her mother in the pub, earlier on. She lives in Laverton.'

She summoned her mental image of the map, showing the local settlements. 'Which is in quite the opposite direction from here,' she added.

'I wanted a tree,' said Juliet. 'I came for a tree.'

Thea smiled at the utter reasonableness. 'There are plenty of them here,' she said. 'But you'll need a saw or axe or something. I suppose you mean a Christmas tree? Haven't you got one yet?'

'They're all the wrong sort. I should have known. I'm not stupid, you know. I just like to follow my ideas. That's not stupid, is it?'

'Ideas don't always work, though, do they?' said Drew, with complete sympathy. It was as if he was saying *The world's at fault here, not you.*

'It would have been too heavy to carry,' sighed Juliet. 'I didn't think of that.'

'Have you walked all the way here?' Thea was still distracted by the geographical implications. 'It must be miles, even using the footpaths.'

'I got rather wet.' Juliet's hair was plastered to her head, and the shoulders of the coat were sodden. 'And it's getting dark.'

'We'll drive you home,' said Drew. 'Maybe your mother's got a tree already.'

'She has,' Juliet nodded. 'But it's too small. I like a big one. Trees make me happy, you see. I love the smell of them.'

'So do I,' said Drew.

'Have you got one?'

'Yes. We put it up over a week ago. Most of the smell's gone by now.'

'Traditionally, this is the day to bring it in and decorate it, you know.' There was reproach in her voice, but she smiled forgivingly at him.

'I know. But I've got two children and they couldn't wait. Listen, why don't you get in with Thea, and she can take you home. Your mother might be worrying. Did you tell her where you were going?'

'I don't have to. I'm a grown woman. I shouldn't even be living with my mother, at my age. It's ridiculous.'

A big Range Rover chose that moment to come past, making a quite unnecessary fuss about squeezing through the space left by the two parked cars. A man in a sporty tweed cap briefly leant out of the driver's window, and asked 'Problems?' He met Thea's eyes in a long lustful appraisal that she had experienced a thousand times before – although less so in the past few years.

'Not at all,' she replied. 'We're just chatting for a minute.'

'Not an ideal place for it,' said the man, with a scornful laugh, and closed his window again.

'And a happy Christmas to you, too,' said Juliet loudly. Thea laughed.

'Bloody Sebastian Callendar,' Juliet added, as the Range Rover drove off. 'Never acknowledges me, even though he knows damn well who I am.'

'Ah – I heard about him. Looks as if it was true what they say.'

'Chases after women like a lion after an antelope,' said Juliet. 'That's what they say about him.'

'You wonder how men like that get away with it, these days.'

'He doesn't,' muttered Juliet. 'Nobody round here's fool enough to take up with him.'

'He's been in prison,' Thea remembered. 'But not for chasing women.'

'He has. But he's out now.' Juliet sounded oddly gratified by this.

'Oh, well.' Thea shook herself briskly. 'That means I've met all the Callendar sons now.'

'Have you? Edwin as well?'

'Oh, yes. Quite a family, by the look of it. All living locally. Do they all work for the family business?'

'Everybody does,' said Juliet absently. 'Its tentacles stretch into all our lives.' It sounded like a quote to Thea. The sort of thing people said to each other so often that its meaning faded from overuse.

Drew called from inside his car, 'Thea, we've got to move. Timmy's desperate for a pee. Can we go?'

'He can do it here,' said Juliet. 'We won't look.'

'He doesn't want to. It's a thing with him. It has to be a proper loo.'

'For heaven's sake,' scorned Juliet.

Drew looked at Thea, saying nothing. She ushered her passenger into her seat, and turned back to Drew. 'Here – this is the house key. You go in and use the loo. Don't let Blondie out of the kitchen. I'll take Juliet home and be back ten minutes after you.' She impressed herself with this display of logistical authority. 'Okay?'

'Um – I turn right here, do I? Then right again at that statue?'

'Yes. You can't go wrong. There's a sign that says Stanton. Hang on, Tim,' she called cheerily at the boy on the back seat. 'Just a few more minutes.'

In the car, it dawned on Thea that here was a chance to ask a whole series of questions about the people of Stanton and how they connected. Juliet might have mental or emotional problems, but she was more than capable of filling in some background. 'What exactly does the Callendar business do, then?' she began. 'Something medical – is that right?'

'They transport supplies to vets. Urgent things. Serum, blood, specimens. It's big business.'

'Stuff for horses, I suppose?'

'Mostly. Dogs, as well. Where the money is. Specially around here. People will pay anything to keep their animals alive.'

'What about Natasha Ainsworth? Did she work for them?'

'Mmm.' Juliet's attention was drifting. 'Who's that man? With the little boy?'

'My friend. He lives in Somerset and very kindly came to visit me when he heard I'd got flu.'

'Have you?'

'It's much better today. I've had two very unpleasant nights. And my head still aches.'

'Eva might have died of it. That's what they thought would happen. But she didn't. She died of something else.'

Thea's scalp prickled gently at this. There had been three deaths in or near Stanton in the past couple of weeks. Two of them had been assumed to be natural or accidental and the third was undoubtedly a murder. 'What was it, then? That she died of?'

Juliet leant towards her, as if afraid of eavesdroppers. 'She choked to death,' she whispered. 'Can you imagine that? She couldn't get her breath, and just *choked*. Her face was all blue when Auntie Barbara found her.'

'How horrible. But what was it that choked her?'

'Just phlegm, they said. That happens, you see, with cystic fibrosis. You have to keep the lungs clear all the time. But Auntie Barbara said she'd done it, only an hour earlier, and there wasn't any phlegm.'

'Did they do a post-mortem?'

'No they didn't. They said there wasn't any need. There was a life-threatening pre-existing condition, and the cause was not in any doubt.'

Thea's mind was grinding into faster action than it had for some days. 'Did Eva work at all? Was she well enough for that?'

'She did some computer stuff at home. Databases. Spreadsheets. She showed me once. Spreadsheets are beautiful, you know. You can do all kinds of wonderful things with them. Lots of people gave her work. Even the council, sometimes. They did a big survey about

266

footpaths, and needed someone to do extra database stuff.'

'Really? And I guess she might have done some work for Callendar Logistics – right?'

Juliet made a growling sound. 'No, she didn't – not any more, anyway. She couldn't stand them, you see. Not since that Sebastian . . .'

'He fiddled the books or something? Is that what I heard?' Too late, Thea remembered Rosa saying that Juliet had been attacked. Had she somehow blunderingly failed to grasp that he, or another Callendar, had been the attacker? Anything seemed possible in this small community, with its long complicated history.

'He tried to blame it on Eva. Thinks I've forgotten, or he'd never have stopped just now.'

'He might not have recognised you.'

'Huh!' scorned Juliet.

'So . . .' Thea had somehow lost any thread she might have thought she was following. 'The point is, I suppose, that you've all known each other for ages and there are plenty of nasty happenings in the past.'

'"Nasty happenings",' Juliet repeated, her voice hollow. 'You could say that. Not just in the past, either.'

'You miss Eva, I expect,' Thea said gently. 'It sounds as if you and she were good friends.'

'Cousins,' Juliet corrected. 'She wasn't very nice, actually. Angry most of the time. We're an angry family. We think we've got a lot to be angry about.'

Thea recalled Juliet's mother, just a couple of hours

earlier, shouting in the pub. Life evidently hadn't been very kind to the Wilsons. The cousins had been victimised in different ways, both Juliet and Eva permanently damaged. There was no way she could ask about the attack that Juliet had suffered, but she knew enough for a sense of waste and hopelessness to grip her, simultaneously with a feeling that however difficult Juliet might find it to function, she was at heart a bright, decent person, full of humour and energy. She had, after all, walked five or six miles along winter paths in a chilly rain. And Thea still heard the delicious rejoinder to the impatient Sebastian Callendar. *And a merry Christmas to you, too.* She smiled again to think of it.

Chapter Fifteen

Juliet navigated the way to Laverton, where Thea dropped her at a handsome old stone cottage that she said was home. The obligation to stop and see the woman safely inside was only briefly acknowledged and then resisted. She wanted to get back to Drew and the dog without any further delay. She had her car back; her flu was receding; the rain had stopped again – there was still an hour or more in which to enjoy the only bit of Christmas she was going to know this year.

At the last minute, Juliet paused. 'That boy – he's not right, you know. I can tell.'

'But you hardly even glanced at him.'

'I did. Let's say it takes one to know one.'

A cold hand squeezed Thea's heart. Was Timmy going to develop some lifelong emotional sickness, as Juliet had done? 'He seems fine to me,' she protested.

'Well he's not. Something's happening to him. I can see it.'

'His mother died.' Thea had not wanted to disclose this fact – it felt like a betrayal. But there didn't seem to be a choice.

'Ah. And his father's too self-absorbed to give him what he needs.' She nodded sagely. 'That makes sense.'

'That's rubbish. Drew's not self-absorbed. He's a wonderful father to both his children.'

'There's another one?'

'A girl. Less than two years older.'

'She'll be bullying him, then,' said Juliet with utter certainty. 'Mental torture. It's what big sisters do.' And without another word, Juliet had moved away, slamming the car door behind her.

The drive back to Stanton took just over five minutes. More than enough time for Thea to remember her own big sister, Emily, and how she had pulled rank, made hurtful remarks, done better at school and made free with Thea's toys. But she hadn't tortured or bullied. Perhaps it was different when you both had an older brother, more powerful than either of you.

Drew had to open the door to her. He seemed awkward and agitated. 'What's the matter?' she asked him before she was properly in the house.

'Nothing. Tim made it to the loo, just in time. It took us a while to find it. The dog's still alive. And there was a phone call just now.'

'Oh?'

'Dennis Ireland.'

'What did he want?' She recalled that Drew had fingered the neighbour as the most likely of all the people Thea had met to have murdered Natasha Ainsworth.

'I'm not sure. He was thrown when I answered. Said he'd heard there's been torrential rain here and hoped there wasn't any flooding. Sounded feeble to me.'

'Did he ask how I was? Higgins wanted him to keep an eye on me, while I had flu.'

'Higgins?'

'Detective inspector. The one who rescued me when my car died.'

'Right. Yes. Did I meet him in Broad Campden?'

'I think not. That seems a long time ago now.'

'Less than a year.' He smiled and she could see he was reviewing their sequence of brief encounters since that windy March when they first met. 'A lot's happened.'

'Too much,' she agreed. 'Too many tragic deaths – especially in Snowshill. That's only a few miles from here, you know. It'd be walkable on a nice day.'

'And Winchcombe,' he contributed. 'Where Maggs tracked you down. She talks about you, you know.'

'Does she?' It felt as if they were on the edge of something, without enough time to give it due attention. It was no surprise that Maggs talked about her – she had a fair idea what was said, too. The question really was – what did Drew reply?

Thea's head was gearing up for another bad evening.

271

The flu had not finished with her yet, and she felt any residual energy draining away. 'Dennis was probably just being kind,' she said. 'I think he's all right.'

'I disagree,' said Drew. 'He was checking to make sure you weren't shopping him to the police in his absence.'

'Rubbish!' She spoke too sharply and Drew recoiled. 'Sorry, sorry. I didn't mean it. My head's aching, and Juliet got me all embroiled just as I was thinking I could forget all about murder. There's something going on about animals and vets. Did I tell you about the canister that Mrs Callendar got from next door? That's got to be important, although she promised me it had nothing to do with the murder. There are hints about some hi-tech research going on, which probably has loads of money invested, high stakes and all that. And I rather think there might have been *three* murders, rather than just the one.'

'"Just the one"?' he repeated. 'Isn't one enough for you?'

'Oh, I didn't mean that, either. Where's Timmy? Is he all right? And Blondie? Has she been out?' Her spaniel had run sniffing to the kitchen door, obviously hoping to be united with the Alsatian. Thea pushed her away, with an irritable word. The dog was still tainted with the needless aggression she'd directed at Blondie.

Drew took hold of her arm and began to steer her into the living room. 'Come on. I'll make some tea. Timmy's back with the rats. Blondie's not going anywhere. I saw a box of mince pies in the cupboard. I'll warm them up and we can have a special Christmas high tea.'

She wanted to tell him about Juliet's remarks – perhaps not those concerning Timmy, but the bits about Eva and her links with the Callendars, as well as the way she had died. Had he deliberately averted such a conversation just then, when she started on the possibility of three murders? Was he not here because he was intrigued by the killing of Natasha Ainsworth? Now he had at least glimpsed the majority of the people she had described, how could he resist the challenge of discovering which of them, if any, had taken part in the ultimate crime?

'Did you say I'd call Dennis Ireland back?' She had to shout to make him hear over the boiling kettle and the clattering china. It sounded as if he was using proper cups and saucers, rather than mugs. There were moments when Drew Slocombe very much reminded her of her mother.

'What?'

'Never mind.' She stroked her dog, at her side as ever. 'Could be worse, Heps,' she murmured. 'You might have got us into even more awful trouble if you'd managed to kill a rat.'

'The rats are thirsty,' came a little voice behind her. Timmy had come quietly out of the back room, and was closing the door carefully. 'There's no water for them.'

'Oh, Lord. There was some this morning – or was it last night? Do you want to do it?'

'I can't get the bottle out of that wire thing. I tried.'

'I'll do it in a minute.' She found she could not face getting up again, now she'd got so comfortable on the sofa. 'Or we'll ask Daddy when he's finished making the tea. We're having mince pies.'

She looked speculatively at the small face. The child was certainly pale, with dark shadows under his eyes, and he seemed somehow pinched, as if undernourished. And yet he had consumed a hearty lunch and taken a normal interest in the proceedings. He had even laughed once or twice. 'Stephanie's going to be jealous of your day out,' she suggested.

He barely reacted at first, then he said, 'She's at Maggs's house. It's nice there. She hangs her cards up the same as these are.' He gazed up at the swags of multi-coloured Christmas cards that Thea had already grown so accustomed to that she barely noticed them.

She remembered a vague implication, months earlier, that Timmy was Maggs's special favourite, in compensation for what she saw as Drew's preference for Stephanie. Everyone agreed that the little boy was suffering more acutely from the loss of his mother, being younger, and having had very little natural mothering since the age of about three. Karen had been shot in the head some years before she died of the eventual consequences of the injury. Even afterwards, Drew had betrayed his little son by falling in with Stephanie's wishes that Karen not be buried in their own field behind the house. Timmy had been promised a grave and suffered acutely when it failed to materialise. Drew's sudden and startling change of heart over that had made little impact on Thea when she first learnt of it. Since then, she had pondered the matter on more than one occasion.

'You'll all be back together this evening,' she said, in an attempt to console. 'And tomorrow's Christmas. I bet Daddy's going to cook a fabulous lunch for you.'

Drew finally made an entrance, carrying a big wooden tray. He distributed drinks and pies and then asked Thea what she had called through to him.

'Did Dennis want me to call him back?'

'No, no. He didn't leave a number or anything.'

'Did you tell him you were going home soon?'

'No. I thought it might be useful if he thought you weren't going to be alone all evening.'

'Thanks,' she said, torn as any modern woman would be between the obligation to be independent and the agreeable sense of being protected. 'But I really can't see him as a threat.'

'You always say that,' he commented. 'You always think you're immune from danger, even when you know there's a killer on the loose.'

'And I've always been proved right,' she smiled, aware of a small boy hearing his father expressing alarming sentiments. 'Don't be melodramatic.'

Timmy ate two mince pies with apparent relish. 'Maggs made some,' he reported. 'But they were a bit burnt.'

'Maggs is no great cook,' Drew agreed. 'She always thinks she knows better than the recipe.'

'That sounds like the woman I know. I imagine she's rather a rebel by nature.'

'She was determined to be an undertaker from the age of about twelve. It was the closest thing I've ever seen to a vocation. And she's never wavered. She finds me quite frustrating these days, with only half my mind on the job. I owe her a better level of commitment, by rights.'

'Broad Campden! You wanted to go there. Gosh, we were only a mile or two away, just now. I completely forgot.'

He shook his head. 'It doesn't matter. What was I going to do, anyway? Just look at it. It would probably be depressing. I know I have to make my mind up about it. It's my primary New Year's Resolution.' He sighed, and fresh shadows seemed to have developed beneath his eyes.

Thea entertained a little fantasy in which she became a full-time assistant in Drew's funeral business, doing the paperwork and drumming up new customers. She had felt for some time that he was missing a lot of opportunities to attract more people to his services. Although ignorant of the arcane procedures in place where nursing homes were concerned, she was convinced that judicious advertising and self-promotion would bear more fruit. 'That's good,' she approved. 'Because I hate to see it going to waste.'

'Yeah,' he agreed. 'Every time I think about it, I feel pathetic and hopeless. There's so much involved in making it viable.'

'I could help,' she said in a breathy whisper, wondering whether that was an offer she'd regret.

'Thanks.' The look he gave her was not eager or excited in the least. He hardly seemed to have heard her. 'But first we have to get through Christmas, and you have to stay here and nurse that dog. What did you mean about there being three possible murders? I can only think of two.'

Had he been puzzling over this ever since she'd said it? It seemed quite probable, from the tone of his voice. But again she was reluctant to talk about it in front of the child. 'Juliet had a cousin, Eva. She had cystic fibrosis, and died a week or two ago. She choked to death. It sounds horrible – a terrible way to die.'

Drew's lips narrowed in a grimace. 'Most of them are pretty bad,' he said.

'Maybe so.' She thought for a moment. 'Not many people manage a really good death, do they?'

'That depends what you mean.' There was a frown between his eyes. 'I used to think I knew all about it. Now I realise what a fool I was.'

Thea went cold. This was really not the moment for any sort of grief-stricken meltdown. 'We'll have to put that off for later,' she diverted him, with a concerned glance at Timmy. Unless she could find some absorbing distraction for him, he was liable to hear and even participate in a conversation that could not possibly be appropriate. 'Let's stick with Eva for now. Her funeral was Friday afternoon, the same as Douglas Callendar's.' She reasoned that Timmy would be entirely familiar with talk about funerals, and by extension, death, but was hardly to be expected to listen calmly to Drew spilling his emotions concerning the death of the child's mother.

'How old was she?' Drew was obviously making an effort to cooperate.

'I have no idea. I assumed thirties or forties. There wasn't a post-mortem. She's buried at a Methodist church somewhere near Broadway. The thing is, she once worked for the Callendar business, doing spreadsheets and so forth. One of the sons – the one that passed us in that Range Rover just now, actually – was embezzling, and tried to put the blame on Eva.'

'And you've got a nice little theory in which there's a conspiracy of some sort? How does that work, if he got caught, which I assume he did?'

She rubbed her head and nodded. 'He went to prison. But doesn't it all seem rather too much of a coincidence to you, that three people closely involved in the same business should all die at once?'

'Maybe. But if the person was clever enough to make one look natural, and one an accident, what went wrong with the lady next door? That was plainly a murder.'

'I know. Although – I do wonder whether it was

intended to look like suicide, and something really did go wrong. It still seems to be a bit doubtful, as far as I can work out. Nobody's told me any details, but Higgins said an artery was severed. They didn't find a weapon, which is the most obvious indication that it was murder. Although, if Natasha had time to crawl to another room, maybe she also managed to hide the weapon after she'd stabbed herself.'

'Why on earth would anybody do that?'

'Precisely. So we draw the obvious conclusion.' Again, she worried about the child hearing such a conversation, but Timmy was contentedly muttering to himself, as he had done in the car, and showed no signs of upset.

'Which raises the question of how someone got in and out of the house,' Drew said. 'Were the doors all locked? Didn't anybody *see* anything?'

'Apparently front and back were both locked, but I don't know if there was a Yale, where you can lock it after yourself. And no, nobody did see anything. There's never anybody out in the street in these villages. A car driving by wouldn't have thought it odd to see somebody coming out of a house.'

'Unless he was covered in blood.'

'Gladwin said there might not have been much, to start with.'

'Is there a back door? The killer probably used that way to escape.'

'Oh yes. Marian Callendar used it yesterday. That's

279

a whole other complication. You can get from this garden into both the others, on each side, quite easily. But I'm not sure how much further you can go.' She sighed again. 'It all makes my head hurt. Literally. It's aching quite badly.'

'But it matters,' Drew said doggedly. 'It could make a huge difference.'

'I'm sure the police will have it all worked out.'

'There's a lady,' said Timmy, staring at the window. The words echoed his earlier alert in the pub and Thea looked round expecting to see a freshly irate Rosa Wilson, with some new reason for being angry with her.

It wasn't Rosa, but Gladwin, with her nose pressed comically against the glass. Thea laughed and waved her towards the door.

'Who's that?' Drew demanded. 'What does she want?'

'It's Sonia Gladwin. Police,' said Thea, heaving herself out of the sofa. Her heart was thumping in cheerful anticipation of finally getting her two friends together in one room. She was in no doubt that they would instantly like each other.

'You've got company,' said Gladwin. 'Sorry to intrude. I thought you'd be feeling all forlorn and abandoned.'

'We are a bit forlorn, actually – both of us. It's Drew. I want you two to meet. It's fantastically kind of you, though, to think of me.'

'Don't be too effusive. It's business as well. I was hoping to run a few things past you.'

'There's a mince pie or two still left and we can make you some fresh tea.'

'Lovely!' The slender dark-haired detective superintendent walked easily into the living room and greeted Drew and Timmy with a friendly nod. 'Heard a lot about you,' she said with a laugh.

'Likewise,' said Drew. They examined each other with interest. Gladwin was tall, very slim and not conventionally attractive. Her dark eyes were deep-set and close together, her nose a bit beaky and her accent unalloyed Cumbria. Drew's boyish charm generally served him well, as did his automatic good manners.

'You don't look like an undertaker,' said Gladwin.

'And you don't look like a police detective. Maybe we should do undercover work together.'

'I thought you already did. I heard the Broad Campden story, don't forget. You were heroic.'

'As were you in Temple Guiting.'

They both laughed, and Thea felt the swell of pride that came from bringing two good people together, along with relief at the timely interruption.

'Now then,' said Gladwin, her eyes on Timmy. 'Who's this young man, may I ask?'

'He's called Timothy, and he's my son,' said Drew with mock formality.

'So, Timothy. I'm going to ask you to be very patient with me while I talk to Thea and your dad. It would be very boring for you, so I wonder whether you'd be interested in having a go on this.' From a shoulder bag she produced a red plastic box slightly smaller than a paperback book. Timmy's eyes widened. 'It's a bit old now, but it's got Pokemon and all sorts of other stuff on it. I expect you know how to work it.'

'No, he doesn't,' Drew began, but Timmy grabbed the Nintendo and had it switched on before his father could say any more.

'They're *born* knowing,' laughed Gladwin. 'Just as they all seem to know all those insane Pokemon characters. I think it must get into their brains from the ether. Not surprising, really, when you think of all those invisible threads flying around all the time.'

'I play with Jake's,' Timmy told his father, without looking up. 'It's exactly the same as this.'

Thea wondered at a woman who carried such a useful toy with her as part of a routine kit. How many male police detectives would have that much sense? Gladwin couldn't have known there would be a small boy on the scene, which made it all the more impressive.

'You won't be able to save anything,' Gladwin warned Tim. 'I'll have to take it with me when I go.'

'Okay,' nodded the little boy.

The three adults settled into the middle of the room, while Tim curled up in an armchair by the fireplace. Gladwin betrayed no sign of urgency, but even so, Thea knew better than to waste any time. 'I saw Juliet Wilson a little while ago,' she began. 'She told me a bit more about the death of her cousin, Eva. It didn't sound altogether straightforward to me. And the man in the bath – we've already agreed that could easily not have been an accident.'

'You're telling me we've got *three* murders to investigate?' Gladwin blew out her cheeks in protest. 'Have mercy!'

'The thing is,' Thea went on doggedly, 'they all connect somehow to Callendar Logistics. I'm sure you'll have delved into all their doings already, but there's something about animals – they donate money for medical research – that could be at the root of it. Them. The murder or murders,' she finished clumsily.

'You've been talking to that vet,' Gladwin accused her.

'Yes.' Thea was impressed. Gladwin had instantly put her finger on the key moment when her suspicions had coalesced into something faintly approaching a theory. 'And Juliet. They said the same sort of thing.'

'Well, I'm sorry to have to tell you this, but we'd more or less arrived at the same conclusion. Natasha Ainsworth was certainly in that same loop even though we've trawled through her computer and can't see anything that would explain why anybody should murder her. Callendar Logistics is basically just a courier service, with a hand in some of the pharmaceutical side of things. They transport drugs, semen, blood – all pretty hi-tech, with dry ice and all that. They have refrigerated vehicles and their own generators, keeping everything at the right temperature. All three of the sons are connected to the business, which is pretty unusual. They all get along, and have their own areas of responsibility. It's a textbook set-up. The only hiccup was when the middle one – Sebastian – turned out to be defrauding some of the customers. That nearly wrecked the whole business. But they came through it, and after he'd done a stint in an open prison they took him back again. Everyone believes he's a reformed character. Nobody has a word to say against any of them. We spoke to a couple of the big stables with fancy expensive racehorses, and they can't speak highly enough of the efficiency and customer care and all that stuff.'

'Even the ones Sebastian swindled?'

'They took their business elsewhere, not surprisingly. Except the one that went bust.'

'Was that down to Sebastian?'

'Probably. We didn't get into the detail.'

'But why not? If Natasha and Eva were both somehow involved as well, that would be a motive for killing them, wouldn't it?' Thea watched the detective's face closely. 'Well, wouldn't it?'

'You're going too fast,' Gladwin told her. 'Making too many leaps. It's much too tenuous to support any sort of arrest or prosecution. And why would the killer wait till now? Why focus on such peripheral people, instead of going for Sebastian himself?'

'Mr Callendar wasn't peripheral. What if he was murdered?' Drew interposed, with a hint of impatience.

'It's too late to have a view on that. Unless someone confesses, it's going to remain an accident forever.'

'And Eva?' Thea asked.

'No idea. It's the first I've heard of her.'

'Somebody – it turned out to be Juliet, actually – stole the flowers from her grave on Saturday. Ask Higgins. He went to investigate. Or rather, he probably sat in the car while Kevin went to talk to the family.' She closed her eyes for a moment, against the throbbing pain in her head that persistently impeded her usual logical processes.

'What's the matter?' asked Drew.

'My head. Every time I think it's getting better, it comes back again, worse than before.'

'Have you taken a paracetamol?' asked Gladwin, already fishing in her capacious bag.

'Not recently, no. Things keep happening to distract me. And I've forgotten where I left them.'

'Here. Have this with a mouthful of tea, if there's any left.'

There was a tepid half-inch in Thea's cup, which she obediently drained, to chase the pill down. 'Thanks,' she said.

'Marian Callendar,' Gladwin pressed on. 'She still has to be top of the list. Except nobody saw her here on Saturday afternoon, and she's got a reasonably tight alibi. If she hadn't come back here yesterday, like somebody needing to finish off a job, I'd have cleared her by now.'

'The thing is, she must have known I'd tell you about it, with everything that implies. So she's either insanely overconfident or innocent.'

'You did say she's got leukaemia, didn't you?' Drew said. 'That might mean she feels she's got nothing to lose. That she's impervious to the usual laws and punishments.'

Gladwin shook her head emphatically. 'She's a *magistrate*,' she said. 'Law and punishment are central to her life. She'd never be able to just ignore them.'

'I think that makes it even more likely, actually,' Drew argued. 'She knows the limitations, the sort of mitigating circumstances that count for something. She sounds rather dangerous to me.'

'Hmm,' said Gladwin.

'But I'm still most interested in the man next door, Dennis Ireland. He phoned here an hour or so ago, and sounded very miffed when I answered. He had easy access to Natasha's house through the gardens, according to Thea. Even if he'd simply walked up to the front door, Natasha would have let him in without a second thought. And he could just have slipped home again without being noticed. It all seems to fit very neatly.'

'Apart from motive,' objected Thea. 'And he's just a fussy old buffer. I quite liked him. He's almost as nice as Ralph Callendar.' She turned to Gladwin. 'I've seen all three Callendar sons now, you know. Sebastian drove past us when we were talking to Juliet, on that little road that runs through Charnal Plantation.'

Gladwin moaned gently. 'I have no idea where that is,' she pleaded.

'Well, I dare say nobody really calls it that. It's what it says on the map, that's all.'

'Thea, I know I've said this to you before, and I'm sure other people have as well – but the whole thing about a murder investigation is about *evidence*. We need *facts*. Admittedly it's important to have some sort of hypothesis to go on, but the moment a fact contradicts the theory, you change it. And gut feelings take a very minor role.'

'Yes, I know. What's your point?'

'You saying you like Dennis Ireland,' Drew answered for the police detective. 'That's got nothing to do with anything.'

'Except I would be interested to know who you *don't* like,' teased Gladwin. 'Just in case.'

'Rosa Wilson and Cheryl Bagshawe,' came the prompt reply. 'Both angry women. Rosa's got a whole lot of emotional problems, which are probably a nasty mixture of cause and effect of her daughter's illness. She's not very nice and I can't see that she's at all good for Juliet. I'm surprised the authorities let them live together, to be honest.'

'And Ms Bagshawe?'

'She's dishonest. Evasive, anyway. Slippery. I thought she was being friendly when she came here on Saturday, but really it was just nosiness.'

'Higgins interviewed her,' said Gladwin thoughtfully.

'She seemed fairly normal, I think. He didn't flag anything up.'

'It's a fair old list of suspects, isn't it?' said Drew with relish. 'A wife, three sons, a mother and daughter, a woman with a Great Dane and a smarmy man next door. And we'll never know if he killed one person or three.'

'He or she,' said Thea firmly. 'There's as many women as men on the list.'

Drew ticked his fingers. 'Four of each, I make it.'

Gladwin snorted. 'Those are just the ones that Thea's met. It doesn't have to be one of them at all.'

'True,' Drew nodded solemnly. 'Perfectly true.'

Gladwin eyed him suspiciously, as if doubting his sincerity. 'So tell me about meeting Juliet Wilson and Sebastian Callendar this afternoon. What happened?'

'Actually, before that we met Cheryl Bagshawe and Rosa Wilson in the pub,' Thea said. 'And Ralph Callendar was there as well.'

'Did any of them say or do anything you think I should know about?'

'Hard to judge. Rosa shouted at me for drawing Juliet to the attention of the police – which I didn't do. Cheryl seemed furtive. Ralph was far too relaxed for a family man on Christmas Eve.'

'I thought he was the one you liked,' Drew accused her. For a crazy second, it occurred to her that Drew might be jealous; that he found it disagreeable to hear her favouring another man.

'I did like him, yes. He was kind and sensitive and

understanding. But now I think he might have been a bit too good to be true.'

'So you've seen everyone today except Marian and Edwin Callendar,' Gladwin summarised.

'And Dennis Ireland – although Drew spoke to him on the phone, so maybe that counts.' Thea glanced at Timmy, bent avidly over the electronic toy. What did they sound like to a child, with their bantering tones and obsessive tossing to and fro of people's names? It was a bizarre conversation by any standards, and she had little confidence that it was furthering the investigation into Natasha's murder.

'So what did Mrs Callendar take from the house next door?' Gladwin went on.

'Haven't you asked her?'

The detective huffed an explosive breath that indicated shocked denial. 'Did you want us to?'

'Why should I care either way?'

'Because she would know where we got the information from and be unlikely to react kindly towards you.'

'Gosh! You were protecting me? As your informant?'

'That surprises you?'

'It does rather. What do you think she'd do to me?'

'That's not the point. It doesn't work like that. There are protocols, guidelines. You don't just confront a person with something another person has said about them. Not if you can avoid it, anyway. It seldom gets you anywhere.'

'It's not *evidence*,' said Drew with something approaching sarcasm.

'Isn't it? Surely it is, if I testify to something I've seen? That must be evidence. What else is it?'

'We discussed it,' said Gladwin, 'and decided not to take further action. Mrs Callendar has a strong alibi for Saturday afternoon. The only way she could be implicated is if others in her family are lying.'

'A conspiracy!' crowed Drew. 'All in it together. So you just need to wait for one of them to crack and drop the others in it. Isn't that what happens?'

Gladwin regarded him with diminished liking. She frowned. She pursed her lips. 'Generally not,' she said tightly. 'When a number of people have a great deal to lose, they tend to very successfully deceive the police and conceal evidence for as long as necessary.'

'But you'd still really like to know what she removed from next door,' Thea said. 'Wouldn't you?'

'Among many other things, yes I would.'

An electronic buzzing made Thea look at Timmy, assuming it was his Nintendo, but Gladwin reached for a phone in her bag and answered it. Within seconds she was on her feet, flapping her free hand at Drew, giving wordless instructions that he failed to interpret. Thea was quicker. 'She wants something to write with,' she said, recalling a device Gladwin had used before – a sort of electronic notepad. Drew widened his eyes helplessly.

'Hang on,' Gladwin told her caller. 'Sorry,' she said

to Thea and Drew. 'I'm being terribly disorganised. I don't really need to make notes. There's some sort of incident at the pub. Higgins thinks I ought to go and see.' She replaced the phone to her ear. 'I'm only a minute away. I'll meet you there, okay?'

'Can we come?' Drew asked like an eager child, when she'd finished.

'Of course not. What about Timmy?'

'What's happening? Did Jeremy say?' Thea was sharing some of Gladwin's impatience with Drew's flippancy. He seemed to grasp this, and subsided with a resigned expression.

'He didn't know. Normally we – CID, I mean – wouldn't be concerned with something like this. It's only because of what happened here that Higgins got the call.'

'Poor old Stanton,' Thea realised. 'They'll be getting special treatment until the whole case is closed. It's probably just a rowdy Christmas sing-song.'

'Probably,' Gladwin nodded, pulling on her jacket. 'I suppose I'd better drive there.'

'It'd take ten minutes at least to walk it. And it's up a steep hill at the end.'

'That clinches it. See you soon.' And she was gone before anyone could say another word.

'It's four o'clock,' noted Drew, a moment later. 'We can only stay another hour at most.'

'And it's dark already,' sighed Thea, feeling an inner darkness that matched the world beyond the windows.

'I suppose you'll be getting excited about Christmas any minute now,' she said to Timmy, who was still bent over the toy, but threw increasingly anxious glances from one adult to another.

'We're not going home yet, are we?' he asked Drew. 'The lady must be coming back.'

'Why must she?'

'She said I had to give the DS back.'

'So she did. I think she might have forgotten about it.'

'Keep playing while you can,' Thea advised.

'Somebody at the door,' Drew observed, as a light tap was heard.

Timmy gripped the Nintendo more tightly, and adopted a mulish expression. 'It's okay,' said Thea, peering out of the window. 'It's not Gladwin.'

'I'll go and see, shall I?' Drew said, with another dash of his earlier sarcasm. Before Thea could apply herself to the question of exactly what was annoying him, he had gone. Had she been patronising him somehow? Had she missed some important remark, or inadvertently said something hurtful? She couldn't think of anything.

He returned followed by a young man who Thea found familiar, but could not immediately place. 'Hello,' he said shyly. 'I'm Richard. I was here on Saturday. I mean – in the street. When—' he looked worriedly at Timmy, 'you know. When there was that trouble next door.'

292

'Of course! Now I recognise you. The student,' said Thea, still staring at him. 'What do you want?'

'How do you know I'm a student?'

'Oh – I just guessed. Home for Christmas?'

'Actually, no. I live in Scotland.' Only then did she register his accent. 'And I'm a postgraduate, doing a doctorate.'

'Good Lord! How old are you?'

'Twenty-four.'

'You look nineteen. What subject?'

'Biochemistry.'

'Why am I not surprised?' said Thea, with a well-worn sense of impending drama.

Drew fidgeted in the doorway, uncertain of his role. Richard had barely glanced at him once he was inside the house, fixing all his attention on Thea.

'You tell me,' he said. 'How can you possibly have expected me to say that?'

'It just seems to be a theme around here. The Callendar connection, basically. I just bet your thesis has something to do with horses.'

'Not directly. It's at a much more molecular level than any particular species. It's essentially to do with the deterioration and preservation of blood cells.'

'Fascinating. So why are you here on Christmas Eve?'

'I wanted to talk to you about Saturday.' Again he glanced at Timmy. 'Except you've got people, so I suppose I should go. Can I come back later in the week?'

'Did you know Natasha?'

'A bit. We did some lab work together a few months ago.'

'What were you doing outside her house that afternoon?'

'Um – I was rather hoping to be the one to ask the questions.' He spoke diffidently, but there was a determined look in his eye. 'I was wondering whether Mrs Callendar has been back here, since the . . . since Saturday?'

'Why?'

'There were some . . . samples . . . that Natasha was keeping safe for me. It's nothing sinister, but I didn't want them to get muddled up with anything in the laboratory, so she kept them in a special storage unit she had upstairs. Marian Callendar knew about it – the samples sort of belong to her, in fact. I doubt whether the police would have found them, so they might well still be there. But if the power gets turned off in the house, then they'll be ruined. I tried to ask Marian what we should do, and she brushed me off. That made me think she'd already been here ahead of me. And if she had, it would make sense for her to go round the back, via this house. I've been all round, and that's the only realistic way to get in.'

'Where do you live?'

'Laverton. I'm lodging with a family.'

'Not the Wilsons?' Thea could not resist asking.

'No. They're called Perkins. Why?'

'Just checking,' she smiled. 'It would be a

coincidence, but I've learnt that coincidences are really very common.'

Richard had no answer to this, but shifted from one foot to another like an awkward teenager. 'Um . . .' he began.

'We can't let him, can we?' said Drew slowly. 'We can't be party to a completely illegal forced entry into a house that's been sealed by the police.'

Thea quailed inwardly at this reminder that she had already committed exactly such a misdemeanour when she let Marian Callendar use the back way. 'Not really,' she said. 'Gladwin could come back at any moment and catch us.'

'Who?' asked Richard.

'She's the SIO, Detective Superintendent Sonia Gladwin. She's been called to some sort of fracas at the pub.'

'Fracas?' It was Drew picking her up on the word. 'Is that what it is?'

'Shut up,' she told him, none too gently. 'It's the word the police use.'

'Sounds as if you know a bit about the way the police work,' observed Richard. 'And you're matey with the top banana lady. Just my luck.'

'Banana lady?' came a little echo from Timmy. He smiled tentatively as if noticing a joke that the others had missed.

'You can sit down if you like,' Thea invited ungraciously. 'If you're staying, that is.'

295

'Why would he?' Drew looked directly at her, searching her face. 'If we won't let him do what he came for, he may as well go again. Unless you want to ask him some more questions.'

She frowned at him in puzzlement. Something had been getting him increasingly irritable for the past hour or more. Ever since Gladwin had turned up. The penny dropped with an almost audible clatter, bringing with it a surge of warm emotion. He wanted her to himself! He wasn't really interested in murders or mysterious samples or even fights in the pub. He just wanted to spend time with Thea on this difficult Christmas Eve when his wife was dead and his daughter unwell.

Except he had been the one to stop and worry about the pale woman in the woods. He had asked Gladwin if he could go with her to the pub. He had given total attention to Thea's account of events since Friday. She'd got it wrong, then. Something else was bothering him.

'I should go,' dithered Richard. 'It's dark. I'll get lost.'

'Why haven't you gone home for Christmas?' Thea wondered. 'Have you *walked* here? Do you know something about Natasha's death?' The questions flooded out of her, almost involuntarily. He had *been* there on Saturday afternoon, slouching boyishly in the background, like a face in a picture that gathered significance the more you looked at it. He might be a missing link, a crucial factor. 'Why were you here when it happened? What were you doing?'

'Steady on!' he protested. 'You're worse than the rozzers. I'm not answerable to you. I've told you everything you need to know. More, if anything.'

'The Scots make more fuss about the New Year than Christmas,' said Drew, answering her first question on Richard's behalf.

The implied support seemed to fortify the young man. 'Listen – just you three stay in here, doing whatever you were doing before I came. Pretend I'm not here. I'm leaving – okay? I'll go. You don't need to show me out.'

Drew was quick to grasp the underlying message. 'Why not?' he asked Thea, in a sudden change of mind. 'What does it matter to us?'

'I told Gladwin when Marian Callendar did it. I'll tell her about you, as well,' she warned Richard.

'Snitch.'

Drew and Timmy both snorted identical laughs at that. Thea felt seriously and unfairly outnumbered. She regarded herself as being firmly on the side of the law and its enforcement agents, but there had been moments when she had sympathised with wrongdoers, or felt the police were misguided. She suspected there could be circumstances where she might add her weight to the balance in favour of a suspect, against the official agencies. There had been times when she'd felt a definite affection for someone who turned out to have done terrible things. This Richard was a likeable fellow, with no sign of malice in him. She remembered feeling sorry for the trauma he appeared to be suffering in the aftermath of Natasha's murder.

'You said when you first got here that you wanted to talk about Saturday. Then you wanted to know whether Mrs Callendar had been into Natasha's house. Now you want to get in there yourself. What's next?'

'I never actually said that. It was you, who gave it away just now.' He raised one eyebrow at her, like a schoolmaster pointing out the subtext of an argument. 'It's all smoke and whispers, isn't it? None of us has said anything for definite.'

'You mean, I haven't got anything concrete to tell the police. No *evidence*.'

'Precisely.' The Scots emphasis gave the word an almost comical force. 'You'd make a terrible witness in a court of law.'

'Fortunately, I've never been called upon to put that to the test,' she said, bravely, closing her mind to the knowledge that recent events in Winchcombe were almost certain to lead to her being called as a witness when the trial eventually took place. By then, she feared, she would have forgotten all but the crudest basic facts. The system was deplorable, with its delays and games and subtle tricks.

'Let's get on with it,' said Drew. 'Timmy and I are going to have to go in a minute.'

A sad resignation gripped her. Drew's visit, so delightfully unexpected, had turned into a fractured series of interruptions. She had only ever seen him in the process of unravelling a crime. All their encounters had been overshadowed by police and violence and fears for their own safety. They'd had no chance to be normal, to sit companionably together in front of a film, or stroll along a Cotswold footpath. The closest they had come had been at Cranham, earlier that year, when he had brought both his children along. Drew's children were always going to be part of the picture, anyway, not to mention Maggs and Den and the constant demands of his business.

She wanted to beg him not to go. She shuddered at the prospect of forced jollity on TV as the only way of passing a long dark Christmas Eve. 'Oh dear,' she said. 'It's been rather a messy visit, hasn't it?'

'It's not finished yet,' he said firmly. 'I vote we let Richard do what he has to do, make another pot of tea, and decide on our New Year Resolutions.' Then he winked at her, which she remembered she'd done herself, for the first time in her life, very shortly after first meeting him. Then, she had meant him to feel included, reassured. Now she drew a very similar conclusion, with the roles reversed. He meant she shouldn't worry, that he wasn't going to abandon her. That he was speaking for Richard's benefit, but his words had a different, deeper meaning for her.

She wondered if something were expected of her – something she ought to say to Richard or Timmy? Some phone call she should make, or crucial detail she should remember. There was something ominous in the air, beyond the imminence of being left all on her own.

'Oh, all right,' she said. 'Off you go, Richard. Let yourself out, will you? I've got myself too comfortable to get up.'

The young man wasted no time. 'Thanks!' he crowed. 'You won't be sorry. See you again, maybe.'

'Bye,' she said, thinking that she very probably *would* be sorry, if only because he'd just said what he did. And thinking, too, that she was highly unlikely ever to see him again.

He went out into the hallway and closed the door behind him. Half a second before he could have had time to get into the kitchen, she remembered Blondie. 'No – wait!' she called.

Too late. There was a throaty bark, a snarl and a cry. 'Oh, God!' cried Thea. 'What's she done to him?'

Drew had moved to his son's side, and was watching his incomprehensible Pokemon antics. He looked up much more slowly than Thea might have wished. 'The dog – she's attacking him. Can't you hear?' Her own dog, who had been at her side on the sofa, as usual, gave a mildly interested yap. 'Shut up!' Thea told her fiercely. 'Drew – go and see what's happening, while I hold her. I've no idea what she might do if we let her join in.' A day earlier, she would have sworn that her spaniel was entirely incapable of wreaking damage on anybody. Now she wasn't so sure.

'Me? She won't take any notice of me, will she?' His reluctance to move seemed perverse and puzzling to

Thea. It increased the panic she was feeling, and she half rolled off the sofa in her haste to set things right. She realised she was more afraid for the Alsatian than the man. He might kick her or touch her bad ear, or slam her in the door.

'Richard!' she called. 'Don't hurt her!' The noise in the hall was not escalating, she realised. When she'd wrenched open the intervening door, she saw the white dog standing there wearing the ludicrous plastic cone, facing the closed kitchen door and growling. 'Blondie. Oh, Blondie – are you all right? Poor girl. Did he give you a shock? Where did he go?'

He had obviously managed to escape the dog and carry on with his original plan. Perhaps he would even have the sense to let himself out of Natasha's house by the front door, or scramble over the garden wall. He was hardly likely to risk coming back the same way, with the angry dog waiting for him.

But the Alsatian was whining more in self-pity than in anger. 'He must have startled her,' said Thea. 'Poor Blondie. What a time you're having. And I've neglected you all day, haven't I? You must be hungry by now. Let's take this nasty thing off you, shall we?'

She half crooned the words, soothing the animal as best she could. Drew had come into the hall, holding Hepzie lopsidedly in his arms.

'Why do I always have to end up holding this dog?' he demanded. 'It was the same in Snowshill.'

'Because she likes you,' suggested Thea fatuously.

Hepzie liked everybody, without discrimination.

'That has nothing to do with it. Is Blondie all right? Where did Richard go?'

'I don't know and I don't much care. I'm going to lock the back door, so he can't get in again. The whole thing's impossible.' She was fiddling with Blondie's collar and finally managed to remove the protective cone. 'Have a look at her ear, would you? It seems better to me. And you can put Hepzie down. I don't think she's going to misbehave again.'

She went into the kitchen and turned the key in the back door. Then she bolted it for good measure. Half a minute later, there was a face pressed against the frosted glass and a persistent knocking. 'Let me in!' Richard called. 'For God's sake, let me in.'

Chapter Sixteen

'You'll have to open it,' said Drew. 'He'll break it if you don't.'

Reluctantly, Thea pulled back the bolt and turned the key. Richard scrambled in as if chased by a bull. 'Quick!' he gasped. 'Out the front. Come and see.'

He led the way across the hall to the sitting room, followed by a bemused Thea, and a grumpy Drew, still holding the spaniel. 'There!' Richard pointed out of the window.

A Discovery was parked twenty yards up the road, attached to a smart-looking horsebox. The head of a horse could just be glimpsed through a small window at the front, thanks to a light from a house window just beyond the vehicle. 'It's Starfleet Sally,' Richard announced. 'I'm sure it is.'

Thea and Drew waited for elucidation. *Starfleet*

Sally, Thea repeated to herself. Must be a racehorse, then, with a name like that.

'She's in foal. Due in a few days. She shouldn't be moved.'

'How do *you* know?' Drew asked him. 'What's it to do with you?'

'Never mind that now. They must be *stealing* her. We'll have to call the police. Or Marian. She's Marian's pride and joy. She's worth a fortune.'

'Come on,' Thea objected. 'They wouldn't be parked in full view in the middle of a village if they were stealing her. Who *are* "they", anyway?'

'That's what I intend to find out.' He strode to the front door and was outside before the others could react. They opted to stay where they were and watch proceedings from the safety of the window.

'A horse,' Drew said wonderingly. 'Didn't you say you thought the whole thing had to do with horses?' He dumped Hepzie on the sofa, none too gently.

'Did I? I suppose I did. It was the vet boy, Toby Something, who made me think that when he was talking about his mother. And then Juliet confirmed it, in a way. It's obvious, really. Oh, look – that's Ralph Callendar.'

'The one you liked?'

'Right. And his brother. The one who was arguing with his mother here yesterday. Edwin.'

The brothers had emerged from the Discovery and were facing Richard with no sign of guilt or annoyance.

They even smiled as they spoke to him. But the younger man was plainly not satisfied. He waved his arms towards the horsebox and was evidently making accusations. 'Oh, I can't stand this,' Thea decided. 'I've got to hear what they're saying.' Before Drew could respond, she had gone outside, shamelessly approaching the three men on no other pretext than curiosity.

'Calm down, man,' Edwin Callendar was saying. This, it seemed, was his role in life – the one who told people to calm down and stop making a scene. He had done it with his mother only the previous day. 'There's nothing for you to get exercised about.'

'But where are you taking her?' Richard demanded. 'That foal . . . you know how much is riding on it.'

'Ha ha,' said Ralph. 'That's a good one.' The others blinked at him. 'Riding on it – pun, see? It's a pun.'

'For heaven's sake,' his brother complained. 'Be serious, won't you. People are going to wonder what's going on.'

Thea's laugh was loud enough to make all three of them turn to her, as if noticing her for the first time. 'What's funny?' Richard wanted to know.

'It's déjà vu,' she said, shaking her head. 'All Edwin seems to care about is what people will think. And yet he gets himself into public displays here in the middle of the village, that might have been designed to attract attention.' She paused, staring hard at Edwin. 'They're not, are they?' she added.

'Not what?' He was visibly struggling with a

powerful urge to tell her to go away and leave them alone, but politeness was so ingrained in him that he couldn't do it.

'Designed to attract attention. Like a smokescreen.' It made irresistibly good sense, as she thought about it, even though she had no idea what he might be trying to hide by diverting attention. 'You didn't stage a fight in the pub just now as well, did you?'

'You've got flu,' Ralph remembered. 'No wonder you're not making any sense. You must be delirious. Go inside, and get warm, why don't you?'

'I'm not delirious. And it's you that doesn't make sense. Why would you park a horsebox containing a pregnant racehorse just here if you didn't want to attract attention?'

'We're waiting for someone, that's all. The horse is perfectly comfortable. We're taking her to another stables, where she'll get five-star treatment. It's nothing for anybody to be concerned about.' He fixed Richard with a reproachful stare. 'Nothing at all.'

'It's a funny time to do it,' muttered Thea.

'That really is none of your business. Either of you,' Edwin joined in with his brother's stance; the two of them, with the same long jawlines and arched brows giving Richard the same accusing look.

'Where?' Richard persisted. 'Where will she be? You know I need access to the foal when it's born. Everything's depending on it. My whole—'

Edwin interrupted him, almost gently. 'We've

changed our minds, old mate. We're backing out of the trial. It's never been right, from the start. The old lady won't stand for it, not with Dad dead. It was his idea, and without him to insist on it, we're cancelling the whole thing.'

'But you can't!' The howl of anguished protest rang through the darkening street and reverberated amongst the quiet stone houses. Richard ran to the back of the horsebox and began to fumble at the catches on the door. 'I've *got* to have it. I won't let you cancel it now. I'll take her somewhere you won't find her.'

Ralph calmly took hold of his hand, in a grip that must have been stronger than it looked. 'Don't be such a fool,' he said. 'It's all over now. All your allies are dead.'

The words cast a sudden stillness over the scene. Then Edwin said, 'God, Ralphy, you make it sound as if they were all murdered. Careful what you say.'

Richard was looking poleaxed, his hand still in Ralph's grasp. 'What?' he stammered. 'My allies? What does that mean?'

'You've lost Natasha, for a start. And Dad. Mum's got cold feet and Cheryl's making everything impossible. Face it, Rick. It's finished.'

'Cheryl? What's to do with her?'

'Good question. She had a word with me today, in the pub, pointing out how careful we need to be. She's got herself in a state about the Shepherds' house-sitter, who she says is likely to cause trouble.'

'That's me,' Thea blurted, desperate for an explanation. 'What did she mean?'

Nobody answered her.

'Tell me,' she repeated.

Edwin gave her a patient look. 'It's really not your business,' he said. 'Do please go back indoors and leave all this to us.'

It was Richard's hysteria that made it impossible for her to just give up and retreat. He really did care about the horse and what happened to it. It obviously mattered enormously to him. And if his allies were dead, that surely meant he was in some sort of jeopardy himself. At the very least, it presumably exonerated him from having committed any violent crimes. 'I think Richard needs somebody on his side,' she said.

'Don't be stupid,' said Edwin. 'Nothing's going to happen to Richard. None of this is about him.'

'So who *is* it about?' Thea wanted to know. 'Apart from Starfleet Sally, or whatever you call her.'

'My mother, if you must know,' came the unexpected reply.

Richard gave a muffled moan of frustration, as if his worst fears had just been confirmed.

Thea rubbed her head, where it still ached in spite of Gladwin's pill. 'Doesn't that make her one of your allies, then? If you both want the horse kept safe?'

'You have no idea what you're talking about,' he said, with polite impatience. 'How could you?'

'So explain.'

But he didn't get the chance, even if he'd intended to, which Thea doubted. A car turned the bend at the end of the street and purposefully approached them. It stopped behind the horsebox, and a familiar woman emerged from it. Thea registered the car after a few seconds. It was silver-grey and had lettering on the door on the passenger's side. 'You work for Callendar's as well then, do you?' she blurted.

Cheryl Bagshawe recoiled slightly, glancing from Edwin to Ralph and back again. 'What's she doing here?' she asked.

'Good question,' said Ralph. 'We told her to go away.'

'She fancies herself as a detective,' sneered Cheryl. 'That's what it is. I told you in the pub she's a menace.'

All around them were beautiful stone houses, restored in loving detail by a philanthropic architect in 1908, containing families and their Christmas trees, their mulled wine and pampered dogs. There would be carols playing, presents being wrapped, excited children going to bed early to hasten the coming morning and all its thrills. If they heard voices outside, they closed their ears to them. If they suspected that some sort of revelation was imminent, that the murder of Natasha Ainsworth might shortly be explained, they had more important concerns to keep them indoors. There would be noise and colour on the televisions, designed to increase the celebratory mood. Let other people solve crimes; it had nothing to do with them.

Thea wondered how loudly a person would have to scream before anybody would open their door and come to investigate.

She even wondered whether Drew could be relied on to protect her if she needed it. His prolonged absence was beginning to feel unnerving. Drew Slocombe fancied himself as a detective at least as much as Thea did. Things just *happened* to her, but he drove all the way from Somerset at the slightest hint of a mystery to be solved. They were very nearly as bad as each other, if you were to make an unbiased judgement about it.

No doubt he felt he couldn't leave Timmy alone in the house. Or perhaps Hepzie had distracted him by trying to get at Blondie again. Or a rat had escaped. Or the telephone rang. Maggs could have called him about Stephanie, wanting to know when he'd be home. The list of possible explanations flashed through her mind as she stood her ground and confronted Cheryl Bagshawe.

Not one of the four people out in the chilly grey village street could be regarded as a friend. Ralph had been kind; both brothers were polite and gentlemanly. Richard was not directly angry with her. And Cheryl was incomprehensible. It added up to a complex situation that she was very far from understanding, but which did not feel especially threatening. 'I thought you were going away,' she said to Cheryl. 'You said you were.'

'I said a lot of things. Most of them were just to shut you up. You ask way too many questions.'

Since the only things she could think of to say were more questions Thea kept silent. There was a surreal, slightly ludicrous tinge to the whole business. The horse in the box was stamping its feet restlessly, making the vehicle rock. Richard was doing a similar little dance of his own, as if in sympathy. All it needed now, Thea thought, was for Juliet and Rosa Wilson to show up and add their own unique contributions. Or Marian and Sebastian Callendar, to complete the family circle.

'We'll have to go,' said Edwin. 'It's nearly an hour each way. I'm supposed to be home by six, and that's not going to happen now, is it? You were late,' he accused Cheryl.

'But *where*?' wailed Richard. 'You've got to tell me.'

'It's over for you, mate – haven't you got that yet? You can just bugger off back to Scotland and give it all up. It was a mad idea from the start, if you ask me. I might as well tell you that Mother has already destroyed that spare embryo she nabbed from Tash's house yesterday, as well. So it really is all over and done with.' It was Ralph speaking, in a sympathetic tone that barely softened the force of his words.

Richard reacted badly. 'How can you say that? Have you any *idea* how much time, money, work, *risk*, I've put into it, this past year? Marian would never harm the embryo – you can't make me believe that. She'll have it safe somewhere. That's all I need to carry on. That's the only thing that matters.'

'She *has* destroyed it, you idiot,' sneered Cheryl.

311

'She'll have chucked it in a ditch five minutes after nabbing it.'

Richard's bad reaction escalated as the possibility that they were telling the truth took hold of him. '*What?*' he howled. 'Why would she do that? What do you mean?'

'Listen, you fool,' ordered Cheryl. 'I never wanted to get drawn into this. I'm not coming with you, after all. You can have this –' she handed Edwin a SatNav '– it'll take you to the vet I told you about. I'm going home. I've had enough. It was never going to work.' She was addressing Richard, but threw looks at everyone else in the group, to indicate they were all included, even Thea.

'How did you know Marian nabbed anything from the house?' Thea asked. 'I never told you.'

'It's not all down to you,' sneered Cheryl. 'Other people have tongues in their heads.'

It was true, of course. Thea opened her mouth to ask another question, but she was drowned out by Richard's anguish. Even she began to worry that the good people of Stanton actually might start showing an interest if the noise kept up. *And where's Drew?* a little voice kept repeating.

'Listen, Rick,' Ralph laid a hand on the distraught man's shoulder, effectively silencing him. 'It's for the best. We never should have agreed to it. You got the old man at a weak moment when you persuaded him to sign up. He was always up for a risk, anyway. He liked your nerve. We all did – of course we did. But we never should have let it go so far. We've flouted too many rules. Sally's foal isn't going to see the light of day either, old chap. It's sad, but there it is. We've carried the cost, and we're losing what might have been a prizewinner, and we're not going to claim any comeback from you. But this is where it ends, okay? No more to be said.'

Thea's mind was darting in all directions, struggling to make sense of this speech. Had Richard somehow genetically manipulated the unborn foal? That's what it sounded like – and yet how could he possibly have managed something so technical? Did the Callendars have their own laboratory somewhere? 'What?' she almost shouted. 'What did he do with the foal?'

'Don't ask,' said Cheryl, with a little rictus of disgust.

Richard had slumped against the horsebox, looking close to tears. Edwin was watching him carefully, like a bodyguard waiting for a suspicious move. He *was* a sort of bodyguard, Thea realised, with the horse the subject of his protection. 'I am asking,' she said. 'So will the police, because I assume it explains why Natasha was murdered.'

The two Callendar brothers stared at her in blank amazement. 'You're joking,' said Ralph, after a moment. 'What makes you say that?'

'It seems obvious,' she said, more defiantly than she felt.

'Well, it's not. If you think Richard's crazy experiments were important enough to warrant killing somebody, you're even crazier than him.'

'He seems to be pretty serious about them,' she argued. 'Look at him.'

'Let me tell you exactly what he was trying to do, then.' Ralph was as patient and polite as ever, despite his brother's obvious wish to get moving. 'His thesis is all about storage and preservation of body parts and blood, essentially. Which is what our business is concerned with, as you probably know. Sally's foal isn't biologically hers. It was implanted in her – embryo transfer, they call it. That's not unusual in itself. But Dicky had been experimenting on the semen beforehand, using various gels and suspensions and I don't know what, to see how long each batch would survive. He got Natasha to look after another foal embryo that he thought was the key to success. The idea behind it all is to avoid having to freeze the semen, or use any system that requires electricity. He's been doing work with sheep and cows and things as well. It's all very worthy stuff, designed to help developing countries improve their livestock out in remote areas where they can't reliably freeze anything. With me so far?'

Thea nodded doubtfully.

'Anyway, he came up with this magic mixture that seemed to keep the sperm alive for over a month in perfect condition. Great, we all thought. Clever old him. But then he pulled a fast one on us, and used this experimental sample on poor old Sally, without permission. She's been used as a surrogate a couple of times now, with another mare's embryo implanted. It's established practice, nothing sinister about it. But young Richard here has been playing a Doctor Frankenstein game with the gametes, testing out his new invention. We didn't find out until months later, long past the point where we could do anything about it. It's incredibly stupid of him, as my mother tried to tell him. It'll invalidate his findings, apart from anything else.'

'It will not,' said Richard hotly. 'Everything's been recorded and monitored. There's no room for any doubt as to what's been done.'

'You deceived us. You knew we'd never have given you permission to switch embryos the way you did.'

'I *had* to,' Richard whined. 'The whole thing has to be tested for real.'

'So what's the problem?' Thea wanted to know.

'We don't think the foal's normal. It was scanned six weeks ago, and its head looks misshapen.'

Thea shuddered. 'Poor little foal. But why take the horse away like this?'

'We're taking her to a top vet near Oxford who'll keep a close eye on her. Costing us, of course. Plus we need to keep the whole thing quiet. There are breeders out there who'd use this to blacken the Callendar name and put us out of business.'

Thea looked at Richard as if she'd caught him in an unspeakable act of depravity. 'It sounds utterly foul,' she spat at him.

Edwin put up a hand. 'Enough,' he said. 'This is wasting too much time. We're going. Now. Cheryl – you can follow us.'

Thea couldn't let it drop there. 'What does *she* have to do with it?' Ralph's explanation had done nothing but raise a host of further questions.

'Another time,' Edwin called over his shoulder. 'We'll explain it another time.'

'No, you won't. You'll explain it now,' came a new voice from across the street.

Chapter Seventeen

It was Drew, who looked as if he'd been standing in the doorway of the Shepherds' house for some time. In the shadowy street he was barely visible. 'You're not the only one who wants to have this settled, and get on with Christmas,' he said, walking towards the group. 'A woman's been murdered, and you all' – he looked from one person to another – '*all* of you have explaining to do. Best get it over with quickly.'

'And just who do you think *you* are, to give us orders?' demanded Cheryl.

Another voice came from a point just beyond the Range Rover. 'He's a very clever chap who called us twenty minutes ago,' it said. 'And we've been here quite a while, listening to what you had to say.' DI Jeremy Higgins materialised from the shadows, accompanied by another man who Thea took a moment to identify.

'So?' Edwin challenged, in a voice gone oddly husky. 'So what?'

'It explained quite a lot – filled in quite a few blanks,' Higgins said.

Thea felt surrounded. On all sides were men who understood considerably more than she did.

'Drew?' she turned to him, reaching out an automatic hand to touch him. 'Do you know what's going on?'

'Sshh,' he said, which simply bewildered her all the more.

'Mrs Osborne,' Higgins addressed her directly. 'We think you must be the key to much of this. Specifically, to what happened here on Saturday. You were on the spot. We think you saw and heard enough to constitute evidence, without fully realising it.'

'Mrs Callendar?' she said uncertainly. 'Do you mean when she went next door? I did see her with something. I told Gladwin. But that was the day *after* the murder. I suppose it was her, all the same. She's arrogant enough.'

She forced her mind to examine the idea. Marian Callendar did seem a likely killer. Hadn't one of her sons implied that she was against Richard's experiments, which would put her against Natasha as well? And she could so easily have made her husband's death seem an accident. 'But she wouldn't kill Eva, would she?' she said aloud. Nobody seemed to understand what she meant.

She wrapped her arms around herself, aware for the first time of how cold it was out there without a coat. She visualised her warm jacket, hanging in the Shepherds' hallway, and how comforting it would be to have it around her now. She almost asked Drew to fetch it for her. Then her mental image expanded slightly, to include the coat hanging next to hers. It was blue, with big buttons. She had seen it that morning, without any conscious registering of significance. But something strange about it had stuck in her subconscious. It ought not to have been there, because it hadn't been there on Friday, when Gloria and Philip departed. There had, instead, been a brown gabardine mac that looked as if it was used for gardening.

'The coat,' she said out loud. 'Go and see the blue coat.'

'What?' Higgins blinked, half excited, half bemused.

'In the hall. Next to mine. Ask Drew.' She wasn't sure why she couldn't just go and get it herself, except that her legs had gone heavy and she felt weirdly breathless. Higgins didn't move, but kept his eyes on her face as if waiting for more.

'Saturday,' Thea murmured. 'Before Natasha was killed. I fainted. Then I was dizzy. I couldn't think properly. It was *you*.'

Everyone followed her wavering finger. The person indicated stood firm, chin held high, saying nothing. 'I remember,' said Thea, greatly surprising herself. 'The coat. It was blue, then brown. The blue one is wrong. There must be blood on the brown one. The coat—' and for the second time in her life, she fainted.

But this time a man caught her and lowered her gently to the ground, mumbling reassurances. He felt big and warm and strong. It had to be Drew. Of course it was Drew. She even came close to saying his name as she emerged from the same pinkish cloud as before. But it didn't smell like Drew. So it had to be Higgins, then. Higgins was a policeman – it would be instinctive for him to jump forward and catch a fainting woman.

Then she opened her eyes.

It was the other man, the one with the waistcoat and the old-fashioned pomposity. It was Dennis Ireland, holding her close and warm and smiling down at her. She felt small against his broad chest, and quite deliciously safe.

Around her things were happening that she couldn't make sense of. It was dark. A man was shouting. A dog was barking. A horse was clattering its hooves on a metal surface. 'Mrs Osborne? Thea?' Another voice was overlying that of Dennis Ireland. 'Can you hear me?'

'Jeremy,' she nodded. 'I'm all right. I must stop doing this. It's embarrassing.'

'Thea?' A third man was there somewhere. The man she'd wanted to be the one to catch her.

'Drew. What's happening? Do you understand any of this?'

'It's all right. We're going into the house. They're making an arrest.'

It wasn't the explanation she'd sought, and she wasn't sure she could get to the house with any vestige of dignity. 'Oh,' she said weakly.

Against all her wishes, she was carried back into the Shepherds' living room and placed carefully on the sofa. More time passed, and people came and went. When she finally surfaced, she could locate only Drew and Timmy in the room with her 'What time is it?' she asked. For some reason, that seemed a very important question.

'Half past five,' said Drew. 'It's half past five.'

'Oh dear,' she moaned. 'It *can't* be that late. You'll have to go. And Edwin's going to get into awful trouble with his wife.' Scraps of conversation returned to her, the crucial and the trivial impossible to differentiate. 'What about Marian? And Juliet? What about the other deaths? Please will somebody *explain*.'

Nobody did. She struggled upright, but didn't leave the safety of the sofa. She was aware of a small boy and two dogs all watching her with round eyes. 'It's okay, Tim,' she laughed. 'I'll be fine in a minute. It's just because I've got flu.'

She was angry with herself at having missed a whole lot of important developments. Frustration gripped her and she sat up straight. 'Who are they arresting?' she asked Drew.

'Richard,' he said.

'*What?*' It was so totally unexpected that she almost fainted again. 'Why? It can't possibly have been him.'

'Listen,' he said, with poorly concealed urgency. 'The Callendar woman phoned here while you were outside. She wanted to know if we'd seen Richard, so I told her some of what was happening outside. She said he was a dangerous lunatic, in effect, with a Frankenstein complex. He's been breaking any number of laws in his research and she's been trying to stop him. Natasha and Douglas had been taken in by him, but she's now got a vital piece of evidence, and has contacted the police about it.'

Slowly, Thea compared this splurge of revelations with what she already knew. It fitted with reasonable credibility. 'So?' she encouraged.

'So I told her she should call the police and tell them he was here – which she did.'

'Did you mention her sons as well?'

'No. I thought it best to keep things simple.'

Thea smiled weakly and nodded.

Drew continued, 'And then you raved about coats and pointed at Richard, and that seemed to be all they needed.'

'I *didn't*,' she almost wept. 'I didn't point at Richard. It wasn't him, Drew. It has nothing to do with him.'

He gave her a severe look which perversely made her want to laugh. 'You did, Thea. You pointed right at him and said you remembered his coat. Or some such thing. Then you fainted and Richard tried to run away and the two brothers caught him and the horse got all excited. You missed rather a lot, actually.'

'You got it all wrong,' she moaned. 'You got completely the wrong person.'

Then Timmy began to cry, for no apparent reason. Drew went to him in concern. 'I want to go home,' the child sniffed. 'We need to go home, Daddy.'

'He's right,' Drew announced. 'Okay, Tim. We'll go in just ten more minutes, I promise. We'll fetch Stephanie and you can hang up your stockings, and have a lovely sleep, and tomorrow will be Christmas.'

'But *Thea* should come as well. We can't go without Thea. She's poorly, like Stephanie.' And his tears flowed afresh.

'Ah,' sighed Drew, as if an important secret had finally been revealed.

'I can't come, sweetie,' she said. 'I can't leave the dogs and rats and everything. I'll be all right.' She remembered a warm chest and a strong arm. 'There's that nice man next door. He'll watch out for me if I get poorly again.'

She stood up, hardly knowing what she meant to do, and went to the door. The loo – she needed the loo, that was it. There was a small one near the front door and she headed for it.

Before her was the blue coat, hanging from its hook as she'd remembered. It seemed to glow with significance. She could visualise its owner inside it. Another coat, brown and probably bloodstained, must be missing. A coat that belonged to Gloria Shepherd, and which had been there on that first afternoon. She

323

almost forgot where she was going, but then decided that whatever happened next would happen better on an empty bladder. She used the thirty seconds productively, rerunning the events of Saturday and the next two days, and the probable motives behind them. When she came out, most of the story was clear in her mind.

'I need to go to Wood Stanway,' she announced to a startled father and son. 'Now.'

'You can't go anywhere. Don't be ridiculous,' Drew snapped.

'I can if I want.'

'You can't, actually. Neither can I, as it happens. Look outside.'

The street was bathed in a strange unnatural light, when she went to look. Numerous people were gathered around a large horse, the group taking up the entire width of the street. Police cars were positioned to prevent any traffic in either direction. 'What is it?' Thea asked. 'What are they doing?'

'The horse is in labour. They had to get her out of the box and keep her as calm as they can. It's been half an hour or more. She's worth thousands. They don't want to take risks.'

'Bit late for that. Poor thing. If the foal's deformed, she might not be able to deliver it. They won't do a caesarean there in the street, will they?'

'I wouldn't be surprised. That woman's a top vet, apparently.'

'It'll be Toby's mother,' she muttered. 'He told me about her.'

'So what's this about Wood Stanway?' Drew was pacing the floor, looking pale and angry. 'I can't decide whether you're delirious and raving, or what. You haven't made much sense in the last hour or so.'

'I'm entirely lucid,' she told him. 'Which surprises me as much as you. It's still not completely clear, but I do know who killed Natasha, and I think I know why.'

'Not Richard?' His expression contained confusion and a lurking hope – probably that she would revise her previous rejection of this proposition.

'Absolutely not Richard. I need to check something on the Internet. Where's my Blackberry?'

'In your bag, I suppose.'

She clumsily accessed Google, and found her way onto the site for the local weekly newspaper. 'Found it!' she triumphed, after barely three minutes. 'September 12th. Meeting of local highways and byways committee. Diversion of the Cotswold Way, at the request of a Mrs Bagshawe. Passionately opposed by walkers' groups . . . dum-di-da . . . yes. I think that's it.'

'Oh, look!' Drew had gone back to the window. 'I think it's born.'

'What?'

'Come here,' he ordered. 'See for yourself.'

She took her phone with her, but forgot it as the small miracle presented itself outside. For the moment she had lost sight of what day it was. 'Oh, gosh!' she exclaimed. 'It looks okay, doesn't it?' The foal was lying beneath its surrogate mother, folded leggily, shaking a head that seemed only marginally larger than normal. All the people stood back, apart from the vet woman who knelt beside the new baby but did not touch it. The mare looked around for the source of her recent discomfort and hard work. When she located it, she turned and began to nuzzle at it. Thea, as well as everyone else, held her breath. The foal successfully got to its feet at the second attempt, and aimed itself determinedly at the invisible udder.

'Ahhh!' breathed Thea. 'Look at that.'

'The road'll be clear again in a few minutes,' Drew said, his voice unsteady.

Thea didn't reply. Her mind was overflowing with scattered fragments of understanding, distractingly competing with each other. 'It's nothing to do with the horse,' she said loudly. 'The horse is a red herring.'

Timmy pulled at her arm. 'How is it?' he demanded. 'A herring is a fish, not a horse.' He shook her, demanding an answer. 'Tell me,' he ordered.

She ignored him and muttered out loud. 'But why were they meeting Cheryl here? That makes no sense. What did she care about foals and biochemistry? Why was she going with them?'

'Thea, we really have to go. But I need to know you'll be all right, first. Promise me you won't go out anywhere. You're not fit to go driving around in the dark. Let it all wait.'

'Wait till when? It's Christmas Day tomorrow. *Christmas Day*.' The enormity of it seemed to swamp her. You couldn't confront a killer on Christmas Day. She slumped in defeat. 'Maybe you're right. I don't seem to be very logical, do I?'

'So will you promise?'

'I suppose so. Am I allowed to make phone calls?'

He didn't laugh or even smile. Instead he groaned. 'Oh, God – I can't just go off and leave you like this. How can I?' He wrapped an arm around Timmy, as if somehow mistaking him for Thea. 'But how can I *not*?'

'Don't be silly,' she said stoically. 'There's really no problem. The minute they let you, you have to be out of here.'

When the knock came, a minute later, they both assumed it was a police officer telling them that things were being tidied up outside and normal life could resume very soon.

Chapter Eighteen

But it wasn't. It was Dennis Ireland, whose broad chest had given Thea her soft landing after her latest faint. 'Can I come in?' he asked. 'How are you now?' He gave her a careful scrutiny, his big face full of gentle concern.

'I'm all right. Drew's just going. You should get back to your sister.'

'All in good time. Let's have a little talk first.' He twinkled at her, a smile that reminded her yet again that this was Christmas Eve and special things were liable to happen.

'The foal's been born, then,' she said.

'Indeed. A fine little filly. Nothing wrong with it, as far as anyone can see. All that Frankenstein stuff got a bit overstated, if you ask me.'

'Did they really arrest Richard?' Somehow that

distressing fact had slipped her mind. 'He didn't kill anybody, you know.'

'Didn't he? Does that seriously matter to you?'

'Of course! Because I know who killed Natasha. It's obvious.' She looked at him intently. 'You were there as well, weren't you? You might have seen it the same as I did.'

'Thea . . .' came Drew's voice, full of warning and worry.

'Oh, Drew. You don't still think it could have been Dennis, do you?' She almost laughed at him.

He stiffened and said nothing. Timmy began to whimper, for no discernible reason. Dennis took charge. 'Come on, chaps. You've had a very long day of it, I can see. Gather yourselves together and leave it all to me. I'll watch out for the young lady here and see she gets a good night's rest. I'll be right next door if she needs anything.'

His joviality was impossible to credit. Thea went to Timmy and bent down to whisper, 'Do you think he might be Santa in disguise?'

The child gazed at the portly man. 'No beard,' he whispered back.

'Ah – that's right. But he's nice, all the same.' She stood up and spoke in a normal voice. 'Now you and Daddy can get off home. I expect I'll see you again soon.'

'Thea . . .' Drew tried again. He looked exhausted, almost to the point of passing out as Thea had done. 'How can we?'

'Easily. As you said yourself, how can you not? You're not needed here any more. Honestly, it can all wait a few days now.' She caught Dennis's eye for a second, confirming what she had begun to suspect.

Drew held out his hand for Timmy. 'All right, then,' he capitulated. 'Go for a wee, Tim, and then we'll turn the car round and head for home. I suppose they'll let us out, now the horse is okay.'

'Can I take the DS?' the boy asked optimistically.

'No,' said Thea. 'Of course you can't.'

He handed it over without complaint. 'Good boy,' she approved. 'You've been an extremely good boy all day.'

Drew didn't touch her before he left. Not a peck on the cheek or even a handshake. He smiled wanly, wished her a happy Christmas, and ushered his son out into the street where the horsebox had just departed and people had all but dispersed. He turned back at the last minute, the car door open, and said, 'But—'

'Go, Drew,' she interrupted. 'Go *now*.'

The tail lights were still etched onto her retinas when she looked up at Dennis and said, 'We're going to Wood Stanway.'

'That we are,' he agreed.

'Your car or mine?'

'Oh, yours, I think. I keep mine in a garage the other end of the village.'

'First I have to feed these wretched dogs. They've had a terrible day.'

He waited in the hallway as she quickly supplied bowls of food for the dogs, giving Hepzie hers in the living room, where she was subsequently confined, to ensure she left Blondie alone. The Alsatian picked daintily at a few morsels, but plainly had little appetite. 'Oh, you poor thing. I'm *so* sorry,' Thea told her. 'But I'll make it up to you, I promise. It'll be much better from now on.'

'Bring some biscuits or something,' Dennis suggested. 'I don't suppose you've eaten anything lately.'

'I had a mince pie,' she remembered, and grabbed the box that still contained two or three remaining cakes.

Activity was proving to be quite restorative and she felt almost normal as she got into her car. 'How much do you know?' she asked him.

'More than you about the background, less about the events of the past two days. I know where we're going, but I have no idea how you worked it out.'

'Footpaths,' she said.

'Indeed. You put your finger unerringly on it.'

She laughed. 'I've met men like you before,' she said. 'Or one in particular. He's called Harry Richmond, and he does exactly this sort of thing, as well. I assumed he was a one-off.'

'I think I should make it plain that I'm strictly a sidekick. Not clever or brave, in any way at all. Just coming along for the ride.'

'Rubbish. You're desperate for a piece of adventure. I bet your favourite books are James Bond or Flashman.'

'Much sadder than that. My father had a complete set of G. A. Henty and I read them all until I was shamefully old. They were written when my grandfather was a boy, so I'm abysmally obsolete when it comes to the practicalities.'

'Well, let's make a plan, shall we?'

They talked intently for the seven or eight minutes it took to reach their destination. Dennis pointed out the relevant house, which was shrouded in darkness. 'We'll have to beware of the dog,' Thea joked.

'Is that supposed to be funny? It's as big as a horse. I imagine it can outrun either of us without any trouble.'

'Maybe she's not here, after all,' said Thea in sudden doubt.

'Oh, she's here all right. Where else would she be?' As if in confirmation the deep hollow bark of the Great Dane could suddenly be heard behind the hedge. 'She's heard us,' Dennis hissed. 'And let the dog out.'

'Forget the dog,' Thea instructed. 'And remember what we planned.'

The plan was essentially simple. Thea and Dennis were to confront Cheryl Bagshawe with their knowledge of what she had done. They would tell her they knew the reasons for it, and the means she had employed. In the car, Thea had said, 'You saw where I was pointing, didn't you? You heard what I was mumbling about the coat. But you never stopped them from arresting poor Richard.'

'I didn't think it was my place,' he defended. 'Besides,

I had my hands full of a fainting lady. And I wanted time to think about it,' he added.

'And you didn't like Natasha, did you? You weren't so sure you wanted her killer to be caught.' The accusation was reckless, but there were still aspects of Dennis Ireland's behaviour that puzzled her.

'Something like that,' he admitted, with a low chuckle. 'How well you see through people, Mrs Osborne.'

'So now you want her to explain it, before it's too late?'

'As do you,' he countered.

'And you're on the highways and byways committee. I saw you listed, when I checked the Internet.'

'Guilty as charged.' He chuckled again.

Cheryl Bagshawe had a dog and probably a lethal knife that she had used once already. Yet Thea felt no qualms as she fumbled her way through the front gate of Old Mill House. She had seen the woman's face just before her most recent faint, had seen the understanding and the flash of admiration at her quick deductions. Cheryl wouldn't try to run and hide, nor would she resist arrest when the time came. At some point over the past few days, the two women had come to a silent understanding that neither could have explained. Cheryl would know, now, that all Thea wanted was a full explanation, and perhaps an apology for the way she had been used.

But if she'd got it wrong, then she had Dennis for protection. Dennis was big and apparently healthy. And he would be a useful witness to whatever might be said.

'Come on,' she whispered. 'Let's do it.'

'Why are we whispering?' he asked in a low voice. 'Why don't we just march right up to the door?'

'Good question.'

The dog barked again, only a few feet away. 'Hello, Caspar,' said Thea as naturally as she could. 'Is Mummy in?'

The response did not come from the Great Dane. It came with a loud aggressive shriek and a flurry of movement that was without warning in the darkness. Air whistled, dog moaned and man shouted. Thea wished desperately that she had thought to bring a torch with her. 'Hey!' she shouted with more force than she thought herself capable of. 'What's going on?'

'For God's sake, woman – what have you done?' The voice was that of Dennis, but enfeebled with terror. Thea had never heard such naked fear before. She could almost taste it like fog or smoke on her tongue.

'How could you be such a fool as to come here?' Cheryl demanded. 'What did you expect would happen?'

The torch might have been forgotten, but the Blackberry was not. It came alive with its own little light, and Thea called the emergency services without the slightest fumble. Then she went to her car and turned on the headlights. They shone mainly on the hedge in front of Cheryl's house, but cast sufficient light to reveal what had happened.

'I would have talked to you on your own,' Cheryl said. 'Why did you have to bring *him*?'

'I thought he might be useful,' she said. 'What's wrong with him?' Thea was kneeling beside Dennis, trying to find where he was hurt. His breathing sounded encouragingly robust, and there was no visible pool of blood anywhere.

'He's a rapist, for a start,' came the bizarre reply.

'*What?*'

'He attacked Juliet Wilson when she was sixteen. She nearly died.'

'So why isn't he in prison?'

'Because there was never any proof it was him. She couldn't identify him, there was no forensic evidence, and he's always been a pillar of the community. She still won't say for sure that it was him.'

'So how do you know it wasn't?' Thea demanded. 'Juliet wanders around the village where he lives. She goes in and out of the house next door. Wouldn't she want to stay away from him, or accuse him, or something? Isn't she frightened of him?'

'It's not that simple.' Cheryl frowned in frustration. 'Juliet has buried the whole thing, as if it never happened.'

'So how do you know about it?'

'He told me, fifteen years ago.' She waved towards Dennis.

'I did not,' the man gasped. 'What the hell are you talking about?'

'You never realised it was me,' she said scornfully.

'You won't even remember, you were so drunk. You'd have liked to have raped me as well, but you weren't capable. You told me enough of the story for me to work out what you were confessing to. I've been looking for a chance to take revenge on you ever since. On behalf of all the women who've ever been raped,' she concluded savagely.

'Rubbish,' he said, followed by a sharp cry of pain. 'You're just a madwoman. You stabbed Natasha Ainsworth, and now you've stabbed me. And I never laid a finger on Juliet Wilson, you stupid bitch.'

'Shut up. You did, and that's an end to it.'

'But you did something even worse,' Thea accused. 'You killed Natasha. You swopped the coats because you didn't want yours to get bloody, and went to her house while I was still semi-conscious after my faint. She must have let you in, and you stabbed her without any warning. You thought she was dead, but she crawled through the house and broke the window. You must have been terrified when that happened.'

Cheryl's display of alarm and confusion outside Natasha's house returned vividly to Thea. 'You really didn't know who had smashed the window, did you? You were scared someone else might have been in the house and seen what you did.'

Cheryl said nothing. Dennis groaned repeatedly, but Thea was cautiously confident that his life wasn't in immediate danger. The knife had pierced his right shoulder, through about three layers of clothes. At worse his lung might be punctured, but from the robustness of his breathing, that seemed unlikely.

'But *why*?' Thea persisted urgently. 'It obviously had nothing to do with the Callendars and that horse.'

'Obviously?' Cheryl sneered. 'How is that obvious, Miss Clever House-sitter? How did you work that out, with your flu and your boyfriend and your idiot dog?' She came closer, still brandishing the knife, bending over the prostrate man as well as Thea as she knelt beside him.

Without warning, Dennis reared up and gave her a powerful punch with his left fist. He must have been tensed in readiness, his legs curled beneath him acting as a lever. The blow caught Cheryl full in the face and she flew backwards, connecting with Caspar and somersaulting over him, to land with a crack on the stone pathway, head first.

'Hey!' protested Thea. Her immediate reaction was frustration at the interruption in what she had hoped would be a full explanation. Then when Cheryl remained ominously silent, she began to panic. 'Bloody hell, Dennis – you've killed her.'

'I doubt it,' he said, struggling to his feet. 'She's as tough as old boots – as they say. Or as tough as Miss Havisham, if not Abel Magwitch.'

'Be quiet,' Thea snapped. The man was demented. Her protector had turned into a rapist and pugilist and she suddenly felt uncomfortably vulnerable. Ambulance and police couldn't hope to arrive for many more minutes yet.

'I can answer your questions, if you like,' he said helpfully. 'I can see you're dying of curiosity.'

'For God's sake – we need to see to Cheryl first. She could have broken her neck for all you know.'

'Serves her right if she has. Please let me explain it to you.'

Thea stumbled to Cheryl's side, trying to grasp the extent of the damage. She was impeded by the Great Dane who was standing over his mistress and whining. The light from her car was filtered through the bare hedge, and not much better than nothing. 'Cheryl?' Thea called. 'Can you hear me?'

A faint hum came in reply, a single note of fear and bewilderment.

'Don't try to move,' Thea ordered. 'There'll be an ambulance in a minute.' She gently pushed the dog aside, but he instantly returned to his position as guard, making it clear that if it came to a contest, Thea was unlikely to win.

Dennis was still talking. He was on his knees, both arms held awkwardly. His words were interspersed with intakes of breath that suggested a severe degree of pain. 'Cheryl never had very much to do with the Callendar business, you know . . .' He gasped. 'She works in Winchcombe, with the National Trust. She doesn't care about horses or footpaths or any of that – although she seems to have been disgusted by that young man's experiments. But that wasn't enough to kill anybody for. All she cares about is Sebastian Callendar. They were lovers, years ago, and she never got over it. His mother did everything she could to break them up, with Natasha's help. Cheryl hated them both . . .'

'So why kill Natasha?' Thea demanded, hooked by his revelations, in spite of herself. 'It would make more sense to kill Marian.'

'She tried to make it look as if Marian was the killer. That way, she'd get her revenge on them both. But she wasn't clever enough . . .' He gasped again. '. . .Were you, old dear?' He leant towards the prostrated woman with a sneer. 'If it had been the other way around, Natasha would have made a brilliant fist of it. You never did have much of a brain, compared to some.'

Cheryl hissed and struggled to sit up. 'Keep still, for God's sake,' Thea told her, feeling sullied by both the injured people, and their blatant mutual hatred. A key factor remained at the forefront of her mind. 'Why didn't you report him for the rape, if he'd admitted it to you?' she asked. 'Didn't you owe that to Juliet? To society in general?'

'She knows it would never have stuck,' he panted. 'She invented the whole stupid story because I resisted her advances. The oldest cliché in the book – the woman scorned.'

It rang true to Thea, but she was still suspicious. 'And how the hell did *you* know so much about everything that's been going on?' she demanded.

'I know most things that happen around here. I'm on all the relevant committees. Finger in every pie. And I can work a computer.'

'So?'

He groaned in pain and failed to respond.

And then the ambulance arrived, without siren or fanfare, and everything was flooded with light and efficiency, and Caspar was unceremoniously bundled into the house by two hefty paramedics.

Three hours later, Thea crawled into bed, having given the dogs and rats the minimum attention required to sustain life until next morning. At least twenty-seven questions threatened to keep her awake until Christmas Day dawned. Did Cheryl kill one, two or three people? Who would take care of Caspar? Could she believe Dennis's assurances that he definitely had not raped Juliet? What was happening to Richard? Where had they taken the mare and her new foal? Where was the brown coat? Had Marian really destroyed the embryo in the flask? And if so, how did Cheryl know about it? How well did all these people know each other? What had happened at the pub to demand Gladwin's presence that afternoon? And a whole lot more. Some answers had been peripherally supplied in the course of arguments and accusations that had flown to and fro since Richard had appeared on the doorstep. The phial had contained a horse embryo, which had to be the most bizarre element in the whole picture. The brown coat, rightfully belonging to Gloria Shepherd and whiffing of cigarette smoke, was probably in a washing machine somewhere.

She had tried in vain to get more information from DI Higgins when he arrived in Wood Stanway twenty minutes after the ambulance and ten minutes after two uniformed officers. He insisted, with some justification, that his own questions took priority. He made her go with him to the police station in Gloucester and tell the whole story of how she came to be in the tiny hamlet with two injured people. He made no allowances for flu or Christmas or events earlier in the week.

But somehow, during the whole process, assisted by the young police officer Kevin, who sat with her for half an hour before her interview, the central question did get answered. Kevin was a born detective, she realised. He knew all the local gossip and how people connected. With no suggestion that Thea was under suspicion of anything other than recklessness, he saw no reason not to chat freely to her. He assured her that Cheryl, who had not broken her neck, but was suffering from a serious concussion, had certainly killed Natasha Ainsworth and for the very simple reason – as Dennis Ireland had begun to explain – that she hated her. She hated her for being everything that Cheryl herself was not. Cheryl had seen the mourners gathering at the house after the funeral, in defiance of any decent moral behaviour, thus providing the final straw. She had heard Natasha rubbish her perfectly reasonable request for a minor diversion of the footpath. Everybody loved her, including Sebastian, object of Cheryl's thwarted devotion. Sebastian had to be fifteen years younger than

Cheryl, if not rather more – a relationship that could at best have been precarious. Natasha was even older, and loved, not as a potential partner but as a lifelong family friend, trusted with their secrets and tolerated as their father's mistress. Cheryl disapproved. She came from Methodist stock and maintained a set of old-fashioned values that alienated her from almost everyone.

'Methodist?' Thea interrupted. 'Like Rosa and Juliet Wilson?'

'They go to the same chapel.'

'Cheryl said Dennis Ireland raped Juliet,' Thea disclosed diffidently. 'That can't be true, can it?'

'Oh, that old chestnut,' scoffed Kevin. 'My dad could set you right on that one, as well as a dozen other people. The fact is, Juliet was never exactly normal. When she was sixteen, she took herself off to Cheltenham one weekend, without telling her mum where she was going. Big hoo-ha, everyone out searching for her. She comes home wild-eyed, mud all over her skirt and a serious problem with men ever since. But when she was examined, there was no suggestion of rape. Not a bruise on her. I don't say she wasn't frightened, maybe even threatened, but nobody's ever believed the wild accusations that flew round.'

'Cheryl said Dennis confessed to her.'

'She's dreaming. He had a drink problem for a while, used to sit in the pub all evening getting maudlin and telling tall stories.'

'And Cheryl sat with him?'

'Something like that. Touch of the Sally Annies about her back then. Didn't last long, when she found that saving souls didn't come easy.'

'Sally Annies?'

'You know. Salvation Army. Methodists can be nearly as bad, given half a chance. Good intentions, obviously. But Cheryl was well out of her depth. Didn't like the things she was hearing. In fact, Cheryl Bagshawe was always hearing things she didn't like, including all that business with the horses.'

'So he *did* tell her he'd assaulted Juliet?'

Kevin spread his hands. 'Who knows? My guess would be he tried to take the girl home one day after the Cheltenham incident – which was kept very quiet, I should add. Maybe he laid a careless hand on her, set her shrieking and imagined he'd done something terrible.'

'I see,' said Thea. 'Thanks, Kevin.'

The long list of other questions would have to wait, she concluded. Some of them would cease to niggle, some would become clear over time, and some would be answered by Gladwin, the next time she saw her.

Meanwhile, there was Christmas Day to deal with. Perhaps, she thought bleakly, she could just spend the entire day in bed.

Chapter Nineteen

Woodside House had no door bell. Instead there was a large knocker in the shape of a fox's head, which connected to a solid lump of metal. It made a sharp disruptive sound that nobody could possibly sleep through. Thea was woken by it shortly before eight on Christmas morning, after barely four hours' sleep.

The Wilson women stood shoulder to shoulder on the threshold, smiling broadly. 'Happy Christmas!' they almost shouted. Thea half expected them to start singing carols.

'We've come for Blondie and the rats,' Juliet announced. 'We've got a cage in the car for them. It's a bit small, but it'll only be for a couple of days.'

'Urghh? Pardon?' mumbled Thea, scratching distractedly at the back of her neck, where the collar of her pyjamas seemed to be causing an irritation. She

345

had not even paused to find a dressing gown.

'Go and get dressed, and then make tracks down to that boyfriend of yours,' Rosa ordered. 'Poor chap – whatever were you thinking of, coming here instead of going to him for Christmas?'

'Boyfriend?' She recalled that Cheryl Bagshawe had used the same word. Had everyone in Stanton been discussing her and Drew, then? How could they possibly know anything at all about him?

'The policewoman told us,' Rosa explained. 'She thinks you need a break, after everything that's been happening here. She knew we were the obvious people to ask,' she added proudly.

'Well, Blondie knows you,' Thea nodded, still befuddled. 'She's got stitches in her ear, though.'

Juliet gave a squawk of distress. 'Why?' she demanded.

'My spaniel did it. Blondie's in season. And she's miserable.'

'I'll soon cheer her up,' promised Juliet.

'It would do us all some good,' said Rosa, with a meaningful look. 'Gloria ought to have asked us in the first place. I don't know why she didn't.'

'But – I can't just show up at Drew's without any warning. He might not want me.' She remembered his coolness in the hours before his departure the day before.

'He wants you. I saw him with you in the pub. That man wants you more than he wants anything.'

'I don't think so,' Thea corrected her. 'His wife's only been dead a few months.'

'Then he needs you as much as he wants you,' said the woman. 'Can't you see that?'

Thea sidestepped the implications of this, with something like terror. 'He'll be wanting to know what happened about the murder,' she said. 'He came because he wanted to do a bit of detective work. He loves all that sort of thing.'

'Oh yes?' The scepticism was like a spotlight shining on the truth. 'Well, however you explain it to yourself, you'd better get going. You might be in time to help him peel some potatoes.'

Still she protested, feeling her face flushing and her heart pounding ridiculously. 'I'm not sure I can find his house. Should I phone him first? How long will I stay? What will the Shepherds think?' She threw questions and objections at random, the whole idea too outrageous to be taken seriously.

Juliet and Rosa worked as a highly efficient team. They ushered her back into the house and upstairs to get dressed. They carried the rats out to their car, and Juliet cradled Blondie's wounded head with infinite sympathy. 'We'll bring them all back on Thursday afternoon,' Rosa said.

Nobody had mentioned the murder. Something in Rosa's eyes indicated a full awareness of the implications and connections. Finally, she voiced some of them. 'We feel bad about Cheryl, you see,' she said calmly. 'She's a member of our church. You're not to think too harshly of her, you know. She's not had an easy life. She helped us when Juliet had her trouble.'

'Oh – you mean when she ran off—' Thea began rashly before Rosa stopped her with a violent gesture and a worried glance towards Juliet, still murmuring over the Alsatian as she attached a lead to her collar.

'You're not to have any silly ideas about our Eva, either,' said Rosa. 'She died as everyone knew she would one day. Poor girl – we won't have much of a Christmas this year, with her so recently gone.'

Thea didn't dare say anything more. She was still too stunned to form proper thoughts, anyway. She was aware that she had misjudged Rosa, as she quite often did misjudge people. 'Thank you for this,' she managed. 'I don't know why you're being so kind.'

'It's as much for Juliet as for you,' said Rosa softly. 'Don't you see that?'

She did not phone Drew. She had a lurking worry that she might reach Staverton, even glimpsing his house, and then turn away again, spending the day driving around with her dog, lonely and frightened. It was a mad thing to do, and dreadfully dangerous. He had given her no indication that he would welcome an invasion on Christmas Day. She doubted that she knew him well enough to have any hope of predicting his reaction.

But she got there. Once in Staverton, which was

a one-street village, with the Peaceful Repose Burial Ground unmissable on its outskirts, there was no difficulty in remembering how to find the house, having been there once before. She parked fifty yards away on a wide grass verge and got out, letting Hepzie follow her without a lead.

There were carols coming loudly from the house, through an open window. The day was mild and grey. Her dog ran up the front path and waited by the door, as if trained to play a part in a film. She sat down and cocked her head, which always made Thea smile. Before she could knock, Drew himself had opened the door, half turned away as something in the house distracted him. When he focused on Thea's face, he was already smiling broadly. The positive current between the two smiling people formed a feedback loop that lifted two hearts and swept aside all impediments.

He stood back, pulling the door wider. Hepzie accepted the invitation and ran waggingly into the house.

They talked for the rest of the day. Timmy and Stephanie sometimes participated, but were mainly content with the many novelties that this particular Christmas was throwing at them. Timmy had hurled himself at Thea with an ecstasy that thickened her throat. She hugged him to her, remembering what Juliet had said about him, and wondering whether she might be allowed to help remedy his troubles. 'Is your flu better?' he asked her, when they detached from the embrace.

'Very nearly,' she said. 'In fact, it's only there when I think about it. So much has been happening that I forgot to be poorly.'

'Huh!' laughed the child with wholesome scepticism.

She slid into an orgy of talk with Drew – about Karen, Carl, funerals, murders, accidents. Grim topics that they discussed easily, uninhibitedly, even in the hearing of Drew's children. Drew wept at one point, reproaching himself for his failings in the way he handled his wife's death. Then he shook himself and asked a dozen questions about Cheryl and Natasha and the fate of the house in Stanton.

Together they puzzled out answers, some of them guesses, most of them very likely to be more or less accurate. The extent of Cheryl's premeditation had them stumped, although Thea suspected there had been a plan from the first day of her time in Stanton. Marian Callendar's exact motivation eluded them, too. They argued gently about Dennis, who was still a minor hero in Thea's eyes, and a figure of suspicion to Drew.

'Cheryl's lucky he isn't suing her for slander,' he remarked, having heard a carefully worded account of the rape story.

'Maybe he will. Can you sue someone who's being prosecuted for murder?'

'I doubt it. And it's probably better just to let it all lie, anyway. Nobody would ever believe it, given how freely Juliet wandered about close to his house. She obviously wasn't scared of him at all.'

Thea's thoughts went back to the previous evening. 'Cheryl really did seem to believe it. It was the main reason why she stabbed him.'

'Main reason? What other one was there?'

'I'm not sure. If she'd been really clever, she might have persuaded the police that he killed Natasha, rather than Marian Callendar,' she mused. 'She might even have persuaded *me*, if she'd told the story convincingly enough, and if Dennis was dead and unable to defend himself. She might have thought that would be the best way of wreaking revenge on him.'

'And so on and so forth,' said Drew with a fond look around the room. Stephanie was in a deep chair with a new toy and Thea's dog. Her flu was receding, but she was low on energy and rather warm. Timmy was sending a remote-controlled car zigzagging around the room. 'Let's change the subject. Let's watch a silly old movie on the telly.'

'Are you glad I came?' she asked.

'What do you think?' he said, and gave her a quick hot kiss on the lips.